A Red Ridge Pack Novel

Web of Lies

Sara Dailey & Staci Weber

TANGLED

Eighteen-year-old Luke Stanton is focused, strong, and intimidating as hell. He has to be. As the future enforcer of Red Ridge, it will be his job to keep the other weres in line. So avoiding close friendships, pack drama, and especially pack females is in his best interest. He witnessed firsthand what love did to his father, so casual human hookups are enough.

Then *she* arrives: Scarlett Reed. She arouses something primal in him, something undeniable. But just as Luke gives himself permission to finally experience something real, the truth bursts free. The were beauty is harboring a secret so devastating it has the power to destroy him. At the same time, the pack is splintering over a battle for leadership, and Luke's strength is needed more than ever. It is a time of upheaval, of the destructive power of lies. Everything he thought to protect is in danger: his family, his friends…and most of all, his heart.

A Red Ridge Pack Novel

Web of Lies

Sara Dailey & Staci Weber

www.BOROUGHSPUBLISHINGGROUP.com

PUBLISHER'S NOTE: This is a work of fiction. Names, characters, places and incidents either are the product of the author's imagination or are used fictitiously. Any resemblance to actual events, locales, business establishments or persons, living or dead, is coincidental. Boroughs Publishing Group does not have any control over and does not assume responsibility for author or third-party websites, blogs or critiques or their content.

WEB OF LIES
Copyright © 2014 Sara Dailey & Staci Weber

Digital edition created by Maureen Cutajar

www.gopublished.com

ISBN: 978-1-941260-53-1

For Shari Hassell, for being...well, for just being damn awesome!

ACKNOWLEDGMENTS

Like all of our books, this story never would have been told without a lot of support from our families. So, many thanks to our parents, in-laws, sisters, husbands, and friends (who feel like family) for keeping us sane.

A special thanks to Shari Hassell for catching all of our crazy mistakes, and to Jordan Mantell, whose beautiful poetry adds so much to our novels.

To the best publisher ever, Boroughs Publishing Group. Thank you! We feel so lucky to be working with you. Many, many thanks to Jill Limber, the best editor ever.

Last but not least, a big thank-you to our husbands for all of their love and support.

CONTENTS

LIES

Mine own breath hath made this bed
Lips stained by tall tales, dripping in venom
Seducing your truth, layer by layer
Exposing its roots, leaving you in a scarlet trail of deceit
I am but a whisper my sweetness
A gentle, seething fable
A temple birthed from a burning myth
A tear filled painting by these blood-spattered hands
A masterpiece of ruin.

—Jordan Mantel

CHAPTER 1

Scarlett

As I pulled the last top out of my closet, I couldn't help but smile. It was tiny, hot, and left little to the imagination. Most importantly, it was sure to bring Luke Stanton to his knees. This was going to be too easy. All it took was one scandalous look during my last visit, and he was practically panting. Yes, Luke may have a reputation of a love-'em-and-leave-'em kind of guy, but I didn't need him to propose. I just needed his attention long enough to complete my mission.

After packing up half my closet and most of my bathroom, I sat down on my bed and surveyed the damage. How long exactly did we plan on being gone? Would I have to start school there after winter break? God, I hoped not.

Squished between my overflowing luggage and the stuff I'd yet to pack, I grabbed my phone and shot a quick text to Drew.

> How long r u packing 4?
> I think I have 2 much stuff?

I sat and waited a few minutes for a response. I really didn't want to have go downstairs and ask my dad. Surely Drew would know. He was our alpha's son after all, and starting today, my pretend brother. Just as I was about to give up, my phone buzzed.

> Not sure. Make sure u have enough for a
> couple of weeks. And don't forget ur
> mission requires ur sexiest winter
> wear. U know u have plenty of it ☺

Asshole. He could only dream of getting his hands on me in my "sexy winter wear." Fat chance. He tried that more than once before his new girlfriend came to town and shimmied her way into his heart, but I always knew that Drew was trouble. And getting involved with the Crescent Hills Pack's soon-to-be alpha might sound like a good idea, but when it didn't work out—and chances were with a guy like Drew it wouldn't—it wasn't good for your status in the pack. Plus, my dad, *the big, bad Fixer*, made it clear before I was even interested in boys that Drew was strictly off limits.

I stood in my half-empty closet and texted him back, giggling to myself as I typed.

    No worries. This snow bunny plans on
    catching herself a jackrabbit ☺

"Hey Scarlett! Come in here real quick," Gavin, my *real* brother, yelled from his bedroom.

I finished up my packing as I shouted back, "No time for lectures, Gavin. We're leaving any minute and I don't want to piss off Dad for not being ready."

I hurried to gather the last of my stuff, but Gavin was determined to do this...again. Before I could zip up my suitcase, he was at my bedroom door. "You really sure you want to do this, Scarlett?"

"Gavin, we've already been through this," I told him.

He ran his hands through his hair and said, "I still don't know why Dad talked you into going back to Red Ridge with him and Drew. This is some serious shit. You realize that, right?"

"Of course I realize this is serious. That's why I agreed to go. If we don't do this, our entire pack will suffer," I reminded him.

"Don't you think I know that? But come on, you seriously don't have a problem with our own father asking you to hook up with a guy in order to screw with his head? I don't know how else to say this, but it kinda sounds like he's whoring you out."

Whoring me out?! He crossed a line with that one. I pushed Gavin toward the door, but he hardly budged, which made me even angrier. "Did you just call me a whore? Are you fucking kidding me right now? He is not whoring me out! How dare you—"

Gavin cut me off and pulled me into a hug. "I didn't mean it like that, Scarlett. I promise. I know you're not a whore. It just pisses me off that Dad wants you messing with a guy like Luke. It's all just so screwed up. You're my baby sister, and I can't help but worry that you'll get in over your head. And I don't agree with how our alpha wants to go about this. There has got to be another way to save our land without destroying another pack in the process."

Jeez, I was so sick and tired of hearing the same thing over and over again. I knew Gavin disagreed with our alpha's decision, and he didn't want me getting involved in pack politics or whatever you want to call it, but it wasn't like I planned on being in the trenches when our pack went to battle with Red Ridge. I hoped it wouldn't come to that if we played our cards right.

I pulled away from Gavin and turned my attention back to my over-stuffed luggage. As I struggled to get my suitcase zipped, I tried to reassure my brother. "Gavin, I want to do this. Dad didn't twist my arm. In fact, I offered. I want to help. This is my chance to do something good for the pack. And for the last time, you don't have to worry about me. I can take care of myself. Plus, Drew and Dad will be there."

"Yeah well, that's what I'm worried about. Drew pretending to be me is freaking ridiculous. He's an asshole and a hot-head, and I wouldn't trust him to take care of a pet rock. And Dad hasn't been the same since he got back from 'fixing' whatever problem needed to be fixed in Red Ridge. They may call him The Fixer, but I'm starting to think that he's the one in need of repair."

Rushing over to close my door, I shushed Gavin. "Don't let Dad hear you say that. He'd beat the shit out of you for just thinking it."

Gavin puffed up like a blowfish and replied, "I'd like to see him try. Ever since I told him I wouldn't be a part of this plan, he's been a total tool."

Oh, my sweet, sweet, blind brother...he hadn't seen *tool*. Dad's spent my entire life treating me like the red-headed stepchild because I never quite measured up to his precious son. No matter what I did, it was never good enough. Gavin would never understand that I'd do just about anything to have my father pay attention to me, and there was no way I would have told him no when he asked for my help. It was the first actual conversation Dad and I had had in almost a year, and I planned on taking full advantage of the opportunity to be there for him when he needed me.

I should probably thank Gavin for refusing to help. Otherwise Dad would have never even considered using me as part of their plan. For the first time ever, Gavin finally got the balls to stand up to him and tell him no, and now my oh-so-perfect brother had the nerve to complain to me about how Daddy's being mean to him? Seriously? Cry me a fucking river. He didn't have a damn clue how *mean* our father could be.

But I didn't say that. No, I would never say something like that aloud. It was definitely in my best interest to keep those kinds of thoughts to myself. I loved my brother more than anyone else in the world, but he was so damn used to being the golden child that it literally sickened me at times.

Instead, I did what I always did. I wrapped my arms around him again, gave him one more big hug, and said, "Don't worry, Gavin. I'm going to be fine."

He squeezed me tight and replied, "I hope so, sis. And I'm sorry for what I said. I just wish you would stay out of it. Promise you'll call and let me know what's going on?"

I pulled away and told him for the millionth time, "Yes, I'll call. And I'll be careful. And watch my back and stay out of trouble. You think I don't listen, but I've heard everything you've said since I told you I was going, so stop worrying."

Our brother-sister-bonding moment was cut short by the sound of Dad's footsteps pounding up the stairs. Dad poked his head in the door, completely ignored Gavin, and said, "We are leaving in five. Get your stuff in the car. Drew is on his way over. He's following us in his car so we have an extra vehicle while we are there."

Dad looked over at the luggage covering my bed and asked, "You planning on moving to Red Ridge indefinitely?"

I replied, "No, but a girl can never be too prepared." Then, I smiled, but he didn't smile back. He never did.

"Well, get your brother to help you with all that. I have my own luggage to load up. I mean it. Five minutes, and we are out of here." He didn't wait for a reply before he headed back down the stairs.

I started to pull my heavy suitcase off my bed when Gavin stopped me, "He'll come around, Scar. He knows that...you know, what happened...it wasn't your fault. You don't have to do this."

I closed my eyes and fought back the memory of her face. Without another word, I took my suitcase and walked out.

CHAPTER 2

Luke

"Cami, are you breaking up with me?" I asked incredulously as I stared into the deep brown eyes of the girl I had been secretly hooking up with for the last few weeks.

I mean it wasn't like I expected us to last forever. Hell, I knew we wouldn't, but I kind of liked Cami, more than most of the girls I'd messed around with over the years anyway. We had fun together, and well, to be honest, I was always the one to do the dumping. Not the other way around.

Cami turned her attention to something off in the distance, but I knew it was because she didn't want to look at me as she dumped me on my ass. "Technically, no. I'm not breaking up with you since we were never really officially together, but I'm done sneaking around. Look, we both know you don't *do* serious, Luke, and if we keep doing what we're doing, things will get serious…for me, at least. Let's just call it quits now before I end up hating you," she admitted, still refusing to look me in the eyes.

She was right. I had never dated anyone longer than a few months. I didn't know why really, but I did tend to split when things got too heavy. I'd never be boyfriend material, and even I had to agree that Cami was smart to end things before I ended up hurting her.

It was stupid on my part to even get involved with her in the first place, but she was just too damn irresistible the night we bumped into each other on a run out in the woods. As wolves, we'd spent hours romping around through the brush like cubs, playing chase for a while until she finally let me catch her. When we shifted back and I wrapped her completely naked body up in a blanket I couldn't seem to stop myself from kissing her.

Unfortunately she'd known me her entire life and was well aware of my *past*. Why she even let things go on for as long as she did was beyond me. The reality is she's a sweet girl and she could do a hell of lot better than me, so I didn't try to convince her otherwise. Besides, I had been texting Scarlett, the Fixer's daughter, ever since she left, and while I wasn't technically cheating on Cami, I wasn't being honest either. It wasn't fair to lead Cami on even if I wasn't quite ready to end things.

"Well…we're okay, right? I mean it's not going to be awkward between us, is it?" I asked, wanting to make sure we wouldn't have to tiptoe around each other for months.

"Oh please, Luke," she said, finally letting her eyes connect with mine. "Get over yourself!"

As she smacked me across my arm, her smile lit up her entire face, and I couldn't help but chuckle, which made her laugh too. To my surprise, Cami grabbed me by the back of my neck and reached up to kiss me one last time, and it was one hell of a goodbye kiss. The kind that made me want to strip off her clothes and beg her to be mine. Damn. I was going to miss kissing Cami.

She pulled away all too soon and asked, "We're all watching the game at the lodge. You coming?" And that was that. Cami dumped me, kissed me, and then asked me to go watch some football. I'll never understand chicks.

Looking off toward the lodge, I replied, "I hope to, but Marcus wants to see me first. I'm heading over there now."

"Sucks to be you! Good luck with Marcus. I hear he's been a little intense lately," she said and headed toward the lodge without looking back. As I watched her walk away, I shook my head, letting everything that had just happened sink in. It wasn't like I ever envisioned a future with Cami, but I certainly didn't see this one coming.

Trudging through the snow, I found myself thinking about how bad it sucked to be me right now. It had been six fucking years since the last time the University of New Mexico's Lobo football team was in a bowl game. I was twelve. Twelve! I had been waiting for this day all goddamned season. So yeah, it totally sucked that Marcus demanded to have an "emergency meeting" with me today. Not yesterday, when I didn't give a rat's ass about who was playing. Not even later on tonight when the UNM game was over and I was trying to put the inevitable slaughter behind me. No. He wanted to meet with me, less than an hour before kickoff. I was going to miss the biggest game of the year, and to top it off, I'd just got my ass dumped for the first time ever.

Walking over to the Walker house, my mind wandered back to all the hearts I'd broken over the years. I knew that I'd hurt them way more than Cami had hurt me today, and for the first time ever, that kind of made me feel like shit. Some girl, a long time ago, should have dumped my ass and done the world a favor. Maybe I would have turned out to be a more sensitive guy. Nah, probably not. I just wasn't cut out for serious relationships.

I didn't need a shrink to tell me that I had relationship issues. I'd put money on the fact that a Dr. Know-It-All would diagnose me with a "fear of commitment" or some shit like that. And then I'd be "encouraged" to go through some intense therapy where I'd find out that it all stemmed from the death of the mother I never got to meet. Dad never got over her, and somewhere deep inside, I was scared that the same thing would happen to me. For good measure, the good doctor would decide that, on some level, I felt guilty for what happened to my mother. Blah, blah, blah. Whatever. It was all bullshit anyways. I just didn't *do* relationships. End of story. No therapy needed.

I barely made it to the driveway before the front door of the Walker's home swung open. "Luke, it's about time. Come on in," Marcus said as I walked up the steps to his house. It felt weird meeting with Marcus alone, like I was betraying Cade. For as long as I could remember, Cade was going to be the next alpha of this pack, and I was going to be his second in command, the enforcer. It was predetermined when we were born. I'd never questioned my future before. It was always supposed to be Cade and me, even though we had never really been friends.

From an early age, I was expected to keep my distance from him socially. It was an unspoken rule, so I ran with a different crowd to avoid getting too close to him for the sake of the pack. According to Marcus and my father, it was better for the pack if we could maintain a "professional working relationship" when we took command. Things could become confusing if the lines between our positions were blurred, or whatever. Personally I'd always thought it was stupid.

Now that Marcus had discovered he had another son, he wanted Aiden to replace him as alpha instead of Cade, just because Aiden was a few months older. I had to be kind of a loner for all these years. I hated thinking about all the parties I didn't go to, all of the invitations I had to turn down, and now some other guy that no one really knew was going to take over. I felt like it was all for nothing and I was being cheated too.

"Have a seat, Luke," Marcus said, moving to the big leather chair behind his desk. Sitting there in his massive office, Marcus looked more like the CEO of some big corporation than the alpha of a werewolf pack. I had a feeling I knew what this little impromptu meeting was about, and I wasn't going to like it.

He crossed his arms and leaned back in his chair. "I need your help, Luke. The pack needs your help."

Oh man, the pack, really? Marcus is pulling out the big guns on this one.

"The situation with my sons is out of control. We cannot continue this way. Not having a clear and accepted heir leaves our pack vulnerable. I need you to help me rectify this issue," Marcus stated plainly.

"I completely agree, sir, but isn't this a family issue?" I asked in my most nonjudgmental, most non-argumentative tone. I almost said more but decided that it wouldn't be in my best interest to mention that this "situation" was entirely his fault. If he had just let Cade take over as planned, none of this would be happening. Aiden would have never fought to be alpha if Marcus hadn't forced it on him. Yes, Aiden was Marcus's first born, but for almost eighteen years, he thought Cade was his only son. While it wasn't Marcus's fault that he didn't know about Aiden, Marcus should have just left well enough alone.

Regardless, he didn't like my response. "It is, but wouldn't you agree that we are all family here? This pack *is* our family, and as the future enforcer of this family, it is your duty to *guide* them in the right direction."

So now we were all one big happy family? I remembered when Cade had turned ten and had a giant sleepover at his house, complete with water-gun fights and tackle football, and I was the only boy his age not invited, for the good of the *family*. "So, what would you like me to do, sir?" I asked, trying to cut to the chase and to hurry our little meeting along.

"I need you to talk to my boys. Get them to come together and do what's right for the future of the pack." He said, being very vague.

"And what would that be, sir? I won't choose sides."

Marcus leaned forward, placed his elbows on the desk, and intertwined his fingers. With his eyes narrowed, he put on his I'm-the-alpha face and stated, "You know how I feel and what I want, but I'm not asking you to choose between them. I'm still sticking to my decision that Aiden should be alpha. It is his birthright, after all. And I plan to stand by him, but I'm at odds with the elders. Something needs to be decided. You were raised to do this. To aid in making decisions that will protect and advance us. Think of this as your first official duty."

That was it? That was what was so important that we had to meet today? Talking to Aiden and Cade. Couldn't one of the elders do that? Someone with a little more clout? What was I supposed to say, *You two need to stop being fucking babies and get over yourselves?* I didn't have the patience or the tact for this kind of assignment, plus who's to say they'd listen to anything I had to say anyway? But that didn't matter. My alpha asked, so I would try, but I seriously doubted I'd have any effect on them. In fact, I would probably just end up pissing them off even more, and then they'd be pissed at each other *and* at me.

Trying to get out of there as fast as I could, I stood up, nodded my head, and reached out to shake Marcus's hand in agreement. After assuring him that I'd do whatever I could, I attempted to make my exit. If I left now and ran all the way to the lodge, I would just make kickoff.

"I appreciate this, Luke. I will call Cade and let him know that you are on the way. I believe both boys are at the Wrights' residence as we speak," he said, stopping me in my tracks. Now? Shit! They better have the goddamned game on!

CHAPTER 3

Drew

"Hey, looking good, baby sis," I teased as I walked passed Scarlett and pinched her cute little ass. She hated it when I did that, but what did I care? She had to put up with me now; well, at least for the next few weeks. Besides, her tight ass was hard to resist, not to mention her huge tits that she proudly displayed every chance she got. Did she really expect me to keep my hands to myself when she dressed like that?

"Pig," she whispered as she rolled her suitcase toward the trunk of my car.

Prying my eyes off Scarlett's mouth-watering body, I glanced over at her brother. "Gavin," I acknowledged just to be polite.

As usual, the golden child didn't respond. One day that jackwagon was going to have to do whatever I said. I may not have been officially the alpha of this pack, but it wouldn't be long before Gavin would be forced to follow my rules. Apparently for now, he still thought it was acceptable to act as if he was above me, but he and I both knew that wasn't truly the case.

After helping Scarlett's dad pack up his car, my father made his way over to us. "Do we need to review the plan one more time?" my father asked, looking directly at me like I was the one who was going to screw it all up. He needed to worry about Scarlett being able to keep the attention of Luke, the man-whore. Not me. I would fit right in. Everyone loves me.

Turning to Scarlett, my father explained, "Scarlett, your job is to get Luke to side with Aiden. Do whatever needs to be done to make it happen. The sooner, the better." Then his attention turned to me. "Drew, you are posing as Gavin. Make sure you don't fuck up with the names. And don't forget that you and Scarlett are supposed to be brother and sister, so make sure you act like it. Befriend both boys. Make them both one hundred percent sure that their being alpha is best for their pack. We need them at each other's throats." Finishing his recap of the plan, he turned to Scarlett's dad and continued, "Brian, you know your role. We don't want you three gone any longer than needed. I'm not sure how long I can keep the mortgage company from foreclosing on our land."

Gavin looked at us with blatant disapproval and then turned to go back inside without saying goodbye. Pouty little bitch!

Scarlett's face fell as she watched her brother storm away, but she recovered quickly and looked more determined than ever. "I've got this, Mr. Barnes. Luke is covered," Scarlett told him, seeming fairly confident.

"See you in a few weeks, Dad," I said, shaking my father's hand before sliding into my car. As I went to close the door, he stopped me and stated firmly, "Whatever you do, make sure this pack crumbles. We need them weak before we can attack. Understand me when I say that pack will be mine, no matter the cost. We don't just need their land; we need their business too in order to keep this pack afloat. I've been able to hide just how bad our situation has become, but I can't keep our council in the dark for much longer."

Shaking off my father's warning, my thoughts quickly turned to the girl I was leaving behind. "I need to make a quick stop," I said when Scarlett said that she was riding with me. If I didn't stop and say goodbye, Avery would kick my wolfy ass. I hated leaving her, but we both knew it was for the good of *our* pack. Avery would rule by my side one day, and this was step one in our plan to be in charge of one of the most powerful packs in North America.

"You are so whipped," Scarlett teased. I knew she was joking; as tough as she pretended to be, she wouldn't dare make a comment like that to me and mean it. Scarlett, if anything, knew her place in this pack, not like her arrogant-ass brother.

As we rounded the corner to my girlfriend's house I said, "Stay here." Scarlett didn't reply as I hopped out of the car. Before I made it to the door, Avery's front door opened and the sexy, leggy brunette stood in the doorway and watched me hurry her way. God, she was gorgeous. Seeing her there made me want to drag her inside and have my way with her right then and there.

"Hey baby, I was hoping that you would stop by one more time," Avery cooed.

I walked up the steps to her and grabbed her around the waist. I pulled her body against mine and kissed her hard. The small little moan that escaped her lips reminded me how much she loved it when I did that.

"I can't stay," I practically groaned, motioning toward my car and Scarlett sitting in the passenger seat.

I saw the pout begin to form on her stunning face, so kissed her again, running my hands down her waist and over the back pockets of her jeans. Squeezing her perfect ass, I pleaded, "I'm sorry, baby. You know I have to get to Red Ridge."

"I know," she said, pressing her body even closer to mine. "Remember what I said about them," she warned again.

"I'll be careful, but I don't know what you are worried about. Nothing can touch me," I teased.

She pulled away a bit and chided, "I mean it, Drew. Don't drop your guard around them. Promise me."

I was just about to kiss the worry off her face when Scarlett honked the car horn.

"Bitch," Avery muttered before she planted a fake smile on her face and gave Scarlett a cute little wave.

"I love ya, babe. I'll be back before you know it," I said and gave my girl one more kiss before I left.

"Love you too. Text me every day?" she asked.

"You know it. See you in few weeks," I replied. I walked back to my car.

"You ready now?" Scarlett asked when I opened the door.

"Yeah, sis, I'm ready."

"God, I hate it when you call me that." She laughed as we pulled out of the driveway and onto the road.

CHAPTER 4

Luke

I walked up to the Wrights' residence just as Aiden and Teagan were pulling up. I stood there with my hands in my pockets waiting for them to grab their packages and walk my way.

"Hey Luke, how was your Christmas?" Teagan asked, walking up to me.

I liked Teagan. She'd been through a lot lately: finding out the hard way that her boyfriend and everyone else on the estate were werewolves, ending up in the middle of a battle between our pack and a crazy werewolf hunter, and worst of all, watching her own father gunned down by the hunter when his plan fell apart. Losing her father had to have been traumatic, but at least she had Aiden and his family to take her in. I wasn't proud of the way the pack had treated her either. Hopefully with time, they will stop treating her like an outsider and more like a member of the pack. Even if she was human, she was mated to Aiden. That had to count for something. I wasn't going to hold my breath though.

"It was good. Yours?" I replied.

"Great," she said looking over at her true mate, Aiden.

I found myself wondering what that must feel like. Finding your true mate. Someone you literally couldn't live without. Not that I would even want something like that to happen to me. I never thought of myself as a one-woman man. The thought of being with only one girl for the rest of my life kind of freaked me out. No, I like it the way I do it. Hook up, have a little fun, and move on.

"What's up Luke? Are you here to talk to Cade? I think he's inside with Alli," Aiden said, knowing I wasn't here to just shoot the shit. It wasn't like I'd ever just come over to hang out.

"Actually, I wanted to talk to both of you. Do you have a minute?" I said. Suddenly, it occurred to me that Aiden may not even know about my role in his future—if he is the next alpha, that is.

"Did Marcus send you?" Aiden asked, the irritation evident in his voice.

Direct, I liked that.

"Yeah, and I'm missing the Lobo game for this. So you got a minute or not?" I knew as soon as the words left my mouth that I was being a jerk, but come on, these two guys are acting like babies and I was going to be the next enforcer, not a goddamned babysitter.

"Sure, come on in. We can talk while we watch the game," he said.

Oh thank God!

I followed Aiden in the house, and he went directly to the family room to turn on the game. He motioned for me to sit, "So, what's Marcus want to know?"

We were already down by ten to San Jose State. Shit!

After watching a short recap, I turned my attention back to Aiden and asked, "So...honestly, why do you want to be alpha? I mean, have you really thought of what it means?"

Aiden didn't hesitate with his reply. "Listen, I know you and Cade are friends, but I'm not backing down. I may not have been sure at first, but I've made my decision. Marcus wants me to take over, I know I can do it, and technically it is my birthright."

Aiden was a lot more serious than I'd ever seen him. Maybe it was because of everything that had happened over the last two weeks, but he's usually more of a jokester. I guess that was why I could never imagine him running this pack, but surprisingly, he looked and sounded a lot like Marcus, which kind of threw me off. How had no one around here noticed the resemblance before?

"Luke and I aren't really friends, Aiden," Cade said as he walked in the room and sat in the chair opposite from Aiden. Cade still looked every ounce the next alpha. He was calm, put together, and had that certain essence about him that demanded attention. He, too, was just like his father, but I would never tell him that. He was right though. We weren't really friends, but only because we were never given the chance.

"My father, well *our* father, never allowed it. He thought that it would be better for the pack when we took over if we didn't have any kind of personal relationship," Cade continued.

Aiden looked a little confused, "Wait, what do you mean *we*?"

"I will be second in command, the enforcer, to whichever one of you becomes the alpha," I explained.

"Marcus never mentioned that," Aiden said as he sat back in his chair. He looked to be contemplating the idea of not running the pack alone, but with me by his side.

"Dad forgets to mention a lot these days," Cade cut in.

I really didn't like being stuck in the middle of these two. The cold, hard look in their eyes made me think that a fight was imminent.

Sitting forward on the edge of his seat, Aiden forced a smile and said, "Well hell, with you helping me out, I'm positive I can do this."

I heard a low growl come from Cade, and I knew that this conversation would be taking a turn for the worse if I didn't stop it.

"Okay, so you know I'm going to have to report back to Marcus. So let me get this straight. Cade are you backing down?" I asked, looking over at Cade.

He crossed his arms over his chest, narrowed his eyes, and shook his head.

"Aiden, I take it you're not backing down either?" I asked.

With a smirk on his face, Aiden sat back and threw his arm over the back of the couch as he replied, "Hell no."

"All right, I guess I'm done here," I said as I stood up, taking one last peek at the game and making my way toward the door.

"Luke, wait a minute," Cade commanded just as I was about to make my grand escape. "I'm sorry my dad is dragging you into this."

I turned back and shrugged my shoulders like it was no big deal. "Whatever you two decide affects my future as well."

"I know it does. It just sucks that my dad is sticking you in the middle of it all. Sorry, man," Cade admitted.

"Forget about it. Listen, I gotta go," I said, heading for the door once more.

My hand was turning the doorknob when Cade's next statement stopped me in my tracks. "Hey, tell that I'm glad he's back."

This time I didn't turn around. I just kept my hand on the knob and asked, "What do you mean?"

Gage was back. That son of a bitch was back, and he didn't bother to tell me.

"Yeah, I heard he showed back up earlier today. Just tell him, okay?"

Without responding, I finally opened the door and headed out.

*****

"Where the hell have you been?" I growled as I opened my front door for Gage. He stood there on my porch with his hands shoved into his pockets and a goofy grin on his face. After Gage had disappeared for more than a month without a single call or text letting me know where he'd run off to, I literally could have killed him if I hadn't been so damned relieved to see my best friend again. He didn't tell any of us he was leaving and didn't answer any of our calls, even when Marcus called. That took some serious balls. I had almost written him off for good, until today.

"Dude, are you going to let me in? It's freezing out here," Gage asked, trying to push his way passed me.

"No. What I'm going to do is kick your ass for leaving like that," I said, blocking his way and making him stand out in the cold.

"Luke! Let him pass. You're letting the cold air in," my dad shouted from his easy chair. Reluctantly, I moved aside and let my supposed best friend come in.

"Hey Mr. Stanton, thanks," Gage said casually, as if he hadn't been missing for the last several weeks.

Gage went over and shook my father's hand before throwing himself into his usual spot on our couch. I stood there completely dumbfounded. Gage just walked in here like he'd never left. Like it was just another day.

Deciding to ignore Gage's unexpected return, I went back to what I had been doing before Gage came over, getting ready to watch the game from the beginning. I should have known my dad would DVR it for me. He rarely lets me down when it comes to football.

I went to the kitchen and returned with my dad's famous homemade salsa, a bowl of tortilla chips, and three Coronas. Finally it was feeling more like a normal holiday around here.

I tried not to be pissed off at Gage, but come on. Who does that? He was here one day and gone the next. He left the pack without any kind of notice, which just didn't happen around here. We weren't raised like that. Pack was pack and you didn't walk out on them no matter what. He had all of us worried, especially his parents, who'd interrogated me for days before they finally decided that I either really didn't know where he went or I wasn't going to tell them.

It wasn't until the game was over and an empty twelve-pack littered the coffee table and my dad had left the room that Gage began to explain. "I just needed to get away, Luke. I wasn't trying to be an ass, but after Cade found his ring in my car…I don't know. I felt guilty for trusting Dylan and pissed that Cade could actually believe that I would kidnap his girl. I mean Cade's known me his entire life, but that didn't stop him from practically trying to kill me because he thought I would hurt Alli. It didn't help that Dylan was my friend. I had let him on the estate, and he almost destroyed everything. I just couldn't look Cade in the eyes after that. So I ran. I know it was a chicken-shit thing to do, but I just needed some time."

I had never even thought about it like that. It never crossed my mind that Gage would have felt guilty for what had happened to Alli, or that he had felt betrayed by his pack. Still, he should have told someone where he was going. What happened with Dylan and Kendall was fucked up, but it wasn't Gage's fault and nobody blamed him. I could have told him that if he would have picked up his damn phone.

"I ran into Cami on my way here. So you hooked up with her and she dumped your sorry ass? Say it isn't so. Did the player get played?" he teased.

"I'm afraid it's true," I admitted with a smile.

"Well what else did I miss?" Gage asked.

"You missed a hell of a lot."

"Grab us some more beer and tell me about it. I'm all ears."

Just as I reached the kitchen, I got a text:

On the way can't wait to see you ☺

Smiling, I thought to myself, *maybe getting dumped won't be so bad after all*…

Walking back into the living room, I handed Gage a beer and said, "Well, I hope you're comfortable because it has been a crazy few weeks." Gage sat wide-eyed as I explained that Marcus was Aiden's biological father, and now I was stuck in the middle of Cade and Aiden's fight for alpha. Then I told him about Aiden's true mate,

Teagan, being a human and how she accidentally led Peter, an insane werewolf hunter, straight to our front door. Luke laughed at first when I told him about Peter but realized just how serious it was when I told him that Peter killed Teagan's father right here in front of all of us when he tried to protect Teagan, and then Peter was killed as well.

Gage sat back on the couch and dropped the back of his head against the wall behind him. I figured he was trying to process all that had gone down while he was gone. After a few minutes, he finally said, "Hey man, I'm sorry I wasn't here…you know, to help."

"Don't worry about it. I'm just glad you're back. Oh yeah, I forgot to tell you the best part, for me anyway. We have a visitor coming from another pack. Her name is Scarlett, and she is hot as hell. But keep your paws to yourself. I plan on keeping her entertained."

Gage chuckled to himself and then leaned back up, resting his elbows on his knees. "Seriously? Are you actually calling dibs?"

"Yeah, I guess I am."

CHAPTER 5

Scarlett

Turning down the familiar dirt road, I actually began to get butterflies. And I don't get butterflies. Ever. What the hell? Was I nervous? No, I couldn't be nervous. This was going to be a piece of cake. Luke would be eating out of my hand by tonight. What did I have to be worried about?

Absolutely nothing. Except, oh I don't know, failing miserably, disappointing my father, having Drew, Mr. My-shit-don't-stink, rub it in my face if I couldn't manage to lure Luke under my spell!

No, I can do this. I'm Scarlett Reed. Hottest werewolf this side of the Mississippi. This may be my first official pack assignment, but I am ready, and I will not disappoint.

My little pep-talk was rudely interrupted by Drew's own words of encouragement. "We are almost there, Scarlett. Smile and don't screw this up."

I bit my tongue—a special talent I'd acquired after years and years of being berated by my father for doing things I didn't even do half the time. It might have taken me longer than it should have, but I finally realized that sometimes it was best to just keep my mouth shut. Now would be one of those times. I needed Drew on my side, which he sort of was, but his cockiness was obnoxious. If I could have Gavin here by my side instead, I wouldn't be so damn nervous.

Shit! Maybe I am nervous.

But there was no time to be nervous because Marcus, Noel, and my father came into view, and I needed to slap a sweet little smile on my face pronto. I could do this. Without a second thought, I pushed aside the butterflies fluttering inside of me, lifted my hand, and waved at the Red Ridge alpha and his scary-beautiful wife. They smiled warmly, and as we pulled up behind my dad's car, they strolled over to greet us.

My father opened my car door and kissed my cheek, apparently already playing the world's-best-father role. He turned to Marcus and Noel and said, "Marcus, Noel, you remember my daughter Scarlett."

The alpha shook my hand, but Noel greeted me with a hug. As she pulled away, she took my hands into hers and said, "Scarlett, we are so pleased to have you here. I think you will be really happy here. Some time away is probably just what you need. If you need anything, you just let me know."

It wasn't until that moment that I remembered our excuse for being here. The story was that I had been depressed and withdrawn ever since my mother passed away, and my father just didn't know what to do with me anymore. He thought a change of scenery might do me some good, and apparently when he divulged his little sob story to the Walkers, Noel jumped at the chance to help him out.

Without missing a beat, my father walked around the car, threw his arm around Drew's shoulder, and continued his introductions. "And this is my son, Gavin. Gavin, this is Mr. and Mrs. Walker."

Marcus gave Drew a solid, two-handed shake and said, "No need for formalities, Brian. Gavin, please call me Marcus."

Drew played his part perfectly, of course. He greeted Marcus with, "Nice to finally meet you, sir," and then turned to Noel, took her hand in his, and added, "And you too, Mrs. Walker. Thank you so much for having us. I'm sure we will have a lovely time while we are here. And please let me know if I can help out around the estate. I'll be glad to be of assistance."

Noel practically melted. *Gross!*

Noel gushed, "Oh, thank you, Gavin. How kind of you. Please make yourself at home. We are so glad to have your family here. And none of that 'Mrs. Walker' stuff." Then Noel turned her attention to the rest of us and continued, "We have set up the guest house for you all while you're here. You are more than welcome to stay as long as you'd like. Marcus and I will show you inside if you'd like."

Noel motioned toward the house next door, and Marcus led the way to its front door. He unlocked it, opened it, and then handed the keys to my father.

Pleasantries were exchanged as Marcus and Noel led us around, pointing out the living room, dining room, family room, and kitchen. This was one mother of a guest house. The quick tour didn't even include the master suite or the three other bedrooms, which we were told were all upstairs. It wasn't as if our house at home was any less lovely, but it was still kind of shocking that they reserved this massive house just for guests. I found myself trying to recall if our pack even had a guest house.

Finally, after reminding my father about a pack meeting that would take place in a couple of hours, Marcus and Noel decided to let us get settled in. Just as they were heading out, my phone vibrated in my back pocket. I waited for the front door to close before I pulled it out to see who had texted me. I had a feeling it was Luke, and I was right.

> Look who's here. We are all meeting
> down by the lake tonight. See u there?

Before I could respond, my father asked, "Who's that? Better be the Stanton kid. Time to get to work on that one, Scarlett. No time to waste."

Then Drew had to add his two cents. "Yep, you have your work cut out for you. I hear he's quite the ladies' man. You sure you're up to the task?"

How the hell was I supposed to respond to that? Having my own father tell me to "get to work" when referring to a guy just felt all kinds of wrong. Maybe Gavin was right after all. But I wasn't about to turn down the one chance to prove my worth. *Thank God Luke is hot.*

With my phone in hand, I turned on my heels, headed toward the stairs, and said, "Someone want to grab my luggage? And no worries, I got this under control. In fact, we are meeting down by the lake tonight."

Surprisingly, my father and Drew each grabbed a suitcase and followed me up the stairs. Honestly I had figured I'd be lugging my own bags up to my room. Interesting.

But from behind me, I heard my father say quietly to Drew, "Perfect time for her to cozy up to Luke. Keep an eye on her and make sure she doesn't screw anything up."

I wanted to say *thanks for the vote of confidence, Dad,* but as usual, I kept my mouth shut and pretended not to hear. They dropped my luggage off at my bedroom door and headed back downstairs. I ignored the urge to tell them both to screw off and texted Luke instead.

    Absolutely! Can't wait to see u.

I'd just have to prove to them both that I could handle this. And I planned to start tonight.

CHAPTER 6

Drew

"The lodge, huh? It's nice, I suppose," I said to Scar as we walked in for our first official meeting of the Red Ridge Pack. Immediately, we were greeted by Marcus and Noel and ushered to the front of the room. We were their special guests, and they wanted to ensure that we were treated as such. Their hospitality was truly annoying, but I slapped a pleasant smile on my face and followed their lead—but not before leaning over and whispering in Scar's ear, "This is going to be devastatingly boring, you know." With furrowed eyebrows, she shushed me and then turned her attention to Marcus as he began to speak to the three of us.

"I'm so glad you've decided to come for a visit, Brian. You and the kids are going to love it here. I'm sure of it. If any of you need anything, please do not hesitate to ask," Marcus said. He politely excused himself and walked up to the podium to begin the meeting.

I have to be honest; Marcus has the alpha thing down perfectly. He managed to switch from friendly host to master of the universe in no time flat. As soon as he stood in front of the pack there was silence, like whatever he had to say was the most important thing in the world. There was no need to bang his gavel. He only had to stand at the microphone and look out over the crowd for a few moments before he began to speak.

"Ladies and gentlemen, please take your seats. We need to get started so you can return home and enjoy the rest of the holidays with your families," he said.

I had to restrain myself from chuckling as there was really no need to ask them to sit. They were already scattering to find their seats when he was on his way up to the podium. Obviously he had no issue with control in his pack, though I couldn't help but notice a few of the elders still whispering among themselves.

Scanning the room, I saw two guys who had to be Cade and Aiden sitting on opposite sides of the lodge. They looked a lot like each other and even more like Marcus. One was sitting between Noel and an extraordinarily beautiful blonde. That must be Cade. I tried not to hate him immediately, but hell, it was impossible. His arrogance and entitlement practically oozed from his pores, and I wanted more than anything to remind him that he was no longer *entitled* to be alpha, and he would never be if I had anything to do about it. I couldn't help but hate him and the blonde bitch with him, who had to be none other than Allison Wright. The half-breed…enough said.

That meant that the other guy had to be Aiden. He was sitting on the other side of the room with his mother, his very obviously human father, and even more noticeably human girlfriend. She stood out even more than the other two blondes in the room. I couldn't deny her beauty, but she looked way too human for my taste. But then again, I would never dream of dating a domestic regardless of what they looked like. Screw them? Yes, but certainly nothing more.

My attention was refocused as Marcus began his speech. "I would like to start tonight's meeting by welcoming back my friend Brian Reed. I'm sure you all remember how helpful he was regarding the situation with the werewolf hunter. He and his beautiful children will be joining us for as long as they would like, and I know you will all make them feel welcome." My pretend father stood and walked up to shake Marcus's hand. As the pack applauded, Marcus requested that Scarlett and I join them at the podium.

"I would like you to all meet Brian's son, Gavin, and his daughter, Scarlett," Marcus continued. I smiled and looked over at Scar who was actually blushing and gazing at a guy nearby, who I could only assume was Luke. Man, she's good. Luke looked as if he was ready to pounce on her right then and there. I had to resist the urge to shout, "Down boy, down."

As soon as we were seated, the questions began to fly.

"Marcus, have you given any more thought to officially naming Cade as your predecessor as the pack wishes?" one of the older members asked, and every head in the room turned to stare at him incredulously.

Maybe control was an issue after all. My father would have that guy's tongue cut out for less than that. The tension in the room was instant and intense.

Marcus's face reddened, and his stance and demeanor stiffened. "Edward, this is not something I plan to discuss at this time," Marcus said through gritted teeth.

Edward, the man with steel balls, stood up and announced, "I, for one, would like to vote on the issue…now." Immediately, the room erupted into a frenzied and heated discussion.

I had to struggle to keep the wicked grin off my face. It was clear this was a serious point of contention, and now everyone seemed to have something to say about it. Not that anyone else was brave enough to speak directly to Marcus. If this pack's meetings were this chaotic, this mission of ours was going to be a walk in the park. We hadn't even begun to stir up trouble, and already the pack was ready to crumble. My father will be thrilled.

Marcus banged a gavel against the podium a few times before the room fell silent once more. "Let me be clear. This is not open for discussion at this time. As long as I am the alpha of this pack, my heir is my choice. End of story. Meeting adjourned. Go home," Marcus shouted. His voiced practically shook the room. With eyes like daggers, he didn't bother to hide his anger or frustration, and I had a feeling that the pack member who misspoke would be punished.

As the room began to clear, Marcus turned his attention to both of his sons. His angry eyes swept back and forth between the two of them. I didn't get it. Marcus and his council of elders, and apparently most of the pack, were at odds. So why not just let Cade and Aiden fight it out? I would. If someone—I don't care who—was trying to take my place. I would beg for the chance to show my entire pack why I should be the next alpha.

We stayed behind a while, waiting for the lodge to clear out. Standing there with Brian and Scarlett, I tried to appear approachable, knowing in my real life I was anything but. Apparently it was working. Aiden and his mate were headed our way.

Aiden reached out his hand as he approached and said, "Gavin, I'm Aiden and this is my girlfriend, Teagan. It's nice to meet you, man."

Teagan reached out to shake my hand as well, and while I'm not a fan of befriending domestics, I shook her hand and replied, "It's a pleasure to meet you both. I hope we can find some time to get to know each other better very soon."

Aiden nodded his head and responded, "Of course." Then he turned his attention to my faux-sister and added, "Welcome back, Scarlett. It's nice to see you again."

"We're all going down to the lake later. Y'all should come so you can meet everyone." Teagan invited us as if it was her place to do so. I smiled warmly and nodded my head, but the whole human-mate thing boggled my mind. She acted as if she belonged, but no human should be allowed to be in this room during a pack meeting. Surely, they didn't consider her as part of the pack. It's just wrong.

"Thanks. Definitely. We will be there, right Scarlett?" I replied trying to sound excited.

"Absolutely! Thanks Teagan," Scarlett added.

"All right, well we will see you there," Aiden said, taking Teagan by the hand and leading her out of the lodge.

"Perfect chance for you to work your magic tonight. But you know, it seems this pack is falling apart without our help. This is going to be too easy," I whispered to Scarlett.

CHAPTER 7

Luke

Tonight's meeting, with the exception of seeing Scarlett, was a complete disaster. I swear our pack was on the verge of ripping each other into shreds over this alpha debacle. Why couldn't Aiden just bow out like a man? Marcus may be irate, but he would have to move past it and then the rest of the pack would be happy.

Not only that, but what the hell was Edward thinking? He wasn't even on the council and certainly had no right to speak out so publicly against our alpha. He had always been an outspoken prick, but now it looked like he had a death wish or something. Our pack may be divided on the issue, but they should know better than to cross Marcus, especially with that damn Fixer in the room. That guy was seriously creepy and looked as if he wouldn't have a problem "fixing" anything, or anybody for that matter.

I couldn't deny the fact that Scarlett's father completely freaked me out. And it wasn't just because of his size or that crazy, messed-up scar on his lip and those fucked-up eyes of his. Mostly it was because no one really knew why or how he came to be known as "The Fixer." It wasn't a title typically given within a pack, but he was well known, and apparently he was called on often from other packs when they needed a problem resolved.

I took a look around the room and quickly decided that it would be best just to get the hell out of there. I wanted to talk to Scarlett, but definitely not with her father standing right there. I'd just have to wait until tonight. *Just smile and keep moving,* I thought to myself as I hurried passed the throng of elders still gathered, still arguing outside the lodge. I could hear some of the elders whispering about me, wondering what I thought of the whole Cade/Aiden alpha situation. Ignoring their stares, I moved quickly past them, hoping they wouldn't stop me to ask.

"Stanton, hold up," Gage yelled as he hurried to catch up to me.

I didn't want to stop there, so I kept walking until I was far enough away from the crazed elders with their prying eyes and burning ears.

"Dude! Wait up! What's up with you?" he huffed.

I stopped abruptly. "Nothing, man. I just wanted to get away from the elders. I'm trying my best to stay as far away from that mess as possible." Gage turned back to check out the animated conversation taking place just outside the lodge doors and then chuckled to himself.

"Are you going down to the lake tonight?" I asked.

"Yeah, I guess. Hey, was it my imagination or was the new girl eye-raping you during the meeting?" Gage asked with a knowing grin.

It was my turn to chuckle now. Scarlett was anything but subtle. Suddenly, I wondered if anyone else had noticed, and my tiny moment of amusement faded fast. I didn't want to be next on her father's hit list.

Gage looked around as if to ensure no one was within earshot. "I'd be careful with that one, man. You did see her scary-ass father, right? He looks like he could be a mob boss or something. Seriously, bro. I'd watch yourself."

It was as if Gage had read my mind. "No shit. That mofo gives me a seriously bad vibe. He's the one who came up to help with the were-hunter situation a couple of weeks ago. That's when I met Scarlett. We've been talking, or rather texting, ever since. But that's it," I explained.

"Talking, huh? Well, I don't think it will take you long to move to the next level with that one. She's freakin' hot. But like I said, watch out for the dad. Anyway, listen, if something comes up and you can't make it tonight, call me. I don't want to go if you aren't."

"No one blames you, Gage. We're all glad that you're back. Cade wanted you to know that. He told me yesterday. Hell, he knew you were back before I did," I said.

He looked skeptical, so I continued, "Just go tonight. I will be there, but don't expect me to hold your hand or anything."

He laughed. "I'm sure your hands will be busy anyway if Scarlett has anything to say about it."

Was it really that obvious? I knew the moment I met her that we definitely had some crazy chemistry, and apparently it was no secret. I'd have to be more careful. I had a feeling Marcus wouldn't be too happy if I hooked up with our new visitor. Plus, I didn't want to end up being a problem that Scarlett's father needed to "fix".

Gage and I had just started walking away from the lodge when I heard my father calling my name. At the same time, we turn back to look over our shoulders. As luck would have it, Dad was waving me over, so I fist-bumped Gage and said, "Duty calls. See you later, man."

Dad ushered me inside and once the door was shut behind us he explained, "Marcus called a meeting with the elders. He wants you, Cade, and Aiden to be there."

"Great. This should be good," I mumbled as we entered a small meeting room. Marcus sat at the head of a long table and the elders were seated along both sides of it. My father took the empty chair next to Marcus, and I wandered over to join Aiden and Cade who were sitting across from each other at the other end, completely ignoring the other's presence. There was an empty seat between Cade and Mrs. Michaels, Cade's grandmother, so I took it. She smiled politely and then turned her attention to Marcus.

Marcus stood and cleared his throat to gather everyone's attention. "I've called you all here today to discuss the situation regarding our future alpha. As you know, I am well aware of the fact that we are not all in agreement, but a decision needs to be made. It is rumored that another pack has made claims of a takeover. We all know that this type of thing doesn't happen often but isn't unheard of. They see our pack as weak. We are divided and the future leadership of our pack is unclear."

Marcus paused for a moment before he continued. "Therefore, we need to come together and be in agreement. We need to make sure this pack is a united force. I'm not an unreasonable man. Many of you have made it known that you will be backing Cade as alpha. However, not all of you feel this way. There are others who have spoken to me in confidence and assured me that they will stand by whatever decision I make. I've made it clear that I am backing my elder son. I could easily use my position of power and make this decision myself. But as I said, I am not an unreasonable man, and I have decided that this decision needs to be ours. As of now, both Aiden and Cade are ready and willing to take on this role." Marcus turned his attention to his two sons and asked, "Correct?"

They both nodded in agreement but neither chose to speak. Marcus nodded as well before he started speaking once again. "Then there are only two options. One, we can vote as a council. Or two, Aiden and Cade will be given the opportunity to fight for the position."

There was a collective gasp among the table as they all began to eye one another, but oddly enough, again nobody said a word. Instead they waited for Marcus to finish his speech. "I know this hasn't been done in a very long time, but it is the way it was handled in the past and has always been an option if someone chose to oppose the alpha's heir taking over. Fortunately our pack has not been in this situation during any of our lifetimes, but here we are. My decision has been made."

Marcus asked his sons to stand. With Aiden and Cade standing side by side at the end of the table, their father addressed them both. "You have one week. The decision is now in your hands. You can fight for leadership or allow your council to decide for you a week from today."

Turning to the elders, Marcus told his council that there was much more to discuss about a possible attack from another pack and assured them that he would address any questions they may have in a moment, but not before Aiden, Cade, and I were excused. I stood and exited the room behind the guys. We were silent as we left the lodge and I figured it would only make things more stressful if I said anything. I wasn't sure what to say anyway, so I kept my mouth shut and watched as they took off in opposite directions.

*****

I couldn't even escape the alpha talk in my own home. The minute I walked in from my workout, my dad stopped me.

"Are you going out tonight?" I had a feeling he only asked as a lead-in to talking about the meeting.

"Yeah, we're all meeting at the lake. It's okay, right?" I knew he wouldn't mind. He never stood in my way and rarely told me what to do, but I always asked permission and he always said yes. It was just the way it was. It had always been just the two of us; my mother died during childbirth, and Dad never remarried. Sure, he'd had a couple of girlfriends over the years, but he was never serious about any of them. Not that I'd ever wanted a stepmother, but I'd always kind of felt bad for him. He deserved to have someone in his life, but he'd never given anyone a chance. Though we'd always been close, we'd never talked about it. It was kind of an unspoken rule, but I knew it was because he'd never gotten over my mother. Regardless, he has always had my back, and I have always tried to stay of out trouble. The last thing he needed was a shitty kid. Don't get me wrong, I was no angel, but at least I tried.

"Of course you can go. You know you don't have to ask," he said, and then, just as I expected, the questions began. "Hey son, have you given any thought to who you would support as alpha. If it comes to that?"

I dropped to the sofa. I didn't want to fight with him. Surely he would support Marcus and side with Aiden. "I don't get a vote, so does it even matter?"

He looked puzzled, which for some reason I found hilarious. He actually wanted me to pick a side. After all these years of staying out of it, of just being the support, the muscle, now I was expected to pick a side. What if I sided with the wrong guy? What then? What if I backed Cade, and Aiden ended up being alpha? How awkward would that be? What would I say to Aiden then? I could see it now: *Sorry, man, I just thought your brother was the better candidate. No hard feelings, right?* Somehow I didn't see Cade or Aiden being cool with that and then trusting me to be their second.

"You must have an opinion, son," my father finally said. "Who do you think would be the better man for the job?"

I didn't even want to go there. "What do you think?" I asked trying to turn the tables on him.

"Cade," he declared without any hesitation whatsoever. That was not what I was expecting. He's the enforcer, our alpha's right-hand man. He was definitely not supposed to go against his alpha.

"Whoa! Are you seriously siding against Marcus?" I asked, unable to mask my shock.

"When it's for the good of the pack, yes," he admitted. "Look, from what I can tell, Aiden is a nice enough kid. And I have never seen anyone stand up to Marcus the way he has, but Cade was raised for this job. It would be like someone coming in and trying to take your place. We cannot allow that to happen to Cade."

"Does Marcus know how you feel?"

My father furrowed his eyebrows and pinched the bridge of his nose. "Not yet. But he will soon enough. This is going to happen soon, so you need to decide what you're going to do."

"Like I said, I don't get a vote, so I really think that I should stay out of it," I told him.

"You might not be able to, son. You may not get to vote, but trust me, the elders are going to want to know who you are backing. I need to know who you are backing. We need to be together on this," he explained.

I never dreamed that my father would ever side against Marcus. Relieved, I finally admitted the truth. "I've always been on Cade's side. It's been my job to have his back since I was old enough to understand what that meant, and things like that don't change." Then without another word, I got up, gave him a tap on the shoulder, and went to get ready for the lake.

CHAPTER 8

Scarlett

I'd barely made it through the front door before Drew cornered me in the foyer. "So, what's the plan, Sis? Tonight is the perfect opportunity to sink your teeth into Luke. I saw you two eyeing each other all through the meeting. Almost got a hard-on watching it."

I backed up a bit and turned around to put my purse down on the console table. God, I hadn't even had the chance to hang up my coat, and he's already up my ass about Luke. What does he expect me to do? Strip him down and screw his brains out right there in front of the bonfire?

When I turned back around, Drew was only inches away. One step closer, and we'd be taking our brother-sister status to a whole new level. Refusing to back away, which I was quite sure was what he wanted me to do since he loved to make me as uncomfortable as possible, I planted my feet and whispered in his ear, "Don't worry, Brother. I can be very convincing when I need to be." Then I let my lips gently graze his ear before I moved away. He sucked in his breath and held it for just a split second.

Two could play that game.

Drew quickly regained his composure and replied, "Well, good. You're going to need to be. You need to get in this guy's head and preferably his pants, too. We need Luke on our side. The sooner, the better. Then we can get the hell out of this town."

I looked around at our new digs, and said, "Oh, it's not so bad. Did you see the hot tub on the back patio?"

Drew shot me a crooked grin, and suddenly I regretted mentioning it. Who knew what dirty little thoughts were going through his mind?

"Hmmm … hot tub? You might want to work that into the *convincing* plans you have for Luke."

As I turned around to head upstairs, I said, "I'll keep that in mind. I'm going to go get ready. Big night ahead."

As soon as I made it to my room, I began rummaging through the clothes I'd packed, searching for the perfect outfit. If only we lived in LA and it was 70 degrees out in December. Life would be so much easier, especially when trying to seduce a guy. You could only look so sexy in a sweater and a coat, topped off with a scarf and mittens if you didn't want to freeze. Even being a werewolf, I still felt ridiculously cold at night. How did domestics survive here in the mountains?

Finally, I settled on a tight, low-cut sweater and my favorite coat. It was form fitting, and when I zipped it up just right, it showed off the perfect amount of cleavage. I'd yet to meet a guy who didn't sneak a peek. Surely Luke would be no different. From what I've heard, he has a hard time resisting anything with a pretty face and a pulse. I just needed to make sure I could hold his attention long enough to sway him to Aiden's side and divide this pack even further. From what I saw at the meeting, it didn't seem as if it would take long.

I only had about an hour before we needed to leave, so I grabbed what I needed and hurried to the shower. I needed to look and smell my best. I had work to do.

Forty-seven minutes later, I had showered, shaved, applied the perfect amount of make-up, curled my hair, and pinned it up into a messy up-do so it didn't look like I was trying too hard. I found my favorite jeans, shimmied into them, and slipped my sweater over my head, careful not to mess up my hair. Then I dug my knee-high boots out of my suitcase and pulled them on over my skinny jeans. Oh yeah, Luke was totally in trouble.

After zipping up my coat to just below the sweet spot, I turned to the full-length mirror on the wall. And there I was, standing there looking just exactly as I had planned. It was me, just somehow not *me*. It wasn't like this was the first time I'd gone out planning to catch a guy's attention, but for some reason, this time it was different. Did I really want to do this? Could I? Truth be told, I wasn't near as "experienced" as everyone one in my pack thought.

It's not like I didn't like Luke. What's not to like? He's super hot and seemed like a decent guy. Maybe that was the problem. I did like him. Would this be easier if I didn't? Definitely not. Then it really would feel like I was "whoring myself out" as my brother so eloquently put it. I took a step closer to the mirror and looked at myself. I mean *really* looked at myself. Staring back at me was a girl I hardly recognized.

I'd never been an angel, and was about as far from the Mother-Teresa type as you could get. All of a sudden, this whole thing just felt wrong. My own father expected me to lure a guy into falling for me so I could screw with his head. Now, after seeing Luke today at the meeting, the way he was looking at me, the way he made my stomach do freakin' flip-flops, I wasn't sure what to think. I tried to remind myself that Luke went through girls like toilet paper. That he probably only wanted to get in my pants. It wasn't like he was going to fall in love with me or anything.

Unfortunately it didn't help. I'd jumped at the chance to help my dad so quickly that I guess I didn't really think about what this all meant. Gavin tried to tell me, but I refused to listen. Suddenly I felt cheap. Slutty. And the girl staring back at me in the mirror only confirmed it.

Just as I was about to find something else to wear, there was a knock at my door. Drew didn't bother to wait for me to invite him in before the door swung open. He stopped in mid-step, and I watched as his eyes made their way up my body. Just as expected, his eyes stopped right at my chest and remained there as he said, "Holy shit, you are smokin' hot! Luke doesn't stand a chance."

I pushed aside the urge to change clothes, grabbed my purse, and said, "Thanks. Let's get out of here." He moved aside only slightly as I walked through the door, forcing me to brush up against him. I tried my best not to outwardly cringe and desperately tried to ignore the fact that he made me feel even sluttier than I already did.

I needed to do this. I *would* do this. I'd made a commitment to my father and to my pack. It wasn't an option, and there was no turning back now.

CHAPTER 9

Drew

Maybe I underestimated Scarlett. She seemed to think that she had everything under control, and seeing the way she looked tonight, I couldn't argue. When we arrived, Luke was nowhere in sight, but Scarlett was sure that he would show up.

Since Luke wasn't my problem, I told Scar good luck and made my way toward the crowd. It was time for me to get to work. Step One – make my rounds. I needed everyone here to know my name and recognize my face. Just as I was getting a bit too flirty with some girl named Becca, I saw Aiden walk up and join the party. Step Two – befriend Aiden. Lucky for me, this step turned out to be a no-brainer. The guy was pretty cool.

After shooting the shit for a while, I finally said, "So…I heard a rumor."

"Oh hell, which one?" Aiden asked laughing.

"That many…huh? Well, I heard that you grew up thinking you were human. Is that true?" I asked, already knowing the answer.

"Yeah, that rumor is true. Pretty messed up, huh?" Aiden laughed, probably at the absurdity of it all.

"That's fucking awesome! I can't believe that. So, how did you find out? Did you wolf out in the middle of school or something?" I asked, feigning interest.

"No, thank God! Actually, it was my sister, Alli, who started to experience things first. Things were getting pretty bad for her back in Texas so Mom told us what we were becoming and moved us here," Aiden explained, not really going into detail.

Even I had to admit that was fucked up. I almost felt bad for the guy. I couldn't even begin to imagine growing up never knowing that I was really a werewolf. I thought my dad was an ass, but he had nothing on Aiden's mom. I mean, that's not even the worst of it. His mother never bothered to tell him who his real father was until the lie finally bit her in the ass. That was a topic I'd have to save for another day.

Looking over my shoulder, Aiden's eyes lit up. "There's my girl," Aiden said. I turned around to see Teagan headed our way. He pulled her against him and nuzzled his face in her hair.

"Hi, Gavin," Teagan said, barely taking her eyes off Aiden to acknowledge me.

"Hey, Teagan, how's it goin'?"

"I'm good, but it's freezing out here. Hey, I hate to steal Aiden away, but I need his help with something."

Aiden didn't argue. Instead, he patted me on the shoulder and said, "Well, nice talkin' to you, man. I'll see ya later." Then he followed his human back toward his house.

Once again, luck was on my side because just as Aiden and Teagan left the party, Cade and Alli showed up. I didn't like Cade, but I could fake it with the best of them, so I put my feelings aside and walked over to him and his mate.

One brother down. One to go.

CHAPTER 10

Luke

Looks like tonight is going to suck ass after all, I thought as I stood near the lake freezing my balls off. We needed to find a warmer place to hang out. Gage wasn't here yet, and I didn't see Scarlett anywhere either. I said a couple of hellos on the way over to the lake, but until I got a few beers in me that was all the small talk I could manage. I've never been much of a fan of hanging out by the lake, but with Gage back and the possibility of seeing Scarlett, I figured I could handle hanging around for a bit, at least until I could get Scarlett inside somewhere warm...and private.

It wasn't long before I noticed Gage wandering my way. "Dude, this party is lame," Gage said, walking over to me with his hands shoved in his pockets and visibly shivering.

That was Gage, for ya. Everything was lame until he had at least a six-pack down him.

"Is there a reason you are so far away from the fire, besides the fact that you are the most unsociable son-of-a-bitch I know?" he asked.

I smiled, or at least I tried to since my face was beginning to go numb. "Occupational hazard."

"You are not the damn enforcer yet, so let's go over to the fire before I lose an appendage," Gage said as he shoved me toward the crowd gathering around the bonfire.

By the time we made it back over to the party, a few more people had shown up. I smiled at Cami, who was standing and chatting with Shari and Sammy. Normally, I would have walked right over to them, but it just felt too soon to go back to being just friends without any awkwardness.

Gage and I grabbed some beers and headed over to talk to Ryder and Becca. I'd never been all that fond of Becca, but she did seem a little less bitchy since Kendall Stuart was kicked out of the pack. Well, with the exception of the shit she'd pulled with Teagan. Since then, she had been on her best behavior. I guess she finally realized that she needed to keep her mouth shut before she became the social outcast of the crew.

"I can't believe I'm admitting this, but it's not so bad out here now that Kendall's not around stirring up drama and shit," I mentioned when Becca wandered off to get herself another wine cooler.

"Yeah," Gage agreed and then looked around to make sure that no one besides Ryder and me could hear him. "Kendall was a piece of work. There is no denying that. And she did have a serious I'm-the-queen-of-the-world complex, but I would have never thought that she was capable of doing what she did. Kidnapping, attempted murder, pack treason—I mean, that's some serious shit. I don't think anyone saw that coming."

He was right. When Cade mated with Alli, I think Kendall went bat-shit crazy. It was like she lost her damn mind overnight.

"Speaking of Kendall, where is Cade tonight? He's coming, right?" Ryder asked me.

"I'm sure he'll be here," I answered. Even though I had no idea what Cade was up to, people always automatically assumed I did.

"Holy shit, bro! Look who is coming your way," Gage said.

I looked over, and my jaw literally dropped. Scarlett was walking toward me. Damn! The girl was built for sin. She was wearing these killer boots over the tightest fucking jeans I have ever seen, and it only got better from there. Her coat fit tightly against her body and was zipped up halfway, exposing the most perfect cleavage I have ever seen. My mouth starting watering from just the sight of her tits crammed into that tiny jacket. My hands twitched at the thought of freeing those puppies from the lace of that bra peeking out from under that sweater.

I barely heard Gage say, "Have fun with that," before he and Ryder took off. I couldn't tear my eyes away from the gorgeous girl headed straight for me.

"Hey Luke, I didn't mean to run your friends off," she said hugging me, pressing her entire body flush against mine.

Shit, those things were now pushed firmly against my chest, making her perfect cleavage bulge even more. I took a quick peek down and tried to hide the fact that I was deeply affected by them. Her tits weren't the only thing bulging at the moment. When her scent hit my nose, I was suddenly in desperate need of a cold shower. Breathing in a mixture of honeysuckle, roses, and perfection, I had to pull away before I led her out into the woods and took care of business. Completely caught up in all that was Scarlett Reed, I couldn't remember what she had said.

"Scarlett, uh, glad you made it," I said trying to recover when she pulled back to look at me.

"I've been here for a while. I didn't see you," she replied. Her eyes traveled down to my lips and remained there for several moments, and I had to resist the urge to cover her mouth with mine right then and there. If she tasted as good as she smelled I would be in serious trouble.

Shifting my focus toward the lake, I said, "I was down by the water. I guess I missed you."

I was prepared for that dreaded moment of awkward silence, but it didn't come. "Where can girl get a drink around here?" she asked with a wicked little smile.

"Come on, I'll get you one."

We walked over to the cooler, and I pulled out both a beer and a wine cooler so she could take her pick. She chose the beer, which made me like her that much more, and went over to sit on the far side of the fire.

"Did you get all settled into your new house?" I asked as I sat down next to her.

She scooted a bit closer to me and shivered. "Oh yeah. The house is great. There is even a hot tub on the back patio. You'll have to come over some time and help me try it out."

"Absolutely," I said and wrapped my arm around her to close the distance between us and to keep her warm. Her leg was touching mine, and all I could think about doing was running my other hand all the way up her thigh while kissing her senseless.

Somehow I managed to push aside, for the most part, all the dirty thoughts I was having about this girl and the fact that her father was probably a trained hit man, and we sat there together for the next hour talking and laughing like we'd known each other for years. Scarlett was more than a hot ass in a tight pair of jeans. She was clever and interesting *and* hot as hell. But suddenly I realized that I not only wanted her, I liked her too—a lot. It kind of freaked me out. No, not kind of. It really fucking freaked me out. Her smile, her smell, her laugh, her damn chocolate brown eyes. Shit! This was not good.

A casual hookup was what I needed right now. With all the shit going down around here, I didn't have the time or energy for something more. I didn't do *something more*. And I had the feeling that things with Scarlett would be anything but casual. Not when all I wanted to do was take her to my bed and stay there for days, maybe weeks. Still, when she ran her hand down my arm and smiled, I was tempted to give it a shot, even if her dad might kill me.

I got so lost in my own thoughts that I didn't hear the last thing Scarlett said to me before she reached over and laced her fingers between mine. I glanced down at our hands together on my leg and my chest tightened. Somehow the simple act of holding hands with this girl felt much more intimate than it should have. More intimate than the countless nights of meaningless sex I'd had over the last year.

Shit, this was so not good.

It was at that moment, sitting there with her fingers intertwined with mine that I decided that this was way too dangerous. I really fucking liked this girl. I could really, really like her, if I let myself, but that couldn't happen right now. I had a feeling this ordeal with Cade and Aiden was about to get ugly, and unfortunately for me, I would probably end up in the middle of it. No, this was not the right time to start anything that could get "real." Not that I even knew what that actually meant. The closest thing I'd ever had to a relationship was screwing the same girl for a month. Did that even count?

"What are you thinking about?" she whispered in my ear, breaking me from my thoughts.

I raised my eyes away from our hands, which turned out to be a big mistake. Her mouth was only inches from mine, and her deep brown eyes were all but begging me to make a move.

I was tempted—*very* tempted. She leaned in even closer to me and I was dying to taste her. To feel the sweet pressure of her lips against mine. To run my hands up her denim-clad thighs, past her tiny little waist and up to those heavenly tits of hers.

I stole one more peek down her shirt. She was so close to me that I could see the rise and fall of her chest. I was no saint. How could I be expected to resist them? When I looked up, I spotted Cami watching me with look on her face that made me feel like a total asshole. I pulled away so fast I nearly fell off the log we were sitting on. *Shit!*

Confusion was plastered across Scarlett's stunning face as I regained my balance. I didn't want to make her feel bad, but this was exactly what I *didn't* need. I didn't need drama with Cami, or Scarlett, or the damn Fixer, or anyone else for that matter. Knowing I could only screw this up even further if I stuck around, I decided to make my escape.

Looking down at my watch, I faked being surprised at the time. "Shit, sorry, Scarlett. I need to go," I mumbled. I walked away before she had the chance to say anything.

CHAPTER 11

Scarlett

What the fuck was that? Did Luke seriously just completely reject me and then get up and walk away?

This is so not happening right now! I do not get rejected! Who the hell does he think he is?

There wasn't a wolf in this pack, besides the two mated idiot brothers, who wouldn't take me out into the woods and screw me senseless given the opportunity.

Sitting there completely flabbergasted, I replayed the night's events in my head. All the right signals were there. He stared at my tits for well past the appropriate amount of time with a hunger in his eyes that spoke volumes. We laughed, flirted, innocently touched each other... One second he looked at me like he couldn't wait to run his hand over every inch of my body and then the next he acted like he couldn't get away from me fast enough. How could he just walk away? More importantly, why? Maybe this wasn't going to be as easy as I'd hoped.

Suddenly my chest tightened, and I had to fight the urge to take off into the woods, strip, shift, and run until I couldn't run anymore. Run until I wasn't pissed anymore. Run until I was too tired to care enough to be pissed. It's not like I even really liked Luke, but having him practically run off when I was sure he was finally going to make a move made me feel like a complete idiot.

No, that wasn't true. Damn it! Who the hell was I trying to fool? Myself, obviously. I did like Luke. And *that* was the problem.

I watched as Aiden and Teagan walked hand in hand in my direction and cringed a bit inside when I realized they were planning to sit next to me. I could only hope the evidence of Luke's rejection wasn't written all over my face. Trapped smack-dab in the middle of completely new territory, I wasn't sure how to handle the feelings brewing inside of me. I *always* got what I wanted—*who* I wanted. I never dreamed Luke Stanton would be any different. His reputation preceded him; he might not be a fan of relationships, but that didn't stop him from making girls swoon right and left. Hell, they knew what Luke was like but that never seemed to stop the revolving door of girls from ending up beneath his perfectly sculpted body. So why wasn't he making me pant right now? Instead I'm sitting here freezing my ass off with a bunch of strangers.

Teagan's voice shook me out of my internal pity party, but I had no idea what she had said. "Sorry, what?" I asked.

She smiled sweetly and replied, "So how do you like it here so far?"

"Oh, it's fine. It's just odd being away from home, you know?"

A sadness crept into her eyes as she responded, "Yeah, I know what you mean." Before she could say any more, Aiden's arms enveloped her, and he pulled her into his lap. She giggled as he planted kiss after kiss all over her cheeks and neck.

I needed to get the hell out of there. My night hadn't gone as planned, and there was no reason to sit out here and torture myself any further. As I made my way to my feet, I said, "Hey guys, I'm gonna get out of here. It's been a long day, and I'm really tired."

Teagan was the first to respond. "Awww, really? Already? You sure you don't want to stick around for a bit?" Her smile was genuine, and there was a kindness about her that seemed to be absent in every wolf I'd ever known.

"Yeah, I better go before I fall asleep out here. But thanks, Teagan. It was really nice meeting you." After the words spilled out of my mouth, I realized that I'd really meant it, and the uncomfortable feelings already invading my body intensified. I didn't want to make friends here. I couldn't. That would only make it more difficult to do what I needed to do for my father...for my pack. Before I escaped, I looked around at the rest of them and said my goodbyes. Just as I turned to leave, Drew caught my eye, and I knew he would be on my trail in no time.

I took off toward our new house, already trying to formulate excuses for what happened with Luke. I should have been off in the woods in the midst of a steamy make-out session, not tromping my way back home with my tail between my legs. Drew would have questions for sure, but there was no way I was going to admit what really happened. He would only make me feel shittier than I already did.

Just as I assumed, Drew called out my name, and I turned to see him jogging my way. "Hey, wait up, would ya?"

Over my shoulder, I called, "Well hurry the hell up. I'm freezing my butt off out here." Before I knew it, Drew wrapped one arm around my waist, pulled me back against him, and grabbed my ass with his other hand. With his lips only a breath away from my ear, he whispered, "Well, give me one minute, and I'll have you warmed up real quick, baby."

My cheeks flushed immediately as I shrugged out of his gasp. "Watch it, Brother! That's no way to touch your sister," I warned, trying to keep the disgust out of my voice. If he were anyone else, I would have kneed him in the balls and told him keep his damn hands to himself, but Drew knew the score. He was going to be the next alpha, and I was just another pretty face among his pack, which meant only one thing. He could get away with just about anything, and he knew it.

Drew let me go, but trailed close by. "Oh come on, Scarlett. You know you want me."

I wanted to slap the stupid out of him. Why did our next alpha have to be such a cocky piece of shit? Picking up my pace, I replied, "Only in your dreams, Drew."

He shot me a wicked grin before asking, "So how'd it go with *Muscles*? I didn't see y'all sneaking off for a romp in the woods, so I'm guessing not great?"

"Shut up, Drew. I'm easing into things. If I just lie down and spread my legs, who's to say he will want anything more to do with me after that?"

As we reached the front door, Drew wrapped his hand around the back of my neck, pulling me toward him so he could whisper in my ear. "Well don't hold out too long. You know, if you do it right, he will be back begging for more. I'd be more than happy to offer you a free lesson or two."

My insides twisted in knots, and if his grip on my neck told me anything, it was that he wasn't joking anymore. I had a feeling that Drew Barnes took rejection worse than I did, so I played the only card I had. The girlfriend card. Cutting my eyes to him, I said, "You know, as tempting as that sounds, I am kind of fond of my limbs, babe, and if Avery every found out, I'm guessing I'd probably lose a few."

A deep, throaty chuckle escaped his lips as I opened the door and we made our way inside. My body flooded with relief when he released his grip, but he reminded me once more, "Don't screw this up, *babe*. I've done my part so far. I'll be best buds with both Aiden and Cade in no time. The groundwork has already been laid, so now it's your turn to figure out your next move."

Before I headed upstairs, I assured him, "Don't worry. I got this. Luke won't know what hit him." Then before he could see the doubt in my eyes, I turned my back and rushed up the stairs. I fell into my bed without bothering to change clothes. I kicked off my boots and curled up into a ball. I couldn't get Luke out of my head. He seemed totally into me, seemed primed and ready to pounce. So what the hell caused him to run for the hills?

I lay there for a while before I finally got up to get ready for bed, but sleep wasn't what I needed. I needed to run. I needed to clear my head and figure out my next move. Maybe I just wasn't cut out for this? No, I could do this. I had to do this. My dad was counting on me, and I couldn't let him down. This was my chance to prove myself. And maybe, just maybe, my father would be able to look me in the eyes again someday.

I sneaked down the stairs and out the back door. Once I made it to the tree line, I quickly stripped, leaving my clothes in a pile by a tree, and shifted. Before all paws hit the ground, I was off, sprinting like my life depended on it.

CHAPTER 12

Drew

The night had gone better than expected. This was going to be too damn easy. Aiden, although a seemingly good guy, didn't have what it took to run a pack of wolves. He was basically a pup, and you couldn't be *that* likeable. A pack is a family, but the alpha should be feared. No one would ever fear Aiden.

Cade, on the other hand, had what it takes. It was obvious the other pack members respected him, maybe didn't fear him yet, but as alpha, respect and fear worked hand in hand. There was a fine line between the two. That made him dangerous to our mission, but he did have a weakness, something that could destroy him: his mate.

Exhausted from playing nice all night, I stretched out in bed and contemplated giving in to some much-needed sleep, but I figured Dad would appreciate—no, expect—an update. He was anything but patient.

"Hello," Dad answered abruptly on the first ring as if he'd been awaiting my call, and I was thankful I called him before he gave up waiting and called me first.

I gave him a detailed play-by-play of my day starting from our arrival on the estate all the way to Luke leaving the party tonight without Scarlett. He didn't sound thrilled about Scarlett, but he did seem pleased when I explained that the pack already appeared to be crumbling before we'd even arrived.

"Listen son, don't let them fool you. Marcus may be an asshole, but he has always been a strong leader. They may look divided, but in order to take them over, we need the pack at each other's throats.

And I'm positive the key to that is through Cade and Aiden," Dad explained.

"I got it. I'm just saying that it won't be as difficult or take as long as we originally thought."

"Regardless, let's just stick to the plan. I spoke to Brian earlier, and he has already set the groundwork for his part. You need to find a way to drive an even bigger wedge between those boys. Create an environment so hostile that they are ready to kill for their position as alpha. Your whole mission there will be in vain if Cade and Aiden aren't ready to take one another down when we make our move," he said, obviously missing my point.

"All right, Dad. Don't worry. I can handle Aiden for sure, and I have a plan for Cade."

"Good. Make sure you keep an eye on Scarlett. I'm having second thoughts about her. We need Luke to do whatever she says. Do you think she can pull that off?" he asked.

I wanted to say, *Hell no! Didn't you hear me when I said that Luke left alone tonight?* But I didn't. Scarlett was trying and, to be honest, she had a good chance with Luke. "She can handle Luke, but I will keep you updated on her progress," I told him.

After I hung up with Dad, I called Avery so she wouldn't be pissed. After a bit of lovey-dovey bullshit, I succumbed to sleep, feeling confident that one day very soon, I would be the alpha of this pack and my own.

CHAPTER 13

Luke

"Back so early?" my dad called as I pushed through the front door of our house and made a beeline for the stairs.

"Yeah, party sucked," I yelled down to him because I knew I had to say something. In truth, the party didn't suck at all. The party really wasn't the problem. My behavior at the party, however, was. Scarlett must think I'm a complete lunatic. I couldn't have explained it if I'd tried. I didn't understand it myself. All I knew was I had to get out of there. There was just something about that girl. But I had too much shit to worry about. I couldn't deal with anything else.

I shut the door to my bedroom and immediately began pacing back and forth trying to catch my breath. Trying to slow my racing heart, I laced my fingers behind my head and took deep breaths in and out. Never before had I been this worked up over a girl. It was like I was having a panic attack, probably brought on by my current state of humiliation. Nothing about the way I acted tonight could be considered normal. It was like someone or something else had taken over and turned me into a raging idiot.

I didn't smile at girls like that. I didn't hold hands in public. I have never whispered in a girl's ear before simply to hear her pulse quicken, to know that it was me who caused it, and I certainly didn't get nervous. What the hell was happening to me? I almost fell off a goddamned log! And that wasn't even the worst part. Scarlett was obviously into me. The signs were there in freaking flashing neon lights. And when she leaned in to kiss me, I don't know... I just flipped out. That was the definitely the worst part. I don't think I've ever turned down the opportunity to kiss a girl before, especially not from someone who looks like her.

Maybe that was it. Maybe I was just intimated by her aggressive approach and her sexy-as-hell boots. No. That was bullshit and I knew it. I liked assertive women. There had to be something wrong with me. Any other girl, any other situation, and I would have had her out of those boots by now.

It had to be Cami. Maybe I just didn't want to hurt Cami by having my tongue in another girl's mouth one day after she broke up with me. Maybe I was being a nice guy. Shit, I was not a nice guy, and Cami knew that. That was exactly why she ended things with me before she got too attached.

Walking into my bathroom, it hit me. I really did like Scarlett, and it had nothing to do with her plunging neckline either. That still didn't explain why I didn't kiss her. Kissing her would have been the natural thing to do. I wanted to kiss her. She wanted to kiss me. But would it have stopped there? I seriously doubted it, and I realized that was the problem.

I always knew it would be a bad idea to get involved with anyone from the pack. I knew my limits, what I was capable of giving someone. I took a big risk with Cami, and I still wasn't sure why I did it. It could have been because Gage took off, and everything was just so screwed up. It could have been because I was between domestics. Hell, it could have been because she wanted it as much as I did. I didn't know, but we'd known each other since we were born. She was my friend, and I used her just like I used the human girls I dated. Luckily she was smart and level-headed enough to realize that I could never be anything more to her than a friend and an entertaining Saturday night.

It would be a mistake to get with Scarlett. Just because she was a werewolf didn't mean that she wasn't just like any other girl when it came to relationships. I could already see how it would play out between us. We would have a little fun together, a few super-hot moments, she would want more, and I would run. That was what I always did. It was my M.O. She would be hurt and I would feel like a dick. And her father would probably kill me but not before Marcus kicked my ass for "disrespecting" our guests. That was why I didn't get involved with pack girls. Sure, she wasn't part of *our* pack, but she was still pack.

I'd made that mistake once. I saw that now. Getting involved with Cami could have turned into a really ugly mess, and I was damn lucky she dumped me when she did. The fact was that I'd probably never have a real relationship, and that was okay with me. I had accepted that a while back, but it wasn't an excuse. Girls knew the score when it came to me. They knew I wasn't the relationship type, but it was still shitty to use girls the way I did. I also knew I hurt them when all they wanted was a little more from me. I just couldn't give them that because there wasn't any more to give. That was it. That was all I was. Shallow. Superficial. A total shithead. I used to try to be more, but I just didn't know how. So somewhere along the way, I stopped trying all together.

I couldn't do that to Scarlett. As much as I liked her and as much as I wanted to be around her, I couldn't. It wasn't smart. With the pack in its current state of uncertainty, I needed to be the enforcer I was raised to be. It was my job to keep the drama of pack life to a minimum, not create more of it. So that was it. The next time I saw Scarlett, I needed to make it clear that we were and would only be friends. That was all...just friends. But good God, if she was wearing another sweater like the one she had on tonight, it may take every ounce of restraint I have.

CHAPTER 14

Scarlett

Upon waking the next morning, I felt uneasy and unsatisfied, but most of all unsure. Unsure of what I was doing. Unsure of what to do next. Unsure of myself. Definitely not a feeling that I was familiar with. My run last night, while it helped clear my mind and ease some tension in the moment, certainly didn't help me figure out what the hell to do about Luke. Staring up at the ceiling, I thought through every single moment I'd spent with Luke: every text message, every flirty exchange, every innocent touch, every single everything. All signs pointed to the fact that he *did* like me or was at least attracted to me, but apparently something was stopping him. I just needed to figure what. I needed a new plan.

I lay in bed for as long as possible, racking my brain for what my next step would be, but eventually my stomach began to grumble, announcing its desperate need for food—especially with all of the energy I exerted the night before. Before heading downstairs, I stopped off to use the restroom and brush my teeth. Looking up into the mirror, I pulled my long brown hair back into a high ponytail. Even my just-out-of-bed look would send most guys into overdrive. There had never been a single guy who, given the opportunity to kiss me, didn't jump at the chance. I usually had to make them slow down, not the other way around.

As I stared at my reflection in the mirror, a small smile crept across my face as an idea popped into my head. It was time for plan B. Bouncing down the stairs and into the kitchen, I thanked the good Lord above that I appeared to be home alone. I didn't need any reminders from my father or Drew that I had business to attend to. After grabbing a protein bar and a bottle of water, I hurried back up the stairs, devoured my crappy breakfast, and hopped in the shower.

Within 45 minutes, I was ready. I had quickly blow-dried my hair, leaving it down to flow in long waves, put on just enough makeup to make my eyes and lips stand out, and found the perfect sweater and skinny jeans to accentuate my curves. Before I headed out, I grabbed one of the earrings I had worn last night off my dresser and shoved it in my pocket. It was time to go to work.

Quickly, I made my way to Aiden and Alli's house, hoping Teagan would be there. She was just the girl I needed to see. Taking a deep breath, I rang the doorbell and reminded myself to smile. I needed this girl to like me, and unfortunately, I'd never been any good at making friends with girls—especially human girls. In fact, I totally sucked at it. Even the girls in my pack, who were usually nice to my face, talked about me behind my back.

Seconds later, the door swung open, and just my luck, Teagan was standing before me. Confusion washed over her face, but was quickly replaced with a friendly smile and a genuine greeting. "Hey, Scarlett. What's up?"

For the first time, I actually took a moment to look at the human girl standing in the doorway. She was cute and tiny, nothing like a female werewolf. Her long, flowing hair was platinum blonde, the color that many women paid an arm and a leg to maintain, but not Teagan. Her hair color was obviously natural and suited her light eyes and skin perfectly. She really was beautiful, and I would assume that the female wolves in this pack weren't too fond of her, being that not only was she human, she was gorgeous and mated to one of the hottest guys on the estate.

I dug my hand in my pocket, pulled out the earring, and said, "Hey, Teagan. I was hoping you would be here." Then I held up the silver hoop and asked, "I lost one of my favorite earrings last night.

Any chance you found it before you left?" Before she could answer, I shivered just a bit, hoping it would score me an invite inside.

It worked like a charm. She opened the door wider as she answered, "No, I didn't see it. Sorry." Teagan paused for just a moment before she continued, "Hey, you want to come in? It's freezing out there."

Perfect! Smiling, I stepped inside and said, "Thanks. It sure is." After an awkward pause in the foyer, I asked, "Hey, are you hungry? I'm starved. All I had was a protein bar this morning."

Turning toward the kitchen, Teagan replied, "Yeah sorta, but I'm not sure what we have to eat."

"Any chance I can convince you to go out to lunch somewhere? I know I've only been here a day, but I already feel like I need to get away for a bit."

Teagan stood there silent for a minute, surely contemplating whether or not lunch with the new girl was a good idea. Finally, she spoke. "Sure, that sounds good, but I need to run upstairs and change clothes real quick and let Aiden and the Wrights know where I'm going."

I had to play my cards just right to pull this off. I needed to somehow get Luke involved in our little lunch date. I didn't have much practice with this kind of thing, but girls confided in each other, right? I mean that's what being girlfriends was all about, as far as I could tell anyway. I took a deep breath and thought, *Here goes nothing.*

I looked over at Teagan pensively. "Can I ask you something?"

"Of course."

Leaning in as if someone might hear, I asked, "Do you think maybe you could ask Aiden to join us? And...maybe he could ask Luke to come too?"

With raised eyebrows, Teagan inquired, "So you like Luke, huh?"

Looking away, feigning embarrassment, I admitted, "Yeah, but I'm not sure if he likes me back. I thought he did, but then last night, he kind of blew me off." With my downcast eyes, I put on my best I-just-don't-know-what-to-do act, hoping she would buy it. When she didn't respond, I glanced back up at her, and although concern was written all over her face.

As soon as our eyes met, she said, "Okay, well let's see what we can do about that. I don't really know Luke, but he and Aiden have been hanging out a bit. I'll text him and see."

*****

An hour or so later, Teagan, Aiden, and I were walking into Happy Harry's Burger Barn, a mom-and-pop burger joint not too far from the estate. Luke would be joining us shortly, and my damn nerves were getting the best of me. With my stomach twisted in knots, I excused myself to run to the restroom. I needed a minute alone to collect myself before I resorted to chewing off my perfectly manicured nails. What the hell was wrong with me? I hadn't been this freaked out about a guy since junior high when I agreed to sneak into a choir practice room during lunch to make out with my first boyfriend, Matt Schaefer.

I ran my fingers through my hair to smooth out my waves, put on a bit of lip gloss, and washed my hands, all the while reminding myself that Luke was just another guy, nothing special. Sure he had a drool-worthy body, with rippling muscles that begged to be caressed. An image of me sliding my greedy hands over his broad shoulder and down his chiseled abs popped into my head. Shit! I needed to get a damn grip. Closing my eyes, I shook the image from my mind.

Before heading to our table, I took one last look in the mirror, adjusted my sweater to ensure my cleavage would catch Luke's eye, and then turned to exit the restroom. As soon as I stepped one foot out of the door, I saw him.

Luke Stanton.

Kicked back in a chair, his eyes danced as he laughed about something Aiden had said. He looked completely relaxed sitting there— faded jeans, leather jacket, his short dark hair combed perfectly to frame his gorgeous face, defining his high cheekbones that any model alive would kill for. God, he was hot. But this was a job, a mission for my pack. After the way I reacted last night, I reminded myself that I needed to keep my emotions out of it.

On my way to the table, Luke glanced my way, and he visibly stiffened but recovered quickly with a small smile. He scooted up a bit so that I could squeeze behind him to get to my chair and said, "Hey, Scarlett. How's day two?"

As I sat and scooted up to the table, I replied, "Good, thanks. Glad you could make it." Before he responded, his leg lightly brushed against mine, shooting tingles up my spine, but instantly, he moved it away.

Luke gave me a generic "Thanks" and then stuck his nose in the menu as if there was anything to order other than a hamburger. I looked over at Teagan, and she shot me a sympathetic grin. By that point, my tingles had fizzled out, and I was left contemplating what to do next.

We ordered, and soon, the small talk that had been taking place before I showed up resumed, and Luke seemed to relax a bit. The Burger Barn was one of those places with white butcher paper on the table so that customers could entertain themselves by drawing on the tabletops with a couple of broken crayons, and Aiden challenged Luke to a game of hangman.

When Luke leaned over to get a better look at what Aiden had written, his leg, once again, leaned into mine. This time he didn't move it. Seconds later, his hand made its way down to lie on his leg, leaving the back of it to rest against my thigh. When it was his turn to write on the table, the back of his hand lightly slid up my thigh before he grabbed a crayon to begin his turn. Stunned by the chill-bumps that broke out all over my body, I involuntarily perked up a bit and noticed Luke cut his eyes in my direction with a wicked grin on his face. Without missing a beat, Luke continued drawing, but his leg remained against mine.

Figuring two could play this game, I leaned over toward Luke, pretending to need something from my purse that I had strategically placed on the floor between our chairs. As I leaned down, the side of my breast pressed against his arm as I slowly slid my way down to reach into my purse. Barely noticeably, and I wouldn't have detected it if I hadn't been looking for a reaction, Luke lightly sucked in his breath. Feeling around in my purse, I felt my cell phone and clutched it in my hand, thankful I had some excuse for fumbling through my bag. But I wasn't finished quite yet. I slowly slid my way back up Luke's arm, making sure to not break contact. I peeked up at him just in time to witness his eyes gazing hungrily down my sweater. Just the reaction I was hoping for.

His eyes finally made their back up to meet my own as I said, "Sorry about that. I thought I had a text."

Clearly shaken, he quickly replied, "No problem," and continued his game with Aiden.

It wasn't long before our food arrived, and as we ate, we all chatted about nothing in particular.

Unfortunately, Luke kept his hands to himself for the rest of lunch, and it almost seemed as if he was making a point to keep things strictly *friendly*. Maybe I'd completely misread the whole leg thing. By the end of our meal, my hopes of finally snagging Luke's attention were spiraling downward at warp speed. Here I thought I could catch this guy hook, line, and sinker, but this little mission of mine was proving to be more difficult than I'd imagined.

But just when I'd decided that I might just be fighting a losing battle, I caught him staring at me while Teagan and I were admiring the butcher-paper artwork of past customers that decorated the walls surrounding the exit. There was a spark in his eyes, and a tiny piece of my hope was restored.

CHAPTER 15

Drew

"Drew, I have a meeting with Marcus today. I think you should come with me. It will give you a chance to hang out with Cade for a while. What do you say?" Brian asked, sitting in the chair opposite the one I was trying to sleep in.

"Sure," I said, feigning interest. "When do we leave?"

"Now, actually," he said which made me want to rethink my earlier response. All I wanted to do today was sleep, but no, Scarlett had to get up at the ass crack of dawn and start slamming doors. Who the fuck does that?

It would be a good opportunity to talk to Cade without Alli around though. They are pretty much inseparable from what I hear, so if I don't go now, I may never catch him alone again.

"All right, I'll be ready in five," I said and dragged my tired ass up the stairs to change.

*****

"Brian, Gavin, so glad you could make it," Marcus said and ushered us into his home. He told me that Cade was upstairs in the game room. That was my cue to leave and let them speak privately. I got it. Being the son of an alpha, I was used to being dismissed. That didn't mean I liked it, but hey, one day soon I'd be the alpha. Then I guess it will be my turn to dismiss people without a second thought.

When I walked into the game room Cade was getting ready to leave.

"Hey, Gavin, what's up?" he said looking a little disappointed to see me. I bet. He was probably heading out to see that hybrid bitch of his. I don't blame him, really. For a half-domestic she's smokin' hot.

"Were you about to leave? I can wait for my dad downstairs," I offered.

"Nah…it can wait. My dad is known for his long, impromptu meetings, so you might be here a while. Call of Duty?" Cade asked.

"Why not," I replied and took a seat in front of the TV.

Cade handed me a controller and excused himself for a minute while he called Alli.

"You sure you don't need to leave? I don't mind," I asked as he walked back into the room.

"No, it's fine really. I told Alli I would meet up with her when the meeting's over."

We didn't talk much at first, but by the time I shot his ass a couple of times he lightened up.

"I guess I'm rusty," he laughed, tossing the controller on the floor.

"From what I've heard you have had a hell of a few months. No time for video games," I said, hoping to get to the reason for my visit.

"You could say that. How much do you know?" he asked.

"Let's see. You mated with a girl who was not your girlfriend. That girlfriend and some rogue tried to kill your mate. You found out that your mate's brother is also your older brother. And your dad wants Aiden to take your spot as the next alpha. Did I get it all?" I said.

Cade leaned back in his seat and seemed to be absorbing every word I just said.

"Hell of a few months is right," he admitted.

That's when the uncomfortable silence seeped in. As I sat there and thought about it, I almost felt bad for the guy. I was actually surprised that he hadn't gone crazy and killed his old man and half this damned pack.

"Can I ask you something, man?" I asked.

Cade just nodded.

"You're not going to let someone, brother or not, who's only been a werewolf for, what, like a month take what is rightfully yours, are you?" That certainly got his attention.

Before he answered, his body visibly stiffened. "It's a little more complicated than that," he said, but the tick in his jaw showed me how he really felt about the topic.

"Is it?" I asked. "Listen, I know it's not my place, and we haven't known each other that long, but you don't seem like the type to just hand over your position without a fight."

"He's my brother...and Alli's brother. That makes it complicated, but I hear what you are saying. And trust me, I'm not going to give up that easily," he admitted.

"Gavin, you ready, son?" Brian yelled from the bottom of the stairs.

I had to give it to that man; he had perfect timing.

"Thanks for keeping me company," I said to Cade as I got up to leave.

"Anytime," he replied, and by the sound of his voice, I knew that I had gotten to him. Yeah, he would be thinking about our little conversation for the rest of the day.

CHAPTER 16

Luke

I had never been so relieved to leave a restaurant before in all of my life. If I had to sit there, that close to Scarlett, for one more minute, I truly believe my hands would have developed a mind of their own. Happy Harry's probably had rules against that sort of thing that I would have broken for sure.

I knew exactly what she was doing too, leaning over to get her phone and brushing up against me. She was not as subtle as she'd like to think she was. What the hell was I supposed to do when her cleavage was right in front of me? Okay, I could have not stared. I could have looked the other direction, but I didn't. Damn it, I couldn't. And that was my fault. I was really going to have to build up some self-control for times like that when I was around her.

I told myself I was going to talk to her. That I was going to sit her down and make her understand that this thing between us, whatever it was, couldn't happen. Obviously I didn't do that. But I needed to, and if I did, maybe she'd understand and take it easy on me. If she knew that I was resisting her for her own good, she would stop going out of her way to touch me, lean up against me, or give me a view that I couldn't resist. Maybe she would even stop wearing those tight little sweaters, those deliciously sexy skinny jeans, and that intoxicating perfume…

Shit, I was getting hard just thinking about her.

I was in so much fucking trouble.

Okay, she was going to be here for what, two, maybe three weeks? Surely I could control myself for that long. If I had to, I could simply avoid her. It would be difficult but not impossible. I could just hang out at home in the morning, spend my afternoons in the gym and my evenings at Gage's or back at home. Yeah, put in some quality time with Dad. If I felt the urge to see her or even think about seeing her, I could run it out of me. That was what I was going to have to do. If not, we'd end up hooking up and nothing good, well in the long term anyway, could come from that.

I was almost home when thoughts of being back at that restaurant flooded my mind. Feeling her leg pressed up against mine, my hand touching her leg, her tits rubbing down my arm. How she caught me staring at her before we left. The look she returned that promised there was more to come. There was no denying that I wanted that girl. I guess my plan to get Scarlett out of my head needed to start now. Trying to hide all the urgency in my voice, I called Gage and told him to meet me at the gym in forty-five minutes. A good workout might take away some of this built-up tension surging through my body. A guy could hope anyway.

*****

Gage was late again. By the time he got to the gym, I was already done with my cardio. Come to think of it, he always *conveniently* missed the treadmill.

"Nice of you to show up," I huffed as I walked over to get a drink.

"You know I hate running with you."

After several gulps from the water fountain, I said, "You are the only wolf in the history of the world who hates to run."

"I didn't say that I hate running. I said that I hate running *with you*," he answered honestly before he shrugged and wandered off toward the free weights.

I knew he did. In fact, I knew that Gage really didn't like the gym at all, but he almost always came with me when I asked. Being a werewolf definitely had some advantages when it came to fitness and muscle tone. Most weres never even stepped foot into a gym because they didn't have to. I, on the other hand, didn't have much of a choice. My dad had me working out long before most boys even started to worry about what they looked like without a shirt on. The enforcer had to look the part. I had to be the biggest, the strongest, and most importantly, the most intimidating. But Gage didn't. He would always be just as fit as the rest of the pack, so I really did appreciate the fact that he came to the gym with me as often as he did.

"So, what's going on with the new girl?" Gage asked as he spotted me on my first set of bench press.

"Nothing," I lied.

Looking down at me, he shot me a look that told me that he didn't believe me and then laughed. "Why the hell not? Send her my way if you're not interested."

I knew he was fucking with me, but that did nothing to prevent the anger and jealousy from boiling up inside me. I tried to cover up my automatic reaction, but it was too late. Gage saw it and ran with it.

"Yeah, I'm between ladies right now. I could use something warm in my bed," he teased and again I tensed. "Damn, Luke, chill! I'm just messing with you."

I put the bar back on the rack and sat up with my head down and my elbows on my knees. I couldn't stand what this girl was doing to me. It wasn't normal.

"She's not making it easy to resist her," I finally admitted.

"Why the hell are you trying to resist her?"

"I can't get involved with another pack girl. I just can't. Not now. Cami and I just called it quits, and it was really stupid on my part to have even started something with her in the first place. It's one thing to jump from domestic to domestic. Chances are they don't know each other, and even if they do, they tend to blame each other and not me. Pack girls are different. You know that," I said.

I didn't know why all of that came spilling out of me, but it did, and there was no taking it back now.

"Bullshit," Gage spat as he pretended to cough.

I lifted my head and glared at him. He started taking off some of the weight from the bar so we could switch places.

I knew there was more he had to say, so I stood above him as he positioned himself on the bench and waited.

He reached up to take hold of the bar but then didn't lift it. Instead, just as I suspected, he started in on me. "That is load of crap and you know it. Cami isn't going to go all crazy-ass ex on you. You're being ridiculous. I get that you don't want to bring your man-whore ways on to the estate, but I've seen that girl. And I've seen the way she looks at you. Now, tell me the real reason you are disappointing that poor girl," he teased.

I couldn't tell Gage the truth. Hell, I could hardly admit the truth to myself. The truth made me feel confused and way out of my element.

"Oh shit! You like this girl," Gage guessed, and when I didn't immediately deny it, he knew he was right.

A change of subject was definitely in order. "Forget it, man. Are you going to lift this shit or what? If not, then get the hell up so I can finish."

A stupid grin spread across his face and he crossed his arms over his chest. "Not until you admit it. You like her."

"What are we, in the third grade? Who cares if I like her? I don't do relationships."

"Who said anything about a relationship? Have fun and see where it goes. Maybe you both will decide that serious won't work. She could decide that she doesn't care for big, muscle-brain assholes and dump you for another werewolf who is, I don't know, taller and way more handsome," he joked, rubbing his hand over his jaw.

When I didn't respond, Gage positioned his hands on the bar once again and suddenly got all serious on me. "You've always sold yourself short, Luke. Just because you're going to be the enforcer doesn't mean you can't have a life."

"What the hell happened to you? Did you grow a vagina while you were gone?" I asked, trying to lighten the mood.

He chuckled and then finally decided to lift the bar as he replied, "Hey, I'm just trying to help. Go ahead and keep pushing her away. Be miserable and uptight until she leaves. I don't care. Or..."

"You're right. I know you're right. There's just too much going on right now," I told him.

After that, we moved on with our workout without any more talk of Scarlett or Gage's new vagina. I thought that a good workout would help clear my head, but as I got in my truck, I was feeling just as confused as I did when I arrived.

CHAPTER 17

Scarlett

More confounded than ever about Luke, I sat there in a daze most of the drive home. It wasn't long before Aiden was pulling up to my new home. Even if the lunch didn't pan out as well as I'd hoped, I did hear one very important piece of information that could definitely prove to be useful. Teagan mentioned to Aiden that Alli was planning a girls' night at their house with her, Cami, and Shari. When Aiden put his car in park to drop me off, Teagan turned to me to say, "I'm sure you could come over tonight if you want. I can talk to Alli."

I was quite sure she was only asking so that I didn't feel left out, but I was smart enough to know that my presence there would just make everyone uncomfortable. I wasn't "one of the girls" and surely Teagan was only asking to be kind. I pushed open the car door and replied, "Thanks for asking, but I have some stuff I need to take care of tonight. Maybe next time."

Stepping out of the car, I wrestled with the idea of asking Teagan for a huge favor. I wasn't used to being so vulnerable, but I finally decided that it was worth a shot. "Teagan, can I talk to you for a minute—alone?" Then I smiled at Aiden, hoping he would give us some privacy.

Teagan looked over at Aiden and said, "Meet you at the house in a few? I'll walk back. It's only a few houses down."

Concern flashed across Aiden's face, but he didn't argue. Instead, he simply nodded his head and leaned over to kiss her goodbye.

Teagan stepped out of the car, and after she watched Aiden drive away, she turned her attention to me. "So what's up, Scarlett?"

Feeling like a foolish schoolgirl, I pushed aside my pride and asked, "Okay, I know you may think this is none of my business, but what do you know about Luke and Cami?" I wasn't really sure why I was suddenly so curious about Luke and Cami, other than the possibility that she may be the reason why Luke was acting so strange. I wanted more than anything to believe that it wasn't because he just wasn't that into me, so maybe I was grasping at straws here, but I was hoping whatever went on between them might shed some light on something.

Standing there looking completely uncomfortable, Teagan replied, "Not much, to be honest. All I really know is that they hooked up for a few weeks, and then Cami broke it off. I'm not really sure if they were ever actually together-together. They tried to keep it on the down-low but most of us knew, though I don't think the adults here ever got wind of it."

Great, she didn't know any more than I did. I needed to know more. What I needed was Cami's perspective on the whole situation, but since I'd barely spoken to her, I knew asking *her* wasn't an option. Cami saw Luke and me by the fire last night, and I was pretty sure she assumed something was going on between us. Hoping Teagan would help me out with my little plan, I asked, "Okay, well I have a favor to ask. Is there any way you could ask Cami about it? I really like Luke, and I don't know..." I trailed off.

Hardly taking a moment to even consider it, Teagan replied, "I don't think that's a good idea. Cami and I aren't all that close, and I don't like to get involved in stuff like that."

"Please just think about it. If the opportunity arises tonight, just consider it. I'd be forever in your debt. Really, I mean it," I groveled. Good Lord, I couldn't believe I was actually begging. What had gotten into me? Suddenly, I felt more pathetic than ever.

But... it was working! I could see the change in her eyes, and I knew before she even spoke that I had changed her mind.

"Okay, I'll try. If the situation is right, I'll ask, but if she doesn't tell me, I am not going to push it."

Before I realized what I was doing, my arms flew around her as I babbled, "Thank you, thank you, thank you!" Teagan's body tensed for the slightest moment but then relaxed, and she returned the hug. Whether I wanted to admit it or not, it felt good. Like I actually had a real friend. I couldn't remember the last time I'd hugged a friend—or anyone for that matter.

*****

My plan was in play, and I could only hope that Teagan would get up the nerve to ask Cami about Luke, but I didn't want to hear Teagan's playback of the conversation. I wanted to hear it for myself. If luck was on my side, I might just be able to get close enough to hear the conversation. It was worth a shot. So once I figured Shari and Cami had arrived at the Wrights' home, I crept out of my house and took to my wolf form. That way I could eavesdrop discreetly and have a better chance of hearing the girls.

Under the cover of darkness, I snuck over to the Wrights' and found the girls huddled around a fire on the covered patio in the backyard. Just as I had hoped, I could get close enough to hear them without being seen. The only thing that could possibly give me away was my scent, but with the fire going, there was a good chance it would go unnoticed. After a few tense minutes, I decided I was in the clear since no one said anything or came looking for me.

Apparently, Teagan's birthday was coming up and Alli invited the girls over to plan her birthday party. Since Teagan was the newest member of the pack, Alli wanted it to be a huge bash, but in truth, I bet she just wanted to do something special for Teagan since it would be her first birthday without her father. That and from what

I'd gathered, Teagan didn't have the best home life before she moved here, so I could only assume that big birthday parties were not exactly the norm, and since her birthday was only a couple of weeks away, Alli seemed determined to make it a night to remember.

I listened as the girls droned on and on about ideas for the party until finally Alli and Shari went inside to make hot chocolate. This was the moment! Teagan was alone with Cami, and if she was going to ask Cami about Luke, this was the perfect time.

I didn't have the best view of the two girls, but I could hear them clearly. A few seconds of silence passed before Cami asked, "So how are things with Aiden?"

"Things couldn't be better, besides the whole alpha debacle," Teagan replied, but before Cami could respond, she added, "So, you can tell me it's none of my business if you want to, but what happened with you and Luke?"

Score! Teagan actually did it. Listening intently, I readied myself for whatever Cami had to reveal.

After a brief silence Cami began. "To tell you the truth, I have no idea what I was thinking getting involved with Luke. I know you don't know him all that well, but I've known him all my life and was well aware that he has absolutely no ability to commit. I mean he goes through domestics—oh sorry, Teagan, I mean human girls— like toilet paper, and there is never a shortage when you look like Luke."

She paused for a moment, and Teagan didn't respond. I could barely see the girls and didn't know what was going on, so all I could do was sit there and silently pray that she wasn't finished yet. I needed to know more.

Seconds later, Cami continued, "This is embarrassing to admit. I've always had a crush on Luke, but I also knew that the second he might actually feel something for a girl, he runs like hell. But when he kissed me for the first time, I couldn't help myself. I was in, despite the risks."

Teagan finally spoke up. "So why did you dump him?"

Cami sighed loudly, and I wished I could see her face. With my heart pounding a mile a minute, I nervously awaited her response. After several excruciating seconds, it finally came. "It was stupid of me to ever think for one moment that there could be something real between me and him. I've always known he was broken, but I guess I kinda hoped that I could be the girl who would fix him. He's never messed around with any of the pack girls, so I actually thought for one very brief moment that maybe I could be the one."

Cami took a deep breath before she admitted, "But I wasn't. I'm not sure Luke will ever be emotionally available to anyone. He's always kept everyone at arm's length, even his friends. I probably shouldn't say this, but you know his mom died during childbirth? His dad never got over it, never remarried, never even had a real girlfriend. I've kinda always figured that was why Luke is so scared to let anyone in. Maybe he's scared he'll end up like his father."

"No, I didn't know about that. How sad. It makes sense though," Teagan said with a hitch in her voice.

"Anyway, when I came to my senses and realized that I would never be that person for him, I broke it off before he broke my heart. He kind of chipped away at it, but it's mostly still intact. It was the last thing I wanted to do, but I had to let him go so that we could still be friends."

Before Teagan could respond, the back door opened and Alli and Shari were back. It was if the conversation hadn't even taken place. The topic immediately switched to more ideas for the party that Alli and Shari must have discussed inside.

I remained there for a few more minutes letting all that I had heard sink in. I knew Luke was a serial-dater, kind of a man-whore, but I would have never guessed the reason. My heart ached for him. Would he ever be able to let anyone in?

I crept away toward the woods knowing there was only one thing that could make me feel better, that could make me feel alive. It was the one thing I'd always turned to. I needed to run. And that was exactly what I did. I sprinted through the brush and the trees until a scent in the air hit me with such force that my legs almost gave out when I came to an abrupt halt. The perfect mixture of sandalwood, leather, and earth filled my senses as my eyes frantically searched the area until they fell upon the most magnificent wolf I'd ever seen. Luke's wolf eyes were staring back into mine.

CHAPTER 18

Drew

I was just about to take a hot shower and call it a night when my phone rang.

"Hey baby," I answered, knowing it was Avery.

"How come you haven't called me?" she demanded in her pouty voice that I love so much.

"Sorry, baby. I've been busy infiltrating a pack," I said sarcastically.

"Very funny. So, how is it going?"

"Well, let's see. I kicked your boy Cade's ass yesterday at Call of Duty."

"What the hell are you doing playing games with him? I'm pretty sure that's not why your dad sent you there," she snapped.

"I have to be friendly, Avery. Besides, I think I got under his skin, so I am doing my job."

"I'm sorry. I know you are. I just hate you being so far away from me and with those people," she whined.

"I'll be home soon, babe. This pack is on the verge of imploding without our involvement, so with us helping things along it can't be too much longer," I assured her.

"Okay, just be careful."

"I will. I love you."

"I love you too. Bye baby," she said before she hung up.

Then I went back to what I was doing before Avery called. The same thing I had been doing all day. Absolutely nothing! It was too damn cold to even think about going outside, and I had no idea where Scarlett took off to. I was about to text her when her father came into the room and wanted to chat.

"How did things go with Cade yesterday?" Brian asked, sitting in the chair by the fireplace.

"I got him thinking, that's for sure."

"What do you think of those boys? Formed any opinions yet?"

"It's obvious right away who's alpha material and who's not. Aiden is a decent guy, but he could never run a pack, and he could never ever take us on. Cade is the one to worry about. He's smart. He's playing his cards just right, and no one has even noticed that he's in the game. He's been able to put himself into the perfect position. If they decide to let the elders vote, Cade's got it. If they make the guys fight it out, Cade's got it. Hell, if they fight for it, he will gain even more respect than if his father just handed him the position. This way, as the pack will see it, he will have earned his title," I said.

Brian seemed to be absorbing my response. "Then we were right to get Luke to side with Aiden. If anyone can help Aiden learn how to fight it's that Stanton kid."

Brian's demeanor instantly changed and a pained expression crossed his face as he continued."I guess I didn't realize it before, but that Stanton kid is huge, isn't he? Naturally, as the future enforcer, I knew he was a decent-sized kid, but he looks like a grown-ass man. I have to admit, I'm a little worried about Scarlett."

"Scarlett can handle him," I answered.

"You think?"

"Don't worry. Luke will be putty in her hands," I told him.

"Where is she anyway?" he asked.

"No idea, but listen, Scarlett and I are going to have a hard time 'making nice' if it's this freaking boring around here. We need to figure out a way for us to spend more time with Aiden and Cade," I suggested. "Maybe even both at the same time. That would be fun, huh?"

We tossed around a few ideas but nothing sounded feasible until the perfect idea popped into my head. "Hey, what's today?"

"It's the 30th," Brian answered.

"Is it too late to put together a little New Year's Eve party?" I asked.

Brian actually thought my idea was great. He offered to go into town and buy whatever we would need. All we had to do was get Scarlett on board and the right guests at the party. We sat for a while and talked about what I could do or say at the party to really stir things up.

Soon the conversation took another turn when Brian let me know that whatever plans he and Dad had for Marcus was well underway. I knew better than to ask questions. If Dad wanted me on the in, he would have told me himself. I'm being kept in the dark, so whatever he has in store for Marcus had to be some pretty serious shit.

"I need to speak with your father, but I was thinking…in order to really weaken this pack, we should probably do something about the enforcer," Brian stated out of the blue.

"Luke's dad?" I clarified.

"Yes. Once Marcus is out of the picture, Phillip will most likely serve as interim until a new alpha is chosen. If Phillip isn't around… Phillip, excuse my language, chaps my ass. Plus, a pack without an enforcer is more vulnerable any way you look at it."

Marcus out of the picture? I started to ask what the hell that meant but decided to hold off, at least for the time being. Instead, I nodded my ahead and agreed. "I can see your point. What do you have in mind for him?"

"Let me worry about that. I'll get in touch with your dad," he said as he stood up to leave. He got to the stairs and then turned back to me. "I will keep you informed on what's going on with Phillip, but let's agree that Scarlett doesn't need to know about this."

"Without a doubt. Scarlett doesn't need to know anything," I agreed.

CHAPTER 19

Luke

My big plan to run until Scarlett was completely off my mind backfired on me within the first five minutes. I had barely made it passed the lake when I first noticed it. Immediately, I slowed to a walk, raising my nose and taking in a deep breath. The scent was faint at first, unrecognizable, but as I continued to follow it, the more and more my heart raced. Then I knew without a doubt who that scent belonged to. It was as fiery and spicy as its owner.

I should have turned and walked away. I should have known what would happen if I followed it, but there was something about that scent that called to me. With every inhale the blood flowing inside of me surged, and my chest tightened. The closer I came to her luscious scent, the more overwhelming the need to touch her, to taste her, to have her scent on my body became. By the time she came into view, my entire body was alive, and I was fighting to control the animal inside me.

Scarlett stood there in the woods, the most beautiful wolf I had ever seen. The current of electricity flowing between us was nearly visible. We stood there just looking at each other, a good fifty feet of forest separating us, but I had never felt closer to anyone before in my life. The moment felt intimate on a level I had never experienced. I was so entranced by her that I was only vaguely aware that she was walking my way.

When she stopped before me, we were so close I could actually feel warmth radiating from her rich, dark fur. The way her eyes were studying me told me that she was as equally intrigued with me as I was with her. She took a hesitant step to the right and continued her examination. As she circled me, I could hear her inhale deeply, taking my scent inside of her. The deep little growl of appreciation that escaped her nearly did me in. It took every ounce of restraint to just stand there and let her be in charge of this. I wanted—no, needed—to dominate, to chase her down and show her exactly who she was playing with.

Needing to move but not wanting to walk away, I sat back on my haunches and watched her. She finished her circle and sat right in front of me. We were nose-to-nose, eye-to-eye. Our breath mingled together in the cold night air. She was so beautiful, strong and lean, and even in this form her legs were long and sexy.

I was waiting for a signal, something from her showing me that she was relinquishing control. I knew she felt like she had the upper hand on me in our human forms; with a body like hers, how could she not? But not here. Not like this. *Come on Scarlett, let go.*

Then it happened. She lowered her eyes first, then her head. She was submitting. What happened next, I had no control over at all. I moved in closer and nuzzled my face in her neck. I think I surprised her because I felt her heart jump. Maybe it was mine. I didn't know how long I sat there, but it was long enough for her scent to burn itself into my memory forever.

It was when I finally did move away from Scarlett that things became real—fast. We were sitting there again simply watching each other when all of a sudden Scarlett leaned in. I thought she was going to nuzzle me back, but she didn't. She bit me, which shocked the shit out of me. It didn't hurt, but it was no gentle nip. No, it was definitely a bite. Afterwards, she sat there with this silly, wolfy grin thing going on like she was proud of herself. She was smiling at me one minute, and she took off the next.

Oh yeah, Scarlett knew exactly what she was doing. She knew that I would not be able to resist the chase. I took off after her as fast as I could. She was fast. With those long legs, she'd have to be, but she wasn't running at full speed because she wanted me to catch her. That was her game, and I was a willing player.

We weaved around the pine trees, jumped over a few large boulders, and slid down snow-covered hills. I stayed behind her, but close...very, very close. We ran further than I had ever run on the estate. When we came to the wall of a cliff, I knew I had her cornered. She had run herself right into a wall. She slowed when she realized that she was in trouble. I followed her lead and slowed as well. Scarlett turned so that she was facing me, but she continued to walk backward toward the cliff wall.

Once again, we were face to face, but this time I had the upper hand. We were no longer running, and I was by far the stronger wolf. She was looking to her left and to her right, trying to find a way around me. *Not going to happen.* I saw a slight tinge of panic on her face when her hind leg hit the wall, and she knew there was nowhere to run. I continued forward, confident that I had her just where I wanted her. Maybe a little too confident because she tried to cut around me, and she almost succeeded.

Before I knew what I was doing, I had tackled Scarlett to the ground. She fought like a champ. At one point, she actually had me on my back, but not for long. In one swift motion the tables were turned, and I had her pinned. She was trapped beneath me, unable to move. I looked down into her eyes and froze.

What the hell were we doing? Scarlett lifted her head off the snow and licked my face. I might have been confused for a moment before, but her kiss shot me straight back into the land of reality. Shit, I was supposed to be avoiding this girl, not running wild through the woods with her. I gave my head a little shake to try to clear my thoughts, but as I did, Scarlett began to wiggle underneath me. I had to get away. If I stayed here with her, we would end up doing something that neither one of us was ready for.

I backed away from her as fast as I could. The look in her eyes felt like a swift kick in the nuts. She looked hurt and maybe a little embarrassed by my retreat. I took a few more steps back, and then she was on her feet. I tried to look remorseful and apologetic, but in this form I didn't know if I was pulling it off. Scarlett took a step toward me and I freaked. I ran. I left Scarlett by the cliff and ran my sorry ass home.

CHAPTER 20

Scarlett

Seriously? Did that shitball actually just take off and leave me standing here like a lovesick cub again?

Lovesick... I am so not lovesick! I am not falling for the like-ya-one-second-running-like-hell-the-next wolf with commitment issues!

Oh God! I am! I am totally falling for Luke Stanton, the freakin' king of commitment issues. Damn it! Damn him! Damn my stupid, stupid heart.

No, no, no. This was not supposed to be happening. I was sent here to screw with Luke's head, not to let him screw with mine. Yet here I stood, in the middle of nowhere, alone and wanting nothing more than to take off after him and finish what we'd started, but I kept my paws planted firmly to the ground. I would not chase him. I would not follow.

My eyes searched the darkness for some sign of life. If I was being honest, I was searching for some sign of Luke. Pathetically hoping that maybe he would turn around. Come back for me. Involuntarily, I took a few steps toward the direction he'd run but reminded myself to stop and think. It took every ounce of restraint I had to force my body to sit. Impulse control was never my strong suit, and in wolf form, it was even more difficult.

What was with his hot-and-cold attitude? I didn't get it. If I had any sense at all, I would allow myself to face the fact that maybe he was just not that into me. But the look in his eyes told a different story. There was a fire there, a want that told me there had to more to it. Or maybe he was just leading me on. Was this all a game to him?

Get me all worked up and then shit all over me? Maybe he wanted to see how many times my pathetic ass would fall for it. He was probably with Gage laughing about our little romp through the woods right now. That sick, twisted mutt.

Oh my God, I'm such an idiot.

It was times like this that I needed a girlfriend. I could spill my heart out and sulk, and then she would tell me what a giant jerk Luke was and how I deserved so much better. How I should give him the cold shoulder and make him realize what he was missing out on.

Come to think of it, that might not be such a bad idea. Maybe I shouldn't be fawning all over Luke. If he was the player he seemed to be, maybe the cold-shoulder act would work. Either way, it was worth a shot. What I was doing wasn't working. Obviously. I wouldn't be standing here all alone if it was.

I was a fool to think for one second that Luke would come back for me, so half-heartedly, I headed back toward the estate, but I didn't run. Instead, I took my time, allowing my mind to process the last few days. Dad was going to want an update, and I wasn't too sure how much longer I could lie and get away with it. I couldn't exactly explain that I'd fallen for the guy and he seemed to want nothing to do with me. Epic fail.

By the time the estate was in sight. I'd decided to give it until after New Year's to admit that I'd failed at my mission. *Operation Cold Shoulder* was my last play. If that didn't work, I'd just have to admit defeat.

After locating my clothes and quickly dressing, I hurried back to what was now my home, at least for the time being. As I looked up at the ginormous house in front of me, it no longer looked as inviting. It no longer held the promise of whatever I'd hoped would happen when I stepped foot on the Red Ridge estate. Somehow, I'd convinced myself that it would all be so easy, but this whole ordeal was anything but.

With both my Dad and Drew's cars sitting in the driveway, I knew what would be waiting on the other side of the door, so I plastered a smile across my face and prayed they couldn't see through my façade.

Just as I'd assumed, Dad and Drew were sitting in the living room. I'd barely stepped foot inside before the questions began. "Have you been with Luke? How are things progressing?" my dad asked.

My eyes darted back and forth between Drew and my dad. Taking a moment to collect my thoughts, I wandered over to the couch. Hoping to appear relaxed, I took a seat as far away from Drew as possible and replied, "Good. It's going just as planned. And yes, I was with Luke." At least I didn't have to lie about that.

"And...?"

"And what?" I asked, avoiding eye contact with the both of them.

Drew let out a sigh as he sat back on the couch. "Well, I spent some time with Cade today. Got in his head a bit about Aiden and the alpha situation. Have you made any headway with Luke regarding backing Aiden?"

"I'm working on it. I had lunch with Luke, Aiden, and Teagan today. Luke and Aiden really seemed to be getting along, and I got to know Teagan better. I'm thinking if Aiden and Luke spend some more time together, Luke may change his mind about Cade."

"Scarlett, you aren't trying to find Luke a new BFF. That's not the enforcer's role. You know that," Dad chided.

"No, I know. I'm working on getting him to open up to me about what's going on with the alpha problem. That takes a bit of time. I can't just start prodding him for information. Once we talk about it, I'll start planting seeds about Aiden."

Another frustrated sigh escaped Drew's lips. "We don't have all the time in the world here. Get the boy between the sheets and after, when he's all satisfied and shit, get him talking about his feelings."

Holy Mother of God! I couldn't believe what I was hearing. *Get him between the sheets? Really?* I kept waiting for my dad to cut in and tell Drew he was out of line, but he didn't. He just sat there awaiting my reply. It was in that moment I knew without a doubt that everything Gavin had said was true. My own father really was whoring me out for the "good of the pack." He was using me just as he expected me to use Luke. And he didn't care if I had to have sex with the guy to get things done.

Well aware that my mouth was hanging open in shock, I couldn't seem to form words, which was probably a good thing being that anything I would have said in that moment probably would have gotten me a one-way ticket back to my own pack. Sign, sealed, delivered, and labeled *Failure*.

Finally, Dad spoke, but it wasn't to defend my honor. It was to give more orders. "Look, Scarlett. We need your head in the game. We are planning a New Year's Eve party for the pack teens, and you have tomorrow to get Luke at least leaning toward Aiden before the party. Drew has plans to shake things up during the party, so you need to do your part."

All I could manage was a nod of my head, and without another word, I headed up to my room. I managed to hold it together until the door was shut behind me. Then I fell to the floor and finally allowed myself to wallow in the sorrow and regret that had been brewing inside me since I watched Luke take off in the night.

CHAPTER 21

Drew

Scarlett made a pretty large shopping list for her father, but at the last minute—after describing pita chips to Brian for the third time—she decided that she'd better go with him. So that left me to make the calls inviting everyone to our New Year's Eve party. Brian made a point to ask Marcus's permission for us to have the party at the house. Marcus thought it was a great idea to keep all the kids on the estate. He agreed it was much safer that way. He even gave Brian a phone list, so that we could call and invite everyone.

I started making the calls as soon as Scar and Brian left for town. It didn't take long and with the exception of Luke and Gage, who I didn't even get a hold of, everyone seemed excited about the party. I wasn't surprised that any of these losers didn't already have plans for tonight.

I tried calling both Gage and Luke one more time but they didn't answer. I thought about leaving a voicemail, but I needed Luke at the party. So I decided to walk over to Luke's and see if he was home and just not answering the phone. I grabbed my coat and hit the road. At least the major players, except Luke, had agreed to be there. Aiden was excited about the party, especially when I lied to him and told him that Cade had mentioned to me how he was hoping that Aiden and Teagan had made other plans and wouldn't be able to come. Aiden fell for it without question, just as I expected. Cade, on the other hand, didn't seem too thrilled about the event, though he accepted the invitation. I didn't give a shit about his lack of enthusiasm as long as he showed up. Now I just had to make sure Luke was there so Scarlett could work her magic.

As luck would have it, Luke and Gage were pulling up just as I got to his house.

"Hey Gavin, what's up?" Luke asked when he saw me coming his way.

"Excellent. You're both here. Scar and I are having a little New Year's Eve thing at the house tonight. Last minute, I know, but it should be fun," I managed, proud of myself for keeping the sarcasm out of my voice. "So, can you make it?" I asked them both.

I noticed that Gage didn't respond until Luke did.

"Sorry man, I have plans tonight," Luke said, but I could tell he was lying.

"That's too bad. We were hoping that you could make it. Well, what about you, Gage?" I asked.

"I'll try to make it," he said, but I knew he wouldn't show without Luke.

"Great! Cade and Aiden seemed pretty excited about it," I lied, or at least half-lied.

"Cade and Aiden are both going?" Luke asked.

"Sure," I said. "Everyone will be there. Well...with the exception of you. Too bad you can't make it."

Luke crossed his arms over his chest, looked over at Gage, and sighed. "I'll guess I can drop by for a while."

The dickhead didn't even try to hide his frustration, but I didn't give a shit. He would be there and that's what matters, so mission accomplished. "All right, man, see you guys tonight then." I said as I walked down the driveway.

I knew that Luke wouldn't be able to refuse if he knew that both Cade and Aiden would be there. He was well aware just how volatile the situation could get between those two. Cade and Aiden in the same room together, both with a few drinks in them? Something was bound to happen. It may be Luke's job to keep them from going at each other's throats, but it was now my job to make sure it happened.

CHAPTER 22

Luke

"Looking good, Pops. Where are you going all dressed up?" I asked when I saw my dad sporting his best suit and tie.

"I'm driving out to Santa Fe with Michelle. You remember her? She runs the Red Mountain Ski resort in town. You met her a couple of months ago when we were snowboarding. Well, the Marriott in Santa Fe is having a New Year's Eve Ball, and she wants to go so we are going to be staying there tonight. I should be back fairly early tomorrow though. Michelle has to be back at work," he explained like he thought he needed my approval.

"Sounds fun," I said, trying not to sound sarcastic. Of course I remembered her. Hot for a domestic.

"What about you? I heard there's a big party on the estate tonight. You planning on going with Cami?" he casually asked, which of course surprised the hell out of me.

"How did you know about Cami?"

Dad gave me look that told me it was his responsibility, and would one day be mine, to know everything that goes on around here.

"Cami dumped me," I admitted, trying not to smile at the thought of it.

"Oh yeah? I wonder why on earth she would do that."

I knew he was fucking with me. We may not talk about it, but he was aware of my track record with girls. He grinned at me as he straightened his tie, and I just shook my head and laughed. Then he turned to look in the mirror and said, "Smart girl."

"I can't believe you just said that!" I slapped him on the back for giving me crap.

"I'm just messing with you. I like Cami. She's a sweet girl. Pretty, too. Oh well, don't let it get you down. You're young, no need to rush things. So what are you doing tonight?"

"I'm going to the party. I don't really want to, but Cade and Aiden are both going, and I feel like something bad will happen if I'm not there to stop it," I told him.

"You're a smart kid. You know that? We're going to have to do something about this situation we are in. I don't like it one bit. It makes us look weak and exposed. Watch those two boys tonight. Don't let things between them get out of hand while I'm gone," he instructed, shaking his head.

"Normally, I wouldn't worry about Cade losing his head around anyone, but lately I just can't read him very well," I admitted, which caused a worried look to appear on my father's face.

"You think it's because of the mating?"

"Maybe. I never really thought about it. Cade is different though. He's more...I don't know how to explain it...real. Does that make sense?" I asked. "It's like he's nicer and more aware of other people's feelings and shit. He completely threw me off guard the other day when he told me that Gage was back in town. He was almost apologetic, and I swear I seriously thought he was going to hug me."

My dad just laughed. "You guys have known each other your whole lives. It makes sense. Maybe he did feel bad for Gage and for you."

"Yeah, but that's what I mean. The old Cade wouldn't have cared about my feelings. It's just weird."

"You think being mated has made him weak?" he asked.

"No, I think it's had the opposite effect. I think it's made him stronger, but more volatile as well. Which is why I'm worried about tonight. Aiden doesn't know when to stop, and Cade is so unpredictable right now. If something were to go down tonight, and since I'm sure there will be some alcohol involved, it's completely possible, Aiden's not going to know what the hell to do."

"Cade's not stronger then you though, right? I'm sure you can handle it. But if you think I should stay, I will." His concern was more than evident in his voice worried.

"Please, he's not even close. Cade would never take me on. No, you go. I can handle them. I would just rather not have to, you know?" I assured him.

"Yeah, but maybe I should stay here just in case something happens."

"No. Dad, I've got this. Really. Go to Santa Fe. Have a little fun. I'm probably overreacting, and if I'm not, then I will step in and squash the situation. You've trained me well." I walked him to the door. He was still thinking about staying, I could tell, but he relented and picked up his overnight bag.

On the way out to his car, he gave me the speech: the one where he tells me not to drink and drive, to be careful about what I say and do around the humans, and to always be smart and protect myself and whoever I'm with. He's been giving me that speech for so long I swear I have it memorized.

Once he was gone, I headed back inside to take a shower and get ready for the party. If only I could bring a date with me tonight, maybe then I could keep my mind off Scarlett for a while. But that was completely out of the question. There was no way in hell I could show up to a party on the estate with a domestic, but that thought gave me an idea. What I needed was an after-party and a date; a night out with some girl with no emotions, no strings, no promises, and no pack. Just a human girl to take my mind off of Scarlett. Without a second thought, I grabbed my phone and made the call.

"Luke! I was just thinking about you!" Taylor, a very hot, blonde cheerleader from my English class answered.

"How's my favorite girl?" I asked.

"Lonely," she moaned. "You haven't texted me all break."

"I'm sorry, babe, but I'm calling you now. Listen, you free tonight?" I asked.

"As it turns out I am free. Which brings me to why I was thinking about you. Want to keep me company tonight? My parents just left to go visit my brother and his family in Albuquerque and won't be back until Sunday, so I'm having some people over to ring in the New Year. And when I kick everyone out, I don't want to be in this big, scary house all alone..."

"Oh, so you need me to come keep you safe?" I teased.

"You know it!"

"I have this family thing that I have to go to, but I'll cut out early. I'll text you when I'm on the way."

"Great! Make sure you're here by midnight so we can celebrate together. I don't want to miss my New Year's Eve kiss," she cooed.

It was that easy. Taylor was one of the hottest girls in school, and we both understood each other. She knew I didn't do the whole relationship thing. Sure, she was looking for someone who could one day whisk her away from her ultra-religious family and this sleepy little town, but until she found him, she was always more than willing to have a little fun with me. I hoped that after the evening was over, I'd be able to forget all about Scarlett Reed... at least for a little while. Just long enough for her to move back to her pack, and then I would be able to move on with my life.

Feeling a lot better about tonight than I did earlier, I took a shower, got dressed, and sent Gage a text telling him that I was on my way to the party.

CHAPTER 23

Scarlett

Surveying the kitchen, I cringed at the thought of playing party host to a bunch of people I hardly knew. Chips, dips, and snacks covered the island, and there was enough alcohol to support a fully functioning bar at a nightclub on a busy Saturday night. Apparently, step one of the New Year's Eve party plan was to get the partygoers hammered.

Knowing this was all a ruse to get Aiden and Cade in the same room only served to intensify the guilt churning inside me. At home, when this whole thing was just a distant plan, it all sounded like such a great idea. Now it just seemed harsh and cruel. More than anything, I wanted to make my father proud. The fact that he actually asked for my help made me feel like his daughter again and not just a body that took up space in his home, a nuisance unworthy of a second of his time. But this was not our pack, and in my heart, I knew we had no business being here trying to ruin them. Suddenly, it was difficult to remember why I'd ever agreed to be a part of this. What was I thinking? Was pleasing my father really worth it? I wasn't sure, especially now that I knew just how far he expected me to go to get things done.

And then there was Luke. The fact that Luke would surely be here didn't help my already frazzled nerves. If only I could flip a switch and turn my feelings off. I wasn't supposed to care about this guy, but I couldn't deny it. I liked Luke— a lot. Too much. This was one hell of a hiccup in our little plan. If Luke found out why we were all really here, he'd never speak to me again. My heart constricted at the thought, and the need to flee overwhelmed me.

I started for the front door, ready to run, to get as far away from this place as I could. It was my go-to response when life became too much to handle. But as if on cue, the door swung open and Drew entered. He looked at me and then at his watch. "What the hell are you doing? Why aren't you dressed? People are going to start showing up any minute now."

Without waiting for a response, Drew practically herded me up the stairs. "Go, go, go!" he demanded. "You have ten minutes to make yourself irresistible, so hurry the hell up."

My legs carried me up the stairs, and I did what I was expected to do. I refused to allow myself to think about anything other than just getting ready for the party. Pushing my conscience aside, ignoring the fact that what we were doing was completely fucked up, I touched up my makeup, ran a straightening iron through my hair, and turned to my closet to find something to wear.

With no time to spare, I stepped back and took a look at myself in the full-length mirror that hung on the bathroom door. An all-too-familiar feeling washed over me. Perfect hair, perfect makeup, and the perfect outfit covered up the real me. Underneath it all, there was a girl screaming to get out, a girl who would make the right decision. A girl who would refuse to be a pawn in her pack's plan. But I couldn't think about her right now. When the doorbell rang, I turned away from the reflection that filled me with guilt and hurried downstairs to greet the first of our guests.

By the time I'd made it to the foyer, Drew was already leading Becca, Shari, Sammy, Ryder, Cami, Teagan, and Aiden into the kitchen toward the makeshift bar. As the group filled their cups, I wandered in to say hello. They all, even Becca, politely replied, but Teagan came over and hugged me as if we were old friends.

Somehow that simple act eased my discomfort, and I almost thanked her.

Teagan smiled and said, "This is your party. Let's get you a drink."

Reaching for a cup, I replied, "That is exactly what I need." I filled my cup to the brim with the Sangria punch I'd made earlier and finally began to relax.

Alli and Cade arrived as I swallowed the last drop of my fruity concoction, and by the time I gotten my first refill, everyone else had arrived—everyone besides Luke and Gage. I may have loosened up a bit, but that didn't stop the fluttering butterflies in my stomach. They were like butterflies on crack, and I cursed myself for being so damn nervous. Teagan must have noticed me surveying the room since she leaned over and whispered, "So have you heard from Luke?"

"No, but I think he is coming." I shrugged my shoulders, trying to appear indifferent.

My father had instructed me to talk to Luke today but that didn't play into *Operation Cold Shoulder*, which after two cups of punch was sounding more and more like a fabulous idea. I had it all planned in my semi-fuzzy head. I'd say a quick hello if he happened to pass by, but other than that, I'd keep my distance. I'd stay in view, so he could see me, but I'd stick to the rules: no eye contact, no flirty smiles, and absolutely no touching.

Seconds later, Teagan nudged me lightly with her shoulder. "Well, speak of the devil." I didn't need to look to know who had just walked into the house. Even if she hadn't said a word, I would have known that Luke Stanton had arrived. It was as if the air in the room shifted, and his presence filled my senses. Every nerve in my body was on high alert as he entered the kitchen to grab a beer.

My hungry eyes drifted his way, and when they met his, it took everything I had to stay on two feet. His dark hair was perfectly disheveled, and his chiseled cheekbones and crooked smile screamed *beware of bad boy*. Add that to his black shirt that couldn't even begin to hide the rippling muscles underneath and the tattered jeans that hung low on his hips, and he was a walking recipe for heartbreak.

My God, he was beautiful.

His eyes held mine for a beat too long before he finally said, "Hey Scarlett." With a beer in hand, he awaited my reply.

Tearing my eyes from his, I focused on Gage, who stood beside him, and replied, "Hey guys. Glad you both could make it." Then, I refilled my cup once again and fled from the kitchen.

CHAPTER 24

Drew

Who the hell knew that there was this many people our age in this pack? By ten o'clock our living room and kitchen were jam-packed. We had the music going, compliments of Aiden's iPod. I swear that fool has the weirdest taste in music, but whatever, people were dancing and drinking, and that's what mattered. I'd asked Brian buy me a bottle of something for shots. Personally, I don't touch the stuff, but I planned on getting Cade and Aiden drunk, so some hard liquor was a must-have.

As I began making my rounds through the party, bottle of Jaeger in hand, I ran into Becca. She was with a bunch of girls dancing to some crazy-ass hip-hop song about Humpty Dumpty or something. She reached out and grabbed me around the waist, pulling me in to dance with her. As she grinded herself against me, I offered her the bottle, and she smiled before seductively placing the bottle to her lips and taking a sip. Instead of handing the bottle back to me, she passed it off her friends. Perfect!

When the stupid song was over, I grabbed the Jaeger out of some girl's hand and went in search of my two new best friends. I saw Aiden first. He was standing near the speaker dock laughing with Teagan and Alli. They all had a beer in their hands, so I let them be and scanned the crowd for Cade. I spotted him talking to Gage and Luke, so I hung back and waited. Cade would be easier to influence without his bodyguard standing next to him.

A few minutes later, Cade was alone and watching the conversation that had his mate smiling and laughing out loud. I walked over and handed him the bottle with a shrug. To my surprise, he grabbed it and took a long pull of the hard liquor. He tried to hand it back, but I put my hands up. "You look like you need that more than I do."

Without responding, he took another swig and then handed it to me.

When "Ice Ice Baby" blasted through the speakers, I seriously contemplated smashing that freaking iPod into pieces, but once again, I told myself that all that mattered was that people were having a good time. I rolled my eyes as almost everyone started rapping along with the song and dancing, even Scarlett.

"Aiden sure is the life of the party, isn't he?" I mentioned to Cade. Aiden seemed to be the only guy in the room who could actually dance, and he successfully got everyone on the makeshift dance floor riled up as he made his way through the crowed rapping every word while he moved to the beat.

Cade kind of laughed a little and reached out for the bottle again. This was my chance, since he seemed kind of pissed already. "I hope you don't mind me saying this, but Aiden can't run this pack. I mean, look at him. He's more cruise director than alpha. And who the hell even has this shit on their iPod?"

Cade took another gulp before he muttered, "It comes down to birth date."

"Screw that. What's he, like a couple months older then you? It should come down to one thing: he doesn't belong in that position and you do."

Cade shrugged. "I hope the elders see it that way."

"You're going to let it go to a vote? Why? Just fight him for it. It'd be an easy win," I suggested.

Cade stared at the crowd. Aiden was dancing and rapping in the middle. Everyone surrounded him, arms in the air, cheering him on.

Cade's jaw clenched before he threw his head back for another shot. Then he took a deep breath and admitted, "It's complicated."

I raised an eyebrow at him while I pretended to take a sip from the bottle he handed me.

"It is," he said. "He's my half brother, my mate's brother, and it would kill Alli if I hurt him." Cade chuckled to himself before he added, "And if he actually ended up hurting me, she'd kill him. I just can't do it…he's family."

"Family? Does he see it that way? He's trying to take something that's yours. It's been yours for eighteen years. Just because he's a few months older than you doesn't make him an alpha," I pointed out and handed the bottle back to him.

Cade took one more gulp and turned toward me. With slurred words, he admitted, "You know man, you're right. He would destroy everything my family worked so hard for if he tried to lead this pack. He doesn't know the first thing about being a wolf, much less the alpha. I just hope that everyone will see that, before it's too late."

His eyes were well on their way to being glazed over, and the way he started talking with his hands told me my plan to get Cade loaded was a success. He handed me the empty bottle. "I need a beer. Want one?"

"Nah," I answered, "but you go on and get you one. Looks like you're going to need it." And that was it. He stumbled toward the kitchen. I didn't know for sure if he was as pissed as I wanted him to be, but he was definitely trashed. Mission accomplished.

CHAPTER 25

Luke

I'd been there for over an hour and "*Hey guys, glad you could both make it*" was all that Scarlett had said to me. I was the one who was supposed to be ignoring her, not the other way around. As much as I tried not to look at her, I couldn't seem to stop myself. Her hair was straight and flowing down her back. I'd never seen it straight, and I couldn't stop imagining what it would feel like to run my fingers through it. To use all those silky, dark strands to pull her against me and force her to stop ignoring me.

Completely absorbed in my own dirty little fantasyland, I didn't see Becca until she fell into me and proceeded to get right up in my face. Already completely smashed to the point of being extremely loud and obnoxious, she laughed at her almost-tumble to the ground and then grabbed my arm.

"Luke!" she yelled as she pressed her body up against mine. "Come dance with me."

I put a bit of distance between us and replied, "Not a chance."

"God…*My name is Luke, and I am so boring. I never want to have any fun*," she whined and then laughed at her own joke.

"Nice."

She turned to Gage, who was standing by my side watching the Becca show. "Gage, tell him. Tell him that he is too damn hot to be so damn borrriinnnggg."

I glared at Gage, warning him with my eyes not to encourage her, but he couldn't help his sorry ass. "Luke, my friend, you are too damn hot to be so damn boring."

That did it. I warned him, but he didn't listen, not that I should be surprised. He never did, but I wasn't going to let him off the hook for this one. It was time for a little payback. "Hey Becs, did you know that this is Gage's all-time favorite song?"

Gage's cocky grin quickly faded, and he looked like he just might kill me when Becca squealed and clapped her hands together. A second later, he was being dragged to the dance floor, and it was my turn to laugh at him. I threw in a little wave just to top it off.

Disaster averted, I wandered into the kitchen to grab another beer. Scarlett was leaning against the counter talking to Shari. As soon as our eyes met, she looked away, not even bothering to acknowledge me, which pissed me off. But that didn't stop me from eyeing her gorgeous body from head to toe. This girl was temptation personified. All I could think about was running my hands—and if I was really lucky, my tongue—over every inch of her. It should be illegal to be so fucking sexy. Just looking at her made me hard, and I couldn't control myself any longer.

"Hey good-looking," Shari teased as I walked up to the two of them.

"Why aren't you in there dancing the night away with Becs?" I asked Shari, but I could barely manage to take my eyes off of Scarlett.

Shari laughed. "Are you kidding? Someone has to stay somewhat sober to make sure she doesn't do anything stupid. Like take advantage of your boy Gage over there. She's practically dry-humping him on the dance floor."

I turned to see if I could spot Gage just as Scarlett grabbed her cup and said, "Will you excuse me for a minute?" She didn't wait for an answer before she took off like the house was on fire.

I stood there completely dumbfounded. Her hot, spicy scent, now completely embedded into my memory, washed over me as she squeezed past. My body responded and begged me to grab her and make her stay, but I somehow managed to control myself. I waited for her to turn around, to give me that look, the one that would tell me that she wanted me as much as I wanted her. It never came.

I figured that was it, then. She wasn't interested. I should have been relieved; it was what I wanted after all. I thought it would be best to pretend that there wasn't that spark, that insanely intense chemistry between us. I'd actually convinced myself that if she would stop flirting with me that I would be able to forget about her, but I swear to God, her walking away just made me want her more.

I watched as she disappeared into the crowd, and this unexplainable, anxiety-ridden pain formed in my chest. I tried to breathe it away, but it just traveled down past my stomach and turned into a pain I knew too well these days. A pain I would have to get Taylor to alleviate for me later.

Shit, Taylor. I looked at my watch to make sure I still had time to get to her house by midnight. I desperately needed Scarlett out of my damn head, and I was hoping that a night with Taylor would do the trick.

Shari decided to go check on Becca so I followed behind her, figuring I'd rescue Gage before I left. On the way there, I noticed Cade and Gavin standing by the stairs sharing a bottle of something. Cade drinking hard liquor was never a good sign, especially since there was an empty bottle of Jaeger sitting on the bottom stair by his foot. I hadn't seen him drink anything except beer since we were fifteen and Gage stole a bottle of tequila from his old man. We all paid dearly for that, both from our dads and from the damn tequila.

"Luke! Man, when did you get here?" Aiden kind of slurred when we approached Becca and her new boy-toy. Gage would never admit it, but he appeared to be enjoying himself. Maybe he didn't need rescuing after all. Aiden threw his arm around me, and announced, "I'm glad you're here. You need a beer." Obviously, he had already had too much to drink because I'd been here for a while, and we had already talked.

He grabbed a half-empty beer off a nearby table and shoved it in my hand. "Come on bro, let's take this party outside to the fire pit. It's hot as shit in here."

Following the guys outside, I was hoping I'd run into Scarlett again, but I didn't see her. I shook the thought out of my head and reminded myself, *Taylor, you know, the smokin' hot piece of ass waiting for me! I'm supposed to be figuring out a way to get out of here for Taylor!*

I decided to stick around for a few more minutes once both Cade and Aiden made their way outside. Before I ran off, I needed to make sure neither of them started any shit. It was surprisingly warm standing around the fire, and thankfully everybody appeared to be getting along and having a good time. Even Cade and Aiden were talking and laughing, not with each other, but in the same vicinity. But all too soon, the entire climate changed as soon as a few girls came outside to join us.

Becca staggered over our way and announced to the group, "Look! Alpha one and alpha two seem to be getting along so well...almost like they were, oh I don't know, brothers." She giggled to herself and slapped Aiden on the back.

I glanced over at Aiden, who was still smiling, but the raging storm in his eyes told a different story. Cade wasn't smiling at all.

"What did I say?" Becca feigned apology. "All I meant was that it's nice to see that you two have finally figured it out. I don't even know what Marcus was thinking. Cade is clearly the only choice for alpha." She turned to Aiden and continued, "I mean really, Aiden. Did you think you had a chance? You may be hot as hell, but alpha material? I think not."

"Stay out of it, Becca. Nothing has been decided yet," Cade warned.

"That's a shame. Oh well, so a fight then? Like they did back in the good old days! I guess it won't be much of a fight though, will it Cade? Poor Aiden doesn't really stand a chance. Just try not to kill him when you're ripping him to shreds," Becca said, looking over at Aiden with pity in her eyes.

And here we go. This is exactly the reason why I needed to be here instead of screwing Taylor's brains out. Fuck!

"Becca," I warned. She looked over to me and smiled innocently. I marched over, and she practically fell into my arms. I picked her drunken ass up, tossed her over my shoulder, and started for the house. As I was carrying her in, I heard some of the guys laughing and then Gage cooed, *"Oh Luke! You're so strong! My hero! I love all your rippling muscles!"* I turned around and flipped the guys off.

I carried Becca straight through the kitchen and into the front room, attracting the attention of some of the girls. I laid her down on the sofa and Shari took over from there. As I turned to go back outside, I saw the time on the television. Damn it! I glanced down at my watch only to have it confirm that I had less than an hour to make it to Taylor's by midnight.

I was just about to find Gage and tell him that I was leaving when I heard shouting coming from the yard. I ran back outside and stood at the back of the small crowd that had gathered since I'd left. I didn't know who had started it, or even how it started, but it had evidently escalated very quickly, and I'd gotten there just as all hell was breaking lose.

"You think just because it's your damn birthright to be the alpha means you actually have the balls to run this pack?" Cade yelled, standing toe-to-toe with Aiden in the middle of the crowd.

Alli pushed herself through the throng and abruptly stopped when she saw what was going on. Her hand flew to her mouth. She stood there frozen as she watched her mate and her brother prepare to beat the shit out of each other. Just then, Teagan came rushing out the back door with Scarlett following close behind. Alli knew better than to get in the middle of two male wolves, but apparently Teagan didn't. Thankfully, Scarlett grabbed her arm and held her away from them.

"What the fuck did you just say to me?" Aiden returned, bumping his chest into Cade's.

"You heard me, bro. You want to fight it out? Let's do this. I'm ready to end all doubt around here. I'm going to be the next alpha, and if I have to kick your ass right here in front of everyone, then that's what I'll do," Cade threatened.

I needed to intervene, but I wanted to give them a chance to decide that this whole thing was ridiculous, that this drunken backyard fight would do nothing to settle things between them. It would only intensify things. But I knew that wouldn't happen when Aiden pushed off of Cade's chest and said, "Well, now's your chance. Come on. Come at me, bro!"

Cade took a step toward Aiden but was stopped in his tracks by Aiden's fist. Aiden landed a hard right across Cade's jaw. Cade took a few steps back, visibly trembling trying to control the change. For a moment, I thought he had it. I watched him take a deep breath, roll his shoulders back, and shake his head a bit, but then without warning he was on all fours growling a bone-chilling warning to his brother standing before him.

To everyone's surprise, Aiden didn't back down. Instead, he smiled wickedly, took off his jacket, and kicked off his shoes. Too soon, I was watching two alpha males ready to attack. I waited, not wanting to overstep, but knowing that it was my job to.

At the first scent of blood I knew I had no choice.

CHAPTER 26

Scarlett

Standing at the edge of the back patio, my mind could hardly wrap itself around the scene taking place before me. It had taken every ounce of willpower I could muster to stay inside when the guys began to make their way out to the fire pit. I had a feeling something bad was bound to happen, especially after watching Drew practically pour alcohol down Cade's throat. That coupled with the way Cade was eyeballing Aiden, I could only imagine the line of bullshit Drew had been feeding him.

I tried to keep Teagan occupied, but it wasn't long before the shouting began and everyone was rushing outside. I'd grabbed Teagan by the arm and pulled her back before she ended up caught between two very angry alphas. As soon as Cade and Aiden shifted, I turned my attention to Luke. With frustration written all over his face, Luke's eyes found mine among the crowd, and seconds later, a menacing growl exploded from deep within his throat and Luke transformed, his wolf form completely looming over the two smaller wolves.

Massive and strong, his muscles rippled under his dark fur as he took off toward Cade and Aiden, who were already well into the throes of a massive brawl. As Luke approached, the wolves separated, but only slightly, just enough for Cade to rear up to attack Aiden once again, but Luke was too close. Instead of striking Aiden, one of Cade's claws caught Luke and sliced its way down the side of Luke's face. Luke let out a sinister snarl, and the rest of the pack began backing away from the fight as Luke lunged for both wolves.

With his teeth, Luke grabbed Cade by the back of the neck and tossed him aside. Cade's body flew through the air and landed in a crumpled pile on the ground several feet away. Turning his attention back to Aiden, Luke slowly prowled toward him, a low growl rumbling from his body. When Aiden backed away immediately, I knew the fight was over. Surely Aiden wouldn't be stupid enough to make another move when Luke looked more than ready to rip someone's throat out.

With a towel in hand, Alli ran over to Cade. She covered him as he shifted back and then threw her arms around him once she was sure he was okay. Teagan followed suit, but I noticed no one was there to help Luke. No one came running to his aid, and for a brief moment, I'd almost convinced myself to just walk away, but I couldn't. *Operation Cold Shoulder* would have to be put on hold for the moment. I hurried inside and grabbed a small blanket off the couch. Rushing to get back, I noticed Cami with a towel headed toward Luke. She gave me a small smile and stopped. She nodded her head toward Luke as if to give me permission to go to him. I didn't need permission, but it was kind of her to let me be the one to help him.

My human eyes met those of the enormous wolf before me, and I held the blanket out in front of me but diverted my eyes so that he could shift back. Seconds later, he took the blanket, and as his hand touched mine, a chill ran up my back. I didn't look at him as I began to walk away, but I didn't get far. His fingers wrapped around my arm, pulling me to a halt.

"Thank you, Scarlett." Luke's husky voice sent me reeling. Feelings I barely understood were brewing inside me, but I couldn't let him see it. I couldn't let him see how much his touch affected me. When he didn't let go, I turned to face him. The blanket was wrapped around his waist, leaving his perfectly sculpted chest exposed. My greedy eyes slowly wandered up to his face, and a small gasp escaped my lips when I noticed the cut along his cheek. Blood ran down the side of his face.

More than anything, I wanted to be the one to help him. Resisting the urge to reach out to touch his cheek, I said, "You're bleeding."

He didn't respond. The softness of his expression shifted in an instance as his eyes left mine to glare back and forth between Aiden and Cade. No words were spoken, but the cold, steely look in his eyes said it all. They needed to get the hell out of there. In no time, Cade and Alli headed off toward Cade's, and Teagan and Aiden were gone just as quickly. The rest of the pack scattered as well, leaving Luke and me standing there alone.

Luke picked up some athletic shorts that someone must have left him from the ground and began dressing. I turned away to give him some privacy and a chance for me to cool down. The anger in his eyes had only dissipated slightly and heat still radiated from his body even though it was freezing outside.

I hesitantly took the blanket from his hand and held it gently to the gash on his face. "Come inside. Let's get you cleaned up." Cade's claw did quite a bit of damage, and even though he'd heal quickly, it needed to be cleaned so that it didn't get infected.

With a small smile, Luke took the blanket from my hand, and he slipped his fingers between my own and led me inside. We walked hand in hand past Drew, who, now that the excitement was over, appeared to be quite content out on the porch with Becca. He came up for air just long enough to give me a nod of approval; I, in turn, shook my head in disgust.

The house was ominously quiet, and as Luke and I passed the huge grandfather clock in the living room, I noticed it was close to midnight. So much for ringing in the New Year.

We entered the bathroom, and under the sink I found some alcohol, cotton balls, and butterfly bandages. With my hands full of first-aid supplies, I turned to face Luke. He let the blanket drop from his hands, and to my surprise, his hands found my waist and lifted me up to the sit on the counter, positioning his body between my legs.

"There. Now you can reach me, Nurse Scarlett."

Heat fired its way through my body, and I felt the blush creeping over my cheeks. Diverting my eyes, I opened the alcohol and wet a cotton ball. Trying to hide the fact that his nearness was all but killing me, I teased, "All right, tough guy. Stay still. I can't promise this won't hurt."

I gently pressed the cotton ball to his cheek. Cringing slightly, he sucked in his breath, and before I could stop it, a smile broke out across my face at the thought of this big, strong guy unable to stand the sting. Unconsciously, my eyes drifted back to his, and his intense gaze caused my already racing pulse to quicken even more.

With his lips only inches from my own, I fought back the urge to lean in and taste him, but I wasn't giving in. I couldn't handle the rejection if he turned away, even though I wanted nothing more than to wrap my arms around his neck and force his body closer to mine. Tearing my eyes from his, I hastily opened the butterfly bandages and gently placed them over the fresh wound. Suddenly, Luke's fingers traced their way across my cheek, then through my hair. With his other hand, he tilted my chin up so that I would look at him once more.

The fire in his eyes caused my body to react in ways I'd never experienced before. Desire pooled deep in my stomach and I suddenly found it hard to breathe. Luke ran his thumb over my needy lips as he leaned in slowly. Staying completely still, I closed my eyes and waited for his perfect mouth to press against my own. Though I couldn't see him, I knew he was only a breath away. I could feel the heat from his closeness, smell that familiar scent that was all his own. I'd never wanted anything more than just one taste of Luke as I stood there breathing him in.

But just before his lips touched mine, Luke's phone went off, alerting him of an incoming text. We both flinched and my eyes flew open. His phone sat on the counter next to me, and I couldn't have stopped myself if I'd tried. Without thinking, I peeked at the screen, and my heart sank at what I read.

> Where ya at, baby? ur going to miss my
> midnight kiss ☺

A stiff moment passed between us and awkwardness filled the air. Trying my best to keep the disappointment out of my voice, I said, "You better go. It will be midnight any minute." As if on cue, the grandfather clock began to chime announcing that midnight was upon us.

With a deep sigh, Luke looked down and slowly closed his eyes. Barely a second had passed when his hand moved toward the phone, and I knew for sure our moment was over. But he didn't pick up the phone. Instead he forcefully shoved it aside, and before I could process what was happening his fingers were tangled in my hair and his lips collided with mine.

His kiss was hard and full of need, causing every nerve ending in my body to awaken. With firm hands, he tilted my head to the side, and when a small moan involuntarily escaped from my lips, Luke took the opportunity to deepen the kiss. With his tongue, he explored my mouth while his hands ran down my arms to my waist. He pulled my body forward and pressed himself against me. I wrapped my legs around him as my head fell back. Trailing kisses down my neck, Luke's hands ran down my thighs and then back up to grab my ass, pulling me even closer. With my fingers entangled in his hair, I gently guided his lips back to mine. I needed more. I needed him. My body ached, called out for him, and I had to force my hands to remain where they were so that I didn't start tearing my clothes off.

Luke inhaled deeply without breaking our kiss, and I knew he wanted me too. If one of us didn't pull away, our clothes would surely end up on the bathroom floor. As if he'd read my mind, he kissed me gently one last time and then whispered breathlessly in my ear, "Happy New Year, Scarlett."

CHAPTER 27

Drew

That was just too easy, I thought as I sat eating my breakfast the morning after the fight. All it took was a little booze to loosen them up and a few encouraging words, and Cade and Aiden did the rest themselves. Well, Becca did help things along. It was freaking fantastic! At first, I thought things were going a little too well at the party, that Cade and Aiden were being too civil, but as soon as Becca opened her big mouth, everything fell into place.

"Morning," I said as Brian came in the room. I couldn't read his expression, but I knew something was up because he didn't seem too happy about last night.

"Quite the party, I heard," Brian replied as he poured himself a cup of coffee.

"It was perfect. I wish someone would have caught it on video because it was freakin' hilarious!" I said, smiling at the memory of those two douche bags ripping into each other. If only Luke hadn't stepped in and ended the brawl.

"Well Marcus is furious!" Brian snapped.

"I bet he is."

"He's called a meeting. We need to get going pretty soon. Is Scarlett up yet?" he asked.

I got up to throw my trash away and place my plate in the sink. "Don't know. Haven't seen her. I do know that she helped patch Luke up last night after he got scratched," I told him, hoping the news might ease the tension in the air.

"She needs to get up. You and Scarlett need to be prepared to take some of the heat from last night. Marcus is mostly upset about the fight, but he was also pissed about the alcohol at the party. Of course, I couldn't tell him that I had purchased it, so naturally he assumed that you did," he explained.

As I washed my hands, I shrugged my shoulders. "Is Marcus blind? Hell, there's more underage drinking going on here than back home. What the hell does he think they're all doing down by the lake all the time? Anyway, I don't care. I'll take the heat. It's a small price to pay. The faster this pack crumbles, the faster we can go home. I'm already tired of being here."

Brian didn't respond. He glanced down at his watch, took another sip of his coffee, and then looked at his watch again. Message received. I headed upstairs to go wake up Scarlett.

*****

Ten minutes later, Brian and I were getting in the car. Scarlett needed more time, so she said that she would meet us there, but Brian wanted to be early. As soon as we were out of the driveway, I gave Brian a play-by-play of the night before, mostly because he needed to know what Luke was capable of.

"Luke is no joke. I knew he was strong, but seriously, I've never seen anything like it. He ended the fight in seconds. He grabbed Cade by the back of the neck and tossed him aside like he was nothing. Shit, all he had to do was look at Aiden, and he backed off immediately."

"What happened then?" he asked.

"Nothing. All three turned back and just stood there. Cade looked at Luke and then left the party without another word. Aiden took a few steps toward him, but Luke put his hand up to stop him. Aiden got the hint and walked away too. That was it. Party over. I tell you, people either are afraid of Luke or they really respect him and his position."

"That is exactly why we should get rid of his father. We go for straight for the jugular and Luke will be such a mess that we won't have to worry about him…or his father."

"How is that going, by the way? Did you speak to my dad about it yet?" I asked. Brian had vaguely mentioned something about taking out their enforcer a couple of days ago. Get rid of the muscle, less to worry about. But that was the last I'd heard of it until now.

"I did, and he agrees with me. We came up with a plan, and it's in place as we speak." "Okay…is that all I get to know?"

"Afraid so. For now the fewer who know, the better. And please remember that Scarlett should know nothing about this," he warned as he kept his eyes trained on the road. "She's far too sensitive to be okay with this part of the mission. I'm beginning to regret ever letting her get involved in this."

I couldn't have agreed more. It was obvious that Scarlett wasn't acting when she was with Luke. She really did like him. Maybe she didn't at first, but there was no denying it now. I didn't plan on letting her father know that though. He would shut it down immediately, and Scarlett's feelings for Luke were a good thing, in my opinion; it made it all more believable, more real. She would of course be devastated when Luke finally found out the truth about her, but that would be her problem. She knew what she was signing up for.

"Back to Luke—should we be concerned about him?" I asked.

"No, we need him to back Aiden. Let's just stay with our plan regarding Luke. It's the best way to cause more distress within the pack. Actually, this might work to our advantage. Let's convince Luke to train Aiden. Aiden needs to learn a little about fighting, so the fight between him and Cade seems fair; plus Luke and Aiden spending time together would help them to build a friendship too, which will piss Cade off."

"I'll mention it to Aiden," I replied.

As soon as we entered the lodge, Marcus was focused on me. It was a good thing Scarlett wasn't here yet. I think she might have cracked under his heated glare. Luckily I'd lived with an alpha my entire life, so this was nothing new to me. I knew how to best handle this. Plead guilty and apologize.

I walked up to Marcus. "Sir, please accept my apologies. It was completely inappropriate for me have alcohol on the estate. This was entirely my fault. I guess I just wanted everyone to have fun," I admitted with as much sincerity as I could muster.

Marcus seemed stunned by my voluntary and immediate apology, and apparently it worked because he put his hand on my shoulder and firmly stated, "Never again, understand?"

After I nodded and vowed to make better decisions from here on out, he turned back to what was really bothering him: his two sons. Cade and Aiden were sitting in the front on opposite sides of the stage with their families. None of them looked happy about being here, especially Cade.

Tension filled the air, and I could only assume that Brian and I had missed something. Maybe Marcus had already said his piece because both boys looked ready to blow...again. Marcus took his seat at the front of the lodge, his arms crossed over his chest while he waited for the rest of the pack to take their seats. It was eerily quiet as Marcus stood and walked to the podium. "I would like to thank you all for coming on such short notice."

Just then, Scarlett landed in the seat next to me. Just to piss her off, I threw my arm over her shoulder and leaned in to whisper, "Took you long enough, but you look so hot, I guess it was worth the wait."

As expected, she swiped my hand away and told me to screw off. I loved that little temper of hers. It would probably get her in trouble one day, but it wasn't like it was any concern of mine. From the corner of my eye, I noticed her scanning the room for Luke and I wondered what exactly went on between them last night. I'd have to bug her about it later.

"I allowed a New Year's Eve party to take place last night here on the estate. It has come to my attention that there was underage drinking going on, which led to a fight between my sons," Marcus announced.

There were a few whispers from the pack, but they were quickly quieted when Marcus cleared his throat. "I can't begin to express how disappointed I am in their behavior and total lack of respect for this pack and our laws."

For several minutes, he raged on and on about disrespectful teenagers and how they take for granted all that is bestowed upon them. Blah, blah, blah. But then suddenly Marcus's face turned beet red and his voice grew louder as he worked himself into a frenzy. One of the elders stood and started to walk toward the podium but stopped in his tracks when Marcus held up his hand to stop him and began to outright shout.

"I blame all of you!" Marcus yelled as he pointed at the elder walking up the aisle and then at the rest of them seated at the front. "All of you!"

The whole pack was clearly stunned by Marcus's outburst, but not a word was spoken. Silence filled the room as the look on Marcus's red face grew even more intense; the veins in his neck were bulging, and he was squeezing the podium so hard his knuckles were white.

"I told you all what I wanted! I was very clear. All of this could have been avoided. I am the alpha of this pack and you should have backed my decision to make Aiden the next alpha. But no! You went against me. You turned against me, turned against your alpha! You were all disobedient! Disobedient, just like Cade!" As he concluded his rant, Marcus panted for breath and drops of sweat slid down his inflamed face.

More elders stood and watched in horror as their alpha swayed on his feet. Clinging to the podium, he nearly collapsed in front of everyone. Lucky for Marcus, the "disobedient" Cade was able to get to him before he fell to the floor. Cade helped Marcus to a chair and ordered a man I didn't know to get him some water. Cade didn't go to the podium. He didn't need a microphone to make his announcement. With a booming voice he declared, "This meeting is over!"

CHAPTER 28

Luke

Walking out of the lodge this morning, I was left with a sense of dread deep in my stomach. I looked around for my dad, knowing that he wasn't back from Santa Fe yet, but after whatever just happened to Marcus in there, I guess it was just an automatic response. The cold January air came as a welcome relief after the suddenly stuffy feel of the lodge. I took a deep breath, hoping the fresh mountain air would ease the tightness in my chest. I think it would have worked too if Scarlett's delicious scent didn't tag along with it. That scent brought back memories of last night, and I had to fight the smile that was creeping across my face. I turned around and watched as Scarlett and her brother walked out of the lodge. When our eyes met, all the fight in the world couldn't have erased the goofy grin on my face.

My feet started moving toward her without my consent. I quickly tried to think of something to say, something that wouldn't sound awkward after what had happened between us last night, but of course my muddled brain failed me.

"Luke, man, how are you holding up? That looks painful," Gavin said, reminding me of the gash on my face. I had forgotten all about it.

"Nah, it's fine really," I responded and then turned my attention to Scarlett. "Thanks again for patching me up last night."

She smiled sheepishly, but before she could answer, Gavin patted me on the back and said, "Well, glad to see you're okay. I'll catch you later, man." He took off after his father, who seemed to be headed toward his car.

Scarlett and I stood there for an awkward moment, neither of us saying a word. I was searching for something to say when thankfully she spoke first. "Are you really okay?" she asked, lightly touching my right cheek. My eyes closed as her soft fingers trailed down the side of my face. I didn't understand, nor did I completely accept whatever was going on between us, but I knew that I had no choice but to give into it. I had never been physically stronger in my life, but standing here with Scarlett, with her tenderly touching my face, I was as weak as a newborn pup.

Fortunately, Cade walked over and saved me from making an ass out of myself. Her touch was testing the limits of my self-control. "Hey Luke, do you know where your dad's at? I can't find him anywhere."

Scarlett tried to excuse herself and give us some privacy, but I took her hand and kept her by my side. "Yeah, he went to Santa Fe for New Year's. He said that he would be back early, but I guess he's running late. I'll give him a call so he knows what's going on, but he should be back soon. Want me to send him over when I see him?"

"Thanks. I don't know what the hell happened in there," he admitted. He was worried, whether he'd admit it or not. There was a tick in his jaw and his fists were clenched down by his side as he shifted his weight from foot to foot.

"Is your father okay now?" Scarlett asked.

"He seems fine now. I think he's just confused about it, you know. He's never lost control like that," he explained. "Luke, about last night, I have to thank you, man. And apologize. Things got out of hand. I can't even begin to think about what would have happened if you weren't there, and I'm so sorry to have put you in that situation."

"It's fine, really," I lied.

"No, it's not. I know how hard that was for you. Things have been so tense between Aiden and me lately. It didn't even occur to me how weird this whole thing must be for you, and it should have. So, I'm sorry, really, for all of it," he insisted and held out his hand.

I didn't say anything as I shook his hand, though I didn't think Cade was expecting me to anyway. He politely said his goodbyes and walked away, leaving Scarlett and me standing in the same unnerving situation we were in when he walked over—except now I was holding her hand.

Remembering that I wasn't going to fight this thing between us anymore, I pulled her into my arms for a quick hug. "Are you busy later?"

She paused for a moment before wrapping her arms around me and saying that she was free for the rest of the day…and night.

CHAPTER 29

Scarlett

After the meeting, I spent most of the day cleaning up after the disastrous New Year's Eve party. This was no way to spend the first day of the New Year, but after what transpired between Luke and me last night, I needed something to take my mind off things.

Unfortunately, even with my workout playlist blaring through my earphones, cleaning wasn't exactly doing the trick. It only gave me more time to replay our first kiss over and over again in my head. I might as well have been lying in bed dreaming about him. But someone needed to clean up this mess, and I seriously doubted Drew or my father would dare get their hands dirty if it involved cleaning products. But it wasn't an issue because they weren't even home.

After the meeting, I wasn't sure what to expect from Luke, but not only did Luke hold my hand in front of Cade and hug me like it was the most natural thing in the world, he wanted to see me later too, which was completely freaking me out, and since nothing was ever set in stone, I wasn't sure what to do. Should I text him? Wait for him to text me? What if he just showed up and I smelled like Pine-Sol? Without a second thought, I stripped my hands of the rubber cleaning gloves, threw my dirty rag in the washer, and ran upstairs to take a shower.

As the hot water washed away the scent of disinfectant, my thoughts turned to what really concerned me. What should I do now? I wanted to be with Luke, and after last night, I could only hope he wanted to be with me too. If he did, I would have to do something. Either I'd have to come clean to Luke or tell my father that I was out, that I wouldn't be a part of their plan to destroy the Red Ridge Pack. One thing was certain: I couldn't be with Luke and lie to him. If I was really being honest with myself, I'd never felt about anyone the way I felt about Luke Stanton. Surely it wasn't love. It was way too soon for that, but something was happening, and I didn't want it to end.

Out of the blue, a storm of emotions, from elation to dread, tore through me. My breathing became erratic, my chest ached, and my eyes burned with unshed tears. I sank down into the tub and covered my face with my hands as the water poured over me. What the hell had I gotten myself into? My father would never forgive me if I turned my back on him, and if I told Luke the truth, I'd most likely be banned from my pack, or worse, and then Luke would hate me for sure for deceiving him. I was trapped in a no-win situation with no way out.

It was times like this that I really missed my mom. She would know exactly what I should do. Actually, if she were still alive, I probably wouldn't be in this situation. Now there was only one person I could talk to about this—my brother. Not Drew, the faux-brother from hell, my real brother, Gavin.

I wasn't sure if I was ready for the earful he was sure to unleash upon me, but I needed to talk to someone. First I needed to see where I really stood with Luke. For all I knew, he could want to meet up to tell me that our kiss was a huge mistake. That he wasn't interested in taking things any further. Or maybe he did want to take things further...a lot further. Maybe sex was all he was after. Then what was I going to do? When we first met, I'd convinced myself that I could hook up with him, no strings attached, but now I didn't think I could do it. Not when I had real feelings for him. I already felt like my father was whoring me out; I didn't need Luke treating me like one too.

Suddenly I wasn't looking forward to our little meeting. There was only this little, teeny-tiny chance that Luke actually cared about me too, and if that was true, I'd be thrilled, but then I'd have to figure out what to do about my pack. No, that wasn't true. Even if Luke wasn't serious about me, I knew I couldn't go through with any of it. I'd tried to make myself believe that what I was expected to do wasn't so bad. All I had to do was get close to Luke and persuade him to side with Aiden. And maybe that wasn't completely horrible on its own, but the truth was, I knew there was much more to the plan. My father and Drew's part combined with mine was unforgivable and just plain wrong. I needed to find a way out of this mess and somehow avoid hurting Luke in the process.

By the time I finally emerged from the shower, I'd decided my best bet was to wait and see where things stood with Luke, and then go from there. There was nothing I could do at the moment anyway. The only thing I was sure of was that I wasn't going to deceive Luke. Whatever happened, happened, but there was no way I would mention Aiden or Cade. I was staying out of it, but like it or not, I'd have to make some tough decisions sooner rather than later.

It wasn't too long after I'd gotten ready that Luke texted me to see if I wanted to meet up. Again, he wasn't clear what "meet up" meant, but I didn't ask. It didn't matter. I needed to see him, so instead, I replied *sure*, and within seconds he let me know that he would be here in thirty minutes.

Time ticked by at a snail's pace as I glared at the clock for torturing me. Needless to say, it was the longest thirty minutes of my life, and the only thing that made it bearable was that my dad and Drew were mysteriously absent from the house. They never came back from the meeting, and I hadn't heard from either of them since this morning.

As I picked up and put away the last of the evidence of the party-gone-awry, the doorbell rang, and immediately a lump formed in my throat. How could I be so ridiculously excited yet so scared to death to see someone? These feelings shouldn't go hand in hand, yet here I stood, petrified and exhilarated.

I swung open the door, and when Luke's eyes met mine, a smile spread across his gorgeous face. He had on the same black hoodie and low-slung jeans as he did this morning, but now wore a red baseball cap turned backward. With his dark hair hidden underneath, his perfect face had never looked more delectable. The desire to pull him inside and finish what we'd started last night coursed through my body, and I could hardly breathe, let alone think straight. Words failed me as I just stood there staring like a complete and utter fool.

But as soon as he reached out his hand and asked, "You wanna get out of here?" I could breathe again. The nervousness drained from my body as I slipped my hand in his and he led me to his car.

Pulling out on the open road, Luke asked, "How about we just go for a drive? Get away from the estate for a while?"

"Sounds perfect," I replied, and I'd meant it. Nothing sounded better than getting far, far away from this place. As we drove past the Red Ridge city limits, Luke visibly relaxed, and I wondered just how hard he was taking this alpha thing or if there was something else going on.

We made small talk as we headed toward an unknown destination, and for the briefest moment, my mind went to that place that tried to convince me that Luke didn't care about me. But those thoughts were quickly squashed as I watched his eyes dance when he laughed at something silly I'd said. Then without hesitation, he reached his hand out and found mine, just like he had this morning, and it felt so natural. With our fingers intertwined, I felt happy for the first time in a long time. I felt secure, and that scared the living shit out of me.

As the foreign feeling washed over me, I turned to look out the window, trying to hide the smile I could no longer contain. Gently squeezing my hand, Luke said, "I'd give anything to know what's going on in your head."

Feeling my cheeks redden, I coyly replied, "Anything?"

With a sly grin on his perfect face, Luke cut his eyes my way for a moment before refocusing on the road to confirm, "Yeah, anything."

"In that case, I'll tell you what's on my mind, but only if you tell me what's on yours first."

When he didn't respond, I thought I'd somehow managed to ruin our flirty moment, but after a minute or so, Luke turned off the main road and into the parking lot of a small park. As he pulled the car into a spot that overlooked the playground, he finally replied, "Deal, but first we do something I haven't done since I was like ten. We play."

"Play? It's already dark and like twenty below out there. You sure you're not just stalling?" I teased, even though in that moment, the gleam in Luke's chocolate brown eyes could have convinced me to scale a mountain.

"Yes, play. Come on, five minutes. It'll be fun." Luke was out of the car and rushing around to pull me out of my seat before I could refuse. I may not be the best at talking, but playing I could do. As soon as my feet hit the pavement, I lightly shoved Luke and yelled, "You're it!" Then I took off running toward the playground.

Hot on my trail, Luke was clearly faster than me but he gave me a chance to get on the other side of the jungle gym before he cut through the middle and tagged me. "Gotcha!" Luke shouted as he took off toward the slide. I followed after, knowing I wouldn't have a chance of catching him if he didn't want me to. Luke climbed up the little rope ladder that led to a ramp. From the top of the ramp, he looked back to see where I was and then waved as he took off down a long, winding tube slide. I'd barely made it up the ramp by the time I heard his feet hit the ground.

I looked out over the edge as he rounded a corner, but I refused to give up. I sat down at the top of the slide and couldn't help but laugh. Years had passed since I'd been on a playground, and a surprising thrill shot through me as I pushed off to slide and sailed down to the bottom.

After the last turn, the tube opened up, and I lifted my head to glance around for any sign of Luke. He was nowhere in sight, but before my feet reached the pebble-covered ground, he emerged from the darkness and scooped me up in his arms like a baby and swung me around. Shocked, a small cry fled from my lips, causing him to chuckle. His entire face lit up, and I realized that before that moment, I'd never seen him look truly content.

Unwrapping his arm from underneath my knees, Luke lowered my feet to the ground. Smiling up at him, I said, "Caught you."

His eyes danced in delight as he replied, "Yes, you have." He leaned down and gently pressed his lips to mine. It was a chaste kiss that was way too brief, yet somehow it was just as sensual as the one from last night.

As he pulled away, he whispered, "Come on. Let's get back to the car and get warmed up." I nodded my head in reply, choosing not to mention that he'd just set my body on fire and the last thing I was thinking about was the weather.

Back in the car with the heater on high, I turned to Luke and asked, "So, what's on your mind, Luke Stanton?"

He looked conflicted, as if he couldn't decide what answer to give. All of a sudden, I wasn't sure if I truly wanted to know. Before he spoke, he took my hand in his, and I was right back to being both terrified and thrilled.

"Scarlett, what's on my mind is you." He took a deep breath and then continued, "There's so much shit going on right now between Aiden and Cade, and now whatever the hell is up with Marcus, but all I can think about is you. I've tried really hard not to want you, not to care about you. But I can't help it. I do. And that's the most honest I've been in a long time."

Honest. He said the one word that managed to squash the joy that was building inside me as I listened to his confession. I might not have been able to tell him everything, but I could be honest about one thing. "I care about you too. But you confuse the hell out of me. One second you seem interested, and the next..."

"I've been an idiot, Scarlett. With everything going on, I convinced myself that I shouldn't get involved because I knew I really liked you, and right now, I need to focus on my pack. But I just want to be with you, and I don't want to deny it anymore."

I didn't know what to say. He said everything I'd wanted him to. He cared about me. He wanted to be with me. The truth was right there in his eyes, and before I realized what I was doing, I turned away, worried that the truth might be in mine as well.

Luke removed his hand from mine, and a chill ran up my spine, leaving me colder than when I'd been running around outside in the freezing weather. But then he reached over, wrapped his arms around me, and pulled me into his lap.

"Say something, Scarlett," Luke pleaded when I refused to look him in the eyes.

I told him the only truth I had in that moment. "I want to be with you too." And then I wrapped my arms around his neck and kissed him.

CHAPTER 30

Luke

I couldn't think about all the things I had just said to Scarlett. I couldn't think about what it meant or what could happen because of my sudden confession. I couldn't think of anything except the way she felt in my arms. This kiss was different. Our lips weren't hurried or demanding like they were last night. Today they were patient, giving...accepting. It was amazing just how much you can learn about someone from a simple kiss. It was obvious that Scarlett was just as fearful of the emotions flowing between us as I was. She trembled under my touch just as I did every time my hands came in contact with her perfect skin.

She let out an incredibly sexy little moan as my hands traveled their way up and down her back, in and out of all that gorgeous dark hair of hers, and around her small waist. Ninety-nine percent of my body was urging me forward, pressuring me to take this to the next level, but there was that damn one percent that was begging me to slow down. Begging me to try for something more. That unsettling one percent managed to get my attention and I slowed down, first my hands, then my breathing, and finally my lips.

With Scarlett still sitting on my lap, I rested my forehead against her chest and listened to the pounding of her heart. Closing my eyes, I breathed in Scarlett's unique scent, now mixed with the heady scent of need, and thought I might come undone right there in her arms. With one last deep breath, I had no choice but to remove my head from her chest, fearing I would lose control and bury my face in the cleavage that had been teasing me all night. Sensing my retreat, Scarlett slid off my lap and left me feeling empty and alone.

Since I had already bared my soul, one more confession wasn't going to ruin anything tonight.

"Scarlett," I said taking her hand in mine, "I don't understand why, and I know I may sound like a silly made-for-TV movie, but for the first time ever, I want us to take this slow. I'm not used to caring. I know that makes me sound horrible, but it's true. I just don't want to screw this up like I seem to do everything else. I want to give whatever this thing is between us a real chance."

The worried expression on her face faded as she leaned in and placed a chaste kiss on the corner of my mouth before she whispered, "Me too."

It was getting late, so I drove Scarlett home in what now could only be explained as a comfortable silence. She was sitting next to me, resting her head on my shoulder. For a moment, I thought she had fallen asleep, but as we pulled up to her house, she gently squeezed my hand and leaned over to kiss me goodbye. Scarlett was halfway out of the truck when she stopped and said, "You know, I had a really good time with you today."

Before I could respond, she'd shut the car door and was walking to her front door. I realized only then that I should have walked her to her door, but it was too late now. *Next time*, I thought. Because there was definitely going to be a next time.

As I drove home, I thought about all the things I needed to learn. I'd never been in an actual relationship before, not a real one anyway. It should have occurred to me to do things like walk her to her door and be the one to tell her that I had a good time, but it didn't. I'd never really tried to act like a gentleman or to make someone feel special before, but I was a quick study, and lucky for me, there was always tomorrow.

I was surprised not to see my dad's car in the driveway when I got home. I looked around the house trying to find any signs that my dad had even come home at all. Nothing looked different than it did this morning. An uneasy feeling crept over me because this was very unlike my father. If he had a change of plans and decided not to come home for a few days, he would have called. Hell, if he was even going to be an hour late, he would have called. My entire body tensed as I picked up my phone and tried my dad's number. The call went straight to his voicemail. After I left a message, I sent him a text asking him to call me and let me know where he was and that he was okay, but no response followed.

*****

Hours later, I was lying awake in my bed. The house was eerily quiet except for the wind that had picked up outside. I knew that I hadn't missed my dad's call, but I checked my phone one more time just to make sure. I had made a deal with myself and with my missing father: I would give him until the morning. If I hadn't heard from him by then, my search would begin.

As I set my phone down on my nightstand, I closed my eyes, and Scarlett's breathtaking face immediately appeared. Why did I listen to that stupid, measly one percent today? Instead of lying here worrying about my dad, who was probably fine and had just decided to spend a couple of days with Michelle, I could have been taking advantage of an empty house with a certain sexy brunette for the entire night. For a brief moment, I contemplated calling Scarlett to tell her just how stupid I was today and to beg her to come over and keep me warm tonight, but that would definitely *not* be taking it slow.

I knew that one day I would inevitably screw this up with Scarlett. Sadly, that was just a given. I tried to push that nagging thought aside, but I couldn't. I'd probably end up taking off when things got too real, but for the first time in my life, I really wanted to give this a try. It may have sounded totally cheesy and lame, but I didn't care. Scarlett Reed made me want things I'd never even dreamed of wanting before.

The sudden realization that I may never be able to give her the happy-ever-after that she deserved to have wreaked havoc on my already tense body. There in the dark, I promised myself that when that time came, I'd let her go, but for now, I just wanted to feel something. Scarlett did that for me. She made me feel something deep inside. What, I wasn't sure, but something. It was there, it was real, and it felt right.

CHAPTER 31

Drew

I finally arrived home after a long day and found Scarlett lying on the couch watching TV all dreamy-eyed and smiling. I couldn't decide if this was a good thing or bad. One, she wasn't locked in her bedroom, and two, she looked like a love-drunk fool. God help us all if she had fallen in love. I stood at the foot of the couch and stared down at her. "What's with the cheesy look on your face?"

"What cheesy look? I'm just relaxing. Where have you and Dad been all day?" she asked.

"We drove back home today. My dad wanted an update, face-to-face. Your dad decided to stay the night and catch up on some work."

"Okay. Well it's late, so I'm going to bed. Goodnight," she replied and started for the stairs.

"Wait," I said, stopping her. "How's it going with Luke? Him and Aiden buddies yet?"

She turned to me and grinned. "Things with Luke are good. We hung out today."

"And Aiden?"

Her gaze fell to the floor as she admitted, "I'm still working on that."

She looked back up, and the doe-eyed, lovesick expression on her face told me it was time for a wake-up call. I walked over to her and slung my arm over her shoulder to lead her to the kitchen.

"Scarlett, Scarlett, Scarlett," I started in my most patronizing tone. I sat her down at the kitchen table before I walked over to the fridge, grabbed us a couple of Cokes, and handed her one.

"Drew, I'm tired. What do you want?" she asked impatiently.

"I'm worried about you. You're not getting too attached to that meathead, are you?"

She crossed her arms over her chest defensively. "I'm fine, Drew. I can handle Luke. You don't need to worry about me,"

She was a bad liar. Time to stop being friendly and open her pretty little eyes. "I can't believe you're so ridiculously stupid."

I paused for a brief moment to gauge her reaction. Her jaw dropped, but before she could respond, I continued. "What do you think is going to happen between you and Luke? He's not your boyfriend. He can never be your boyfriend. You are using him and that's all. You can pretend for now if you want, but get your head out of your ass for a minute and think. When Luke discovers the truth about us, about you, what do you think he's going to do? You think he's going to forgive you? Tell you that it doesn't matter that you lied and manipulated him?"

I thought that she would yell back or throw her Coke at me or something, but she didn't. She just sat there staring at the can in her hands.

"Maybe your dad was right. Maybe you aren't cut out for this. He should send you home before you screw this up any further."

She looked up then. Finally, something I said was at least sinking into her thick skull, but I wasn't finished just yet.

"Is that what you want? You want to go back home with everyone knowing that you failed?" I asked, my voice seething with pity. "Haven't you screwed up enough?"

That did it. She was pissed now. Good! She needed to be furious. If she messed this up, our entire pack would suffer. If she couldn't do this, I would rather her just leave now before it was too late.

"I can handle this," she said, standing up and pushing in her chair.

"I hope you can for your sake, but I don't know. I'm not convinced. Maybe you should just go and leave Luke to me," I threatened.

Scarlett smiled, but her eyes narrowed and stared into my own. "In your dreams. You may be our next alpha, but you saw what Luke did last night to Cade and Aiden. What makes you think he couldn't do the same to you?" she stated defiantly.

She started to leave the kitchen, but there was no way in hell that Scarlett was going to have the last word. I stood in the doorway, blocking her exit. "You're right, Scar. Sure, Luke could kick my ass. No doubt about that, but you know me. I've never played by the rules."

"Let me pass," she sneered.

I moved in closer. Scarlett knew better then to turn away from me, but I could tell that she wanted to. I made her uncomfortable, and I was going to use that fact to my advantage.

"I need to believe you, Scarlett. I need to be able to trust that you will do what is best for our pack. Can I trust you, Scar?" I asked softly in her ear as I pressed my entire body against hers. "Tell me, Scarlett. Tell me I can trust you."

Her body quivered slightly, but she didn't move away. She didn't respond either, so I kept her there close to me. I would be her alpha one day soon, and she needed to know her place.

"Repeat after me," I commanded. *"Luke is not my boyfriend."*

Scarlett remained silent, so I wrapped my arms around the small of her back and pulled her even closer, so close that the lengths of our entire bodies were completely enmeshed. When I felt her body stiffen, smelled the fear that was building inside her, and heard her heart rate increase, it instantly made me hard as a rock. I pressed myself against her to make sure she could feel it. With my lips only a millimeter away from hers, I whispered, "Say it, Scarlett."

She relented, knowing I wouldn't back down. "Luke is not my boyfriend."

"I will not get attached," I said.

"I will not get attached."

I grinded against her again before I continued. "I will do what is best for my pack."

"I will do what is best for my pack," she repeated.

My lips almost touched hers as I looked into her eyes and whispered, "Good girl."

I lingered there a while longer, sensing that her fear and agitation were only increasing. I smiled and then brushed my lips lightly against hers. Her body tensed even more. Deciding that she'd had enough, I stepped aside and let her pass. In true Scarlett form, she held her head high, looked me right in the eyes, and walked passed me.

Just as she reached the stairs I said, "Hey, Scar."

She stopped but didn't look at me.

"Want me to come up and tuck you in, baby?"

Scarlett turned around, gave me the finger, and went upstairs. I stood there and waited for what I knew would come.

Once her door slammed and I heard it lock, I smiled triumphantly and went into the living room to watch TV.

CHAPTER 32

Scarlett

Flattening my back against my bedroom door, I slid to the ground and wrapped my arms around my knees. I dropped my head and finally allowed the tears I'd been holding back to fall freely. I'd refused to let Drew see me cry, but with his body pressed against mine, it took all I had not to break down right there in front of him.

I needed a shower to wash away his stench, but fear kept me bound to the safety of my room. I didn't have the strength to face him again tonight. It was bad enough that I'd have to wake up in the morning and act like nothing had happened. There was nothing I could do about it. Drew knew that, and I hated him for it. *Evil son of a bitch.*

As I crawled into bed, I couldn't get Drew's words out of my head. As much as I despised him, he had one thing right. If I told Luke the truth, he would never speak to me again. But he was going to find out at some point whether it was me who told him or not. Either way, I'd lose him. There would never be a future for us, no matter how much I cared about him, no matter how much I regretted what I'd willingly agreed to do.

Once again, tears stung my eyes, and I clinched them shut, desperately trying to stop the pain coursing through me, but it did no good. The vice grip around my heart tightened, and I gasped for air as I sobbed uncontrollably. I hadn't wept like this since the night my mother died. That night, I thought my endless tears would never dry up, and now I felt as if I'd been cast right back into that dark, dreadful place I thought I'd never escape from.

Trying to calm myself, I took deep breaths, inhaling and exhaling slowly. But then my mind would turn to Luke, and I'd lose it all over again. If I told him the truth, he'd hate me forever. I wouldn't be able to go back home. Betraying my pack…if it didn't get me killed, it would most certainly get me banished. My father would never speak to me again. I'd lose everything, everyone. Everyone except Gavin. He would never turn his back on me.

Before I realized what I was doing, I'd reached for my phone, found his name, and pushed the call button. Seconds later, Gavin answered, concern filling his voice. I tried to disguise my tears as I said his name, but I knew it would be in vain.

"Scarlett, what's wrong. What happened?"

"Gavin, I've screwed everything up. I don't know what to do," I cried into the phone, gripping it tightly as if it was the only lifeline I had left.

"Slow down. Tell me what's going on. Do you need me to come there? I can be in the car in five minutes."

"No! You can't. It will just make things worse. Drew is supposed to be you. I just…"

"Hey, it's me. You can tell me. What happened?" Gavin pleaded.

Now that he was on the phone, I had no idea what to say. How to tell him how badly things had turned out, how wrong I was to agree to infiltrate the Red Ridge Pack. Gavin had warned me, but I refused to listen. Convincing myself that he was just jealous that Dad wanted my help, I'd completely ignored Gavin's advice. I needed it now, and this time I would listen.

"I don't know what I'm doing here. I'm stuck. No matter what I do, I'll lose him, Gavin."

"Who? What are you talking about?"

"Luke. I think I might love him." It wasn't until the words were out of my mouth that I knew in my heart that it was true. I was falling in love with the one guy I could never have, not after what I'd done. The sobbing started all over again, this time with vengeance, but I focused on my brother's voice as he tried to calm me down.

"Breathe, Scarlett. You have to breathe. You are going to be okay, I promise. I won't let anything happen to you, but right now, you have to breathe."

I did as he said, inhaled and exhaled over and over again. He gave me a moment to settle down before he told me what I needed to do. "Listen, this may not fix everything, but it will get you out of there in one piece. Just come home, Scarlett. Pack your shit and get out of there. Do not tell Luke about Dad and Drew. Do not tell anyone that you are leaving. Wait until Drew is asleep, and go."

"What? You think I should just leave? But what about Luke?"

"I know what you're thinking. You care about this guy, I get it, but you can't tell him what's going on. If you do, who knows what our alpha will do? Banishment will be the least of your worries. I need you safe. That's what is most important. Please just come home."

I couldn't believe what he was saying. Just leave, like nothing had happened. I couldn't. "No Gavin, I can't just take off. What will Luke think if he wakes up tomorrow, and I'm gone?"

Sounding completely panicked, Gavin begged, "Just come home. There is nothing you can say or do to make this better. But if you stay, if you tell him, you're putting your life at risk. And Dad's too. You don't think he will be blamed for this? Of course he will. I'm sorry, it's not what you want to hear, but it's the truth. You don't have a good option here, so you need to choose the one that's best for you, for our family. You need to leave tonight."

I hardly recognized my own voice as I spoke. "Yeah, okay... okay, I will. I'll leave tonight."

Over and over again, Gavin assured me that everything would be all right, but we both knew he was lying. I promised that I'd call him as soon as I was off the estate. His voice cracked as he told me he loved me. I hung up the phone, but I didn't get up and pack. Instead, I lay in bed for over an hour, thinking about every possible option and every possible outcome. Gavin was right. I needed to leave, but not before I saw Luke one last time.

CHAPTER 33

Luke

My heart dropped into the pit of my stomach when I woke up in the morning and my Dad was still not home. He didn't come home. He didn't call. Something was wrong. May dad would never be that thoughtless or irresponsible, and he would never leave his pack unprotected.

I couldn't sit around and wait any longer, so I threw on some jeans and a hoodie and went looking for him.

It was only a twenty-minute drive from the estate into town, but it seemed to take forever. I had to see if Michelle, the woman my dad went out of town with, was back at work. I was really hoping that when I pulled up to the Red Mountain Ski Resort that she wouldn't be there. Maybe the assistant manager would tell me that Michelle just called and said that she had fallen in love, ran off to Vegas, and gotten married or something crazy like that. That she and her new husband were staying there a few days for their honeymoon. I knew it was a stupid thought. I knew my dad, and Dad would never do anything like that, but all the other scenarios that were running through my head were too devastating to think about.

I may be eighteen years old, technically an adult, but I couldn't stop myself from thinking that if something did happen to my father, I'd be all alone. Sure, I'd have my pack, but it wouldn't be the same.

I pulled up in front of the resort just in time to see Michelle pulling into her parking space. I sat there stunned; my little fantasy about Dad and Michelle may have been ridiculous but for that brief moment, it gave me a tiny ounce of hope. Now that hope was gone.

Michelle saw me and waved as she walked over to my truck, "Hey handsome. What are you doing up this early?"

"Hi, Michelle. Just grabbing some breakfast. Did you and Dad have a good time in Santa Fe?" I asked trying to pry some information out of her.

"Oh, honey, it was great. Didn't your daddy tell you about it?"

"You know Dad. He never says much," I replied with a smile and a shrug.

"Oh Luke, it was wonderful! The Marriott was all decorated for the holidays. We had this fabulous dinner, we danced, we drank champagne…well, I just wished I didn't have to be back so early on the first. We were having such a good time. I hated to leave, but he was so sweet to wake up early and drop me off here where I'd left my car," she gushed, completely unaware that she was confirming my worst fears.

I looked down at my hands, hoping to hide my concern. "I'm glad the two of you had fun."

Michelle snuggled into her coat and then glanced at her watch. "Gotta go, honey. Tell your dad to call me, okay?"

"Sure Michelle," I replied and watched her walk into the resort. That was it then. Dad was safe in his car in this parking lot twenty-four hours ago. Sometime between then and now, somewhere between here and home, he'd disappeared.

The car behind me honked, breaking me from my daze. I rolled my window up and pulled out of the resort.

I had taken the main road into town to get here and didn't see any signs that maybe Dad had car trouble, so I took the back roads home to the estate.

Nothing. I was grasping at straws, and I knew it. Even if Dad's car had broken down, and his cell had died, he could have easily made it to the woods where no one would see him. He *is* a werewolf. He could have simply changed and run home…unless he was hurt.

I was almost home when I decided that I couldn't do this on my own, and Marcus needed to know that his second in command was missing. I probably should have told Marcus sooner, but I really hoped that Dad was fine and just having a good time.

I pulled up in front of the Walker house, turned the truck off, and just sat there. I could feel the weight of the last few days bearing down on me. The fight between Cade and Aiden, my relationship with Scarlett, and my missing father was all heavy stuff and threatened to suffocate me. Who knows how long I sat there, but it must have been long enough to draw attention because Cade actually came out to get me.

Cade opened the passenger door and slid into the seat. "Is everything all right, Luke?" "My dad never came home," I blurted out without looking his way.

I heard Cade take a deep breath, like he was processing that information and what it might mean before he asked, "When was the last time you saw or heard from him?"

"New Year's Eve."

"Let's go inside. Dad will want hear all of this. He was just complaining that Phillip hasn't been around."

Once inside, Noel insisted that I join them for breakfast while I told Cade and Marcus the whole story, or what I knew of it anyway. She set a huge plate of eggs, bacon, and fried potatoes in front of me and squeezed my shoulder as she went back into the kitchen. I'd never considered how much I missed out on not having a mother, but for some reason, at that moment, I realized I had. It was probably just because Dad was missing and I was worried, but out of nowhere, a stabbing pain shot through my chest as I imagined what it would have been like to sit at our table with my Dad as Mom brought us a hot breakfast and smiled at me the way Noel smiled at Cade. Pushing the painful thought aside, I dug into the scrambled eggs.

Between forkfuls, I told Marcus and Cade about Dad's New Year's Eve plans, how he and Michelle had gone to Santa Fe for the night, but Marcus was already aware of that. I told them that I had tried calling and texting Dad several times, but he never responded. Without hesitation, Marcus grabbed his cell and tried, but it too went straight to voicemail. That was a very Marcus thing to do, I thought. As if my dad was would answer his call but not mine. Then I told them I'd tracked down Michelle this morning, but she didn't appear to have a clue that anything might be wrong. Obviously, I avoided telling her that he never came home as she would surely insist on calling the police.

Marcus took one last sip of his coffee and stood abruptly. "I don't like this one bit. Phillip is in trouble. He would never take off without telling anyone. Something is wrong, and he definitely needs our help. I can feel it."

He paused for a moment, then said, "Luke, go home and get something of your father's, a shirt or jacket, something with his scent on it. Come straight back here. I will form a search party. If he's out there hurt, we will find him."

As I got up to leave, Noel came back in the room and gave me a big hug. "It will be okay, honey. We'll find him."

"Thank you, Mrs. Walker. I'm sure we will. And thanks for breakfast. It was perfect."

"Cade," she said, "go with Luke. He doesn't need to be alone right now."

I was about to say that I would be fine, but Cade was already slipping into his coat.

*****

It felt weird going through my dad's things. Cade suggested something from his hamper would be best, something that hadn't been washed yet. So I grabbed the t-shirt Dad had on New Year's

Eve before he changed to get ready. I held it up to my nose to make sure his scent was strong. It was, and my eyes filled with tears. I hadn't shed a single tear since the age of five, and for the first time in so long, I felt weak. Completely helpless.

"Ready, Luke?" Cade called from the living room.

Shit! I quickly dried my eyes with the back of my hand and went to meet Cade. Avoiding eye contact, I nodded toward the door. I didn't want anyone to see me like this, especially not Cade. Weakness was not an option for an enforcer.

But as soon as I opened the front door, I came face to face with yet another major weakness. Just the sight of her made my pulse quicken. Apparently, this day was hell-bent on breaking me down. Scarlett was walking toward me with two steaming cups of coffee, one in each hand, and a beaming smile on her face. Seeing her this morning, so oblivious to my new situation, I tightly clinched my jaw as my eyes threatened to fill again.

Her eyes shifted quickly between Cade and me, and her smile faltered. "I hope it's okay that I just stopped by."

"I'll go on ahead. Want me to take that?" Cade offered.

I handed him my dad's shirt and assured him that I wouldn't be far behind. Then Cade smiled and said a polite hello to Scarlett before leaving.

With genuine concern in her eyes, Scarlett asked, "Is everything all right?"

When I didn't reply immediately, she handed me one of the cups, but instead of taking it, I took both. I sat them on the railing to the porch and pulled Scarlett to me. I held her tightly, and without question, she let me. Breathing deeply, trying to control the all-consuming emotions that I had no idea how to handle, I stood there, inhaling her scent and letting it run through me. She didn't let go, but finally asked, "What's going on, Luke?"

I pulled away and let go of the words I'd been holding in. "My dad is missing."

Her eyes widened as she latched onto my arms. "What do you mean *missing*?"

"I haven't seen or heard from him since he left here on New Year's Eve. I'm heading over to the Walkers' right now. Marcus is putting a search party together."

Her head collided with my chest and she let go of my arms to hug me around my waist. "Oh Luke, I'm so sorry. You must be going out of your mind with worry."

"Please let me help," she said into my chest before she stepped to look up at me. "I'm going to run home and get my dad and I'll meet you there, okay?"

I couldn't have said no if I'd wanted to, so I nodded and walked her to her car. Before she left she reached up and whispered, "Don't worry. We'll find him." Then she gave me the quickest of kisses and left.

CHAPTER 34

Drew

Scarlett came barreling in the house like Leatherface was chasing after her with a chainsaw in his hands. She didn't stop to say anything to me; she just ran upstairs and slammed her door shut. *The bitch has some serious issues,* I thought from my usual spot on the sofa in front of the TV. It was about two minutes later when she hurried back down wearing a sweat suit and flip-flops, not really appropriate attire for the bitter-ass cold outside, but they were her toes, not mine. Then I realized that she must be going for a run. I thought about going with her. Maybe that was what I needed to shake the boredom from my body.

If only Avery were here, I definitely wouldn't be so sexually frustrated. Sure, I could convince Becca to spread her legs at any given moment. She'd been all over me since we got here, but if Avery ever found out, she'd probably beat Becca within an inch of her life, give her time to heal, and then do it again. And I would very likely lose my favorite appendage. Best I just stay bored.

Scarlett stopped in front of the sofa, blocking my view of the TV. "Drew, I need to ask you a question. And I need you to be honest."

This sounds promising, I thought. "You know honesty isn't my strong suit, but go ahead, ask away."

"Did we have anything to do with Luke's dad disappearing?"

Here was where my semester of drama in high school would pay off. I shot up to a sitting position and widened my eyes in shock. "What? He's missing? What happened?"

"He never came home. The last time Luke saw him was New Year's Eve. Please tell me that my dad wasn't responsible for that," she pleaded, looking very suspicious. "I know we're trying to cause issues here, but we're not kidnappers. Surely you wouldn't go that far, right?"

I stood up and, channeling my inner Johnny Depp, I placed my hands on her shoulders and vowed, "I swear I don't know anything about Luke's dad. If we had anything to do with it, someone would have told me."

Scarlett chewed on her bottom lip, obviously trying to decide if I was lying. The minute I felt her shoulders relax, I knew she'd bought it.

Just then, Brian walked through the front door and instantly shot me a look that screamed, *get your hands off my daughter*! What the hell had gotten into him? It was perfectly acceptable to pimp your own daughter out to Luke, but I wasn't allowed to touch her? To prove I didn't give a shit what he thought, I tugged Scarlett closer to me and wrapped my arms around her in a big hug, and not a brother/sister-type hug either. Turning my head to Brian, I said, "Scarlett just told me that Mr. Stanton is missing."

"I heard. Marcus called and asked me to help with the search."

I released Scarlett from our embrace but kept one hand on the small of her back. "I was just reassuring Scar that we had nothing to do with it when you walked in," I explained.

Brian, who was an even better actor than I was, walked over to us, and looking his daughter straight in the eyes promised, "Honey, I swear to you we were not involved. When Marcus called me, that was the first I'd heard about it."

Scarlett's face paled as her eyes studied both her father's and my own, surely searching for some sign that we were lying. Her attention was diverted when her phone buzzed, and Brian and I both watched as she read the text. "That was Luke. I'm heading over there now. Do you want me to wait for you?" Scarlett asked her father as she squirmed out of my reach.

Brian, shaking his head, told her to go ahead and to tell them that he would be there soon. Scarlett nodded her head and took off out the door.

Brian stood by the window and watched until Scarlett was far enough away before turning his attention to me. "Everything went exactly as planned."

I followed Brian as he turned on his heel and marched into the kitchen.

"My men followed Phillip from the Marriott in Santa Fe to the ski resort in Red Ridge. After he dropped the domestic off, my guys forced Phillip's Mercedes off the road. Once they took in his imposing size, they decided to go ahead and tranq him and just be done with it. When I left our land, he was still unconscious. They will most likely need to keep him drugged while he is there just to be on the safe side," Brian explained.

"I don't understand. Why didn't they just kill him? It could have easily been made to look like a car accident. Why keep him alive?" I asked.

"Leverage. Your dad wants to make sure that things with Marcus are handled. Once he's out of the picture, we'll dispose of Phillip. We might need him if our cover is blown or my plan for Marcus falls apart. So we're keeping him alive until then. Don't worry. Phillip doesn't pose a threat. He is sedated and locked in the jail cell beneath our meeting room."

"Sounds too risky to me. A guy like Phillip is dangerous."

"Not my call. That's the way your dad wants it," he said as he shrugged. "I just do what I'm told and don't ask any questions. You know how your father is. He's never been one to take advice from anyone."

"All right, you have a point there. Should I go with you and help with the search?" I asked.

"Nah, stay here. I'm going to make sure they don't stumble upon any scents or evidence that could lead them to us."

I felt an anxious tick start up in my jaw. "I thought your guys handled it. Why would there be anything to stumble upon?"

"There isn't," Brian stated defensively. "We covered our tracks very well since we expected that there'd be a search once they realized Phillip wasn't coming home. We should be fine but it won't hurt to get out there with them and see what they find. It's just a precaution, and it's not like I can tell Marcus no, right?" Brain stopped for a moment and looked around the kitchen. "If you need something to do, how about you clean this mess up?"

I chuckled at the thought. "Yeah, right!" I hadn't cleaned a day in my life and certainly didn't plan to start now. I pushed off the counter and headed back to the couch.

Five minutes later, Brian left and I was flipping through the TV channels in search of something decent to watch. Man, this sucked. I could be home right now buried between Avery's hot thighs. Hmmm, maybe she'd be up for a little fun. I grabbed my phone and shot off a text.

> Baby, I hate it here. And I miss you so
> bad.
> Tell me what you're wearing and then
> take it off and send me a pic.

Seconds later, my phone dinged, and I looked down at the message and smiled. Oh yeah, I could work with that.

CHAPTER 35

Scarlett

With shaking hands and a stomach full of nerves, I walked to Marcus's house, hoping it would give me time to collect my thoughts and calm myself down. Tears stung my eyes as I considered the possibility that my pack was behind Luke's father's disappearance. I wanted nothing more than to believe that my own father would never do such a thing, to trust that even Drew wouldn't stoop that low. But my gut told me otherwise. This was no coincidence.

I was supposed to be making my grand escape from Red Ridge, but now I had no choice but to stay. Gavin was going to kill me for not leaving, but with all-consuming guilt and grief running through me, I knew I had to stay, had to see this through. I couldn't leave Luke, not like this. I'd never forgive myself for walking out on him. In the end, he would hate me either way. I knew in my heart that even if I ran, he would eventually find out about the part I played in all of this. The least I could do was stay and help in any way I could.

As I stood in front of the Walkers' home, I swallowed back the lump in my throat and decided what I must do. First, I needed confirmation that my pack was indeed behind Phillip's abduction. Only then could I come clean to Luke. I had to be sure, and then I'd be ready to make whatever sacrifice I needed to. This time, my pack had gone too far. It's one thing to infiltrate the pack, mess with Cade and Aiden's head, and stir up trouble; it's another to hijack their enforcer.

I'd almost made it to the front door when my phone buzzed again with another incoming text. I didn't have to look to know it was Gavin…again. He'd been blowing up my phone all morning after I texted him to tell him I wasn't coming home. I didn't offer any explanation because I knew he would flip if I told him that Phillip was gone. He definitely wouldn't want me involved. Before I went inside, I took a look at my phone on the off chance that it was Luke.

> If you don't answer me, I'm getting in
> the fucking car and driving down there!
> I'm not kidding, Scar! Don't test me.

Damn it, Gavin! I couldn't let him do that. Things were already screwed up enough. Quickly, I responded, my fingers trembling as they moved over the letters.

> I promise I'm fine. I'll leave as soon
> as I can but something came up and I
> can't get away. I'll call and explain
> asap. Just stay home!

Silently praying Gavin would stay put, I knocked on the door ready to face the pack I had betrayed. Would they see through my lies? When Luke looked at me, would I crumble? I wanted to crumble, needed to, but I couldn't. Not yet. Soon, I'd tell Luke everything, but I knew when I did, he'd push me away. He'd never want to see me again, so before the inevitable, I had to do what I could to help bring his father home safely.

The door swung open, and Luke stood before me looking as breathtaking as usual, but the hopelessness in his eyes caused my heart to constrict. Not caring who else was there, I threw myself into his arms, needing to be close to him. Luke enveloped my body in his arms and gently kissed the top of my head. "I'm so glad you're here. Thank you for coming, for wanting to help."

I pulled away and looked up into his desolate eyes. "Thank you for letting me. Right here is where I need to be." And it was true. This was exactly where I needed to be right now. I only wished my father wasn't coming. I could hardly look at him without wanting to claw his eyes out. I may not have proof, but I knew in my heart that he was lying to me. Soon he would be here, pretending that he didn't know exactly what had happened to Phillip, and somehow, I would have to act as if my own father wasn't a kidnapper. But he was. He was The Fixer. If there was a problem, he "fixed" it, and it appears as if someone decided that Phillip was a problem.

Suddenly the urge to divulge all my secrets overwhelmed me, and I opened my mouth prepared to confess everything I knew, but as if on cue, a car drove up, its door slammed, and my father's voice filled the air. "Luke, I'm so sorry to hear about your father. But don't you worry. We will find him. I'm sure of it."

He shook Luke's hand and patted him on the back with such sincerity that even I found it hard to believe that he could be behind the abduction. After a quick thank you, Luke moved aside so my father and I could enter. Without waiting for further instruction, my father headed toward voices coming from the living room with Luke and me following close behind.

As my eyes scanned the room, the nervous energy coursing through me intensified, but my father didn't bat an eye. If he'd had any part in the abduction, no one would suspect it. His no-nonsense attitude commanded the room as he got right down to business. "Good, you are all here. The sooner we get out there, the better. There are a few things we need to go over before we head out."

A very disheveled Marcus made his way over and shook Dad's hand. "Thanks for coming so quickly, Brian." My father nodded and then proceeded to go over the most productive ways to search and to cover the most ground. We may have been wolves, but we didn't have nearly as much experience with tracking as my dad, so he quickly went over a few important tips.

Just as my father was wrapping up his brief lesson on search and rescue, Marcus intervened, "We are going to split into two groups.

One group will search the main road; the other group will take the woods and the back roads.

Dad used the pat-on-the-back routine with Marcus as well. "That sounds like a good plan."

"Let's split up and get started," Marcus commanded.

At the sound of the words "split up," I grabbed Luke's hand and glued myself to his side. The last thing I wanted was for us to be separated during the search. When my father began calling out names for the groups, I implored him with my eyes to keep us together. "How about in the first group, we have Cade, Marcus, Gage, and Noel? That will leave myself, Aiden, Luke, and Scarlett in the second." Without waiting for approval from Marcus, which did not go unnoticed by the way, he then turned to Alli and added, "Alli, you can stay here with Teagan and wait by the phone in case someone calls. And since we will be in wolf form, it would be good to have someone here to open the door when we return."

Marcus didn't say a word about my father suddenly ordering people around. Instead he simply nodded his head as he moved to stand with his group. An alpha rarely relinquished control over anything, but my father acted as if this was completely normal. Maybe they had an understanding that we didn't know about, or since my father took a lead role when the psycho were-hunter came to town, Marcus was allowing him to step up. Either way it was quite odd, and apparently I wasn't the only one who noticed. With the exception of Marcus, everyone in the room looked a bit confused.

Ignoring the elephant in the room, my father walked over to pick up the shirt that was draped over the arm of the couch. He took a deep whiff of the shirt and then passed it to Marcus for him to do the same. As the shirt was passed around so everyone could take in Phillip's scent, my dad continued to give instructions. "Marcus, your group can take the main road. Be sure to stay in the tree line. You don't want to be seen. My group will stick to the woods, and the back roads into town. Let's meet back here within two hours. Obviously we won't have a watch, but be mindful of how much time has passed."

Finally Marcus spoke up. "Thank you, Brian. Make sure you all stay close to your group. And of course, stay hidden. I'm not all that comfortable going out in the daytime, but time is of the essence, and we don't have any to waste, so please be cautious." He held out his hand and asked for Luke's phone. "Let's leave your phone with Alli in case your father calls. You never know." Hope glimmered in his eyes, and for the first time, I felt bad for Marcus too, and I turned away, worried someone would see the guilt in my own eyes.

With as much privacy as we could find, we all took wolf form and headed out to begin the search. Once we reached the dirt road, we separated, and my dad took the lead in our group. Throughout the search, I stayed close to Luke. I kept my nose to the ground but never let him out of my sight. Before long, we were deep into the woods and well into the Red Ridge city limits but still no closer to finding Phillip. This came as no surprise to me. If my father was behind this, it would take more than a search of the surrounding areas to find him.

Noticing the mounting tension in Luke's rigid body, I blocked his path and consoled him in the only way I knew how in this form. I nuzzled against him, sweeping my nose across his neck. When he returned the sentiment, my heart swelled within my chest. His dark eyes bored into mine, and I so badly wanted to be able to erase the pain that filled them. He kept his eyes trained on me until Aiden came into view. Simultaneously, we both turned toward Aiden, watching as he jerked his head to the side, motioning for us to follow.

After thoroughly exploring the end of our search area, we followed my father as he headed back to the estate. The entire way back, we spread out, still holding out hope that we might catch a hint of Phillip's scent in the air. But we came up empty, and after we made it back to the house and shifted back, we soon learned that the other group had no luck finding Phillip either. There was no trace of him anywhere.

CHAPTER 36

Luke

Every second that passed without a word from my father, the more desperate the situation became. I knew the chances of finding him on the search were slim, but I was hoping for something. Maybe a clue, or a scent, or something that would give me an ounce of hope that he was alive and well. If Dad went missing just after he dropped Michelle off at the resort, then it had been roughly thirty-two hours. I've watched enough *The First 48* on A&E to know that we were running out of time. After searching the routes to town and most of the area surrounding Red Ridge, we'd come up empty.

I didn't know what to do next. We couldn't call the police. They wouldn't be any better at finding someone than a pack of werewolves anyway. As far as I knew, there was no official werewolf organization where I could report him missing. The only thing I could do was trust that Marcus could solve the mystery of my missing father. Last year that would have been enough for me. A few months ago even, but now, with Marcus behaving so erratically and out of character, I just didn't feel confident that he was up for the job.

After Noel served everyone some ice water, we all gathered in the front room of the Walkers' house waiting for someone to say something. Finally after guzzling the entire contents of his glass, Marcus broke the silence. "Brian, you have connections with the surrounding packs. You need to make contact with them. See if they know anything. At least make them aware that one of our kind is missing."

"Of course," Brian agreed.

"See if they know anything. Anything! At least let them know that Phillip…"

"Dad?" Cade questioned.

We all looked on horrified as Marcus, glassy-eyed and sweating profusely, swayed on his feet as he continued to repeat himself over and over again. Cade tried to take his father's arm, but Marcus swung out wildly stopping any offer of assistance. On his own, Marcus made his way to the arm chair by the fireplace and collapsed.

Suddenly, the air in the room felt thick and suffocating. Something was definitely wrong with our alpha. What were the chances that Marcus was sick or losing his mind during the same time that my dad went missing? Suspicions filled my head, and by the look on Cade's face, he was coming to the same conclusion. We needed to figure out what happened to my dad. And somehow convince Marcus to see the pack's doctor. Could this be the work of the mystery pack that was supposedly after us? I couldn't argue that it was possible, but it didn't explain Marcus's outbursts. He hadn't been off the estate in several days.

A moment later, Marcus took a deep breath and pushed himself to his feet. "I will make some calls and work with Brian to get the word out. Luke, I'm going to need you to go home and stay by the phone in case Phillip calls." He straightened his clothing and smoothed back his hair as if nothing had happened.

Unsure how else to respond, I simply nodded as he continued, "Let's all meet here at the same time again tomorrow."

Scarlett took my hand and whispered, "Want me to come with you?"

Of course I wanted her to come with me. I wanted to drown myself in all that was Scarlett Reed and forget about everything else. But I knew I needed some time to process, to focus on what to do next. Turning to face her, I pushed a piece of hair behind her ear and asked, "Is it okay if I just call you later? It's been a really long day, and I'm not going to be good company."

"I understand," she assured me before kissing my cheek.

Quickly, I thanked everyone for helping with the search before walking out the door. The skies were darkening as I made my way home alone. My thoughts were scattered all over the place, and the last thing I wanted to do was sit idly by the phone. There had to be something more I could do. I just didn't know what.

With only the slightest glimmer of hope, I opened the front door but noticed all too soon that the house was exactly as I'd left it. I checked the voicemail, but there were none. Needing to do something, I headed into my dad's office and went online to log into our bank account. I thought maybe there would be some unusual purchases or questionable charges that might point me in some kind of direction. But all I'd learned was that the last time Dad used his debit card was at the Marriott in Santa Fe. Nothing after that. There weren't any suspicious charges before that either.

Since I was already going through our finances, I grabbed the credit card statements from Dad's office and called to get the most recent transactions. I was on a roll then, and I started pilfering through everything. Every file my Dad had, every folder in the cabinet and every document on his laptop, every box of photos and mementos from his life. Nothing was left out.

I was sitting on the floor of the office surrounded by papers holding the very last box, the box labeled Victoria Stanton 1976-1996, when the doorbell rang. Saved by the bell was an understatement. With Dad missing, it was probably not the best time to be looking at all of my mother's things. I carefully placed the box aside and went to answer the door.

"I hope you don't mind, but we are keeping you company tonight," Aiden said, holding five pizza boxes out in front of him.

"I don't give a shit if he minds or not. Move it Stanton, I'm freezing out here," Gage announced as he squeezed past me, carrying a pack of sodas in each hand.

Surprised by their arrival, I moved aside, and they all came in one by one. Aiden entered carrying the pizzas. Teagan followed him in with a stack of movies in her hands. Alli was next with a couple of blankets tucked under her arm. Cade was by her side with a box of microwave popcorn. Last but certainly not least, Scarlett was standing on my doorstep. The one person I actually wanted to see tonight. She was holding a plastic bag full of every different candy bar imaginable.

"Sorry, I succumbed to peer pressure. I know you wanted to be alone tonight," she said shyly as she walked in.

I put my hand on her waist to stop her at my side. "You are the very best distraction I could ever ask for," I whispered in her ear before my lips found the soft and fragrant skin just behind it. I felt her body come alive from the simple touch of my lips, and suddenly I wished we were all alone.

"Find anything helpful?" Cade asked, pointing to my mess on the office floor. Not thinking, I'd left the door wide open. "No, I thought maybe I would find something, like a strange charge on his credit card or a withdrawal from our back account, but I didn't find anything," I explained as I wandered over to shut the door. By the time I'd made it to the kitchen, everyone had made themselves at home. I thought that I had wanted to be alone, but as I looked around at the room full of friends, I knew I was wrong.

CHAPTER 37

Drew

"So how did the 'big search' go?" I asked, making exaggerated air quotes with my fingers as Brian came in the house and began to warm his hands in front of the fireplace. I already knew the answer of course. It went great for us, but not so great for poor Luke. I didn't expect it to take so long though.

"The search went as predicted, and they found nothing." He looked at me over his shoulder, "The real excitement came after the search."

"Oh yeah?" I asked, hoping he'd elaborate.

"Marcus lost it. He started rambling on, repeating himself over and over again, swaying on his feet. He even took a swing at Cade. That's what took so long. Well, that and when Marcus finally did get himself together, he asked me to contact some of the other packs. He asked me to stay and make my calls from his office. I wasn't really comfortable with that, but I couldn't see a plausible way out of it, so I went along. No harm done I guess. I know my men and nothing will be found that can be traced back to us, but now, thanks to my assistance, every pack in the West is on alert for the missing enforcer."

"Let's just hope your guys did as good of a job as you think they did."

"Trust me, they did," Brian said with confidence as he turned to face me.

He better have been right. I was about to inherit a pack that was up to its testicles in financial problems. The last thing I needed was for us to get caught in this scandal. Then we really would lose everything. When my father told me about Mr. Langley, our pack's ex-treasurer, taking off and disappearing with almost every cent of the pack's money, I couldn't believe it. I couldn't believe that my dad was stupid enough to allow one single person access to all of that money.

Without money, our business failed, and with no way to make more money, we were going to losing our land. Land that has been in our family for generations. All because my father did the unthinkable without any consultation or discussion with the elders. He mortgaged the property thinking that he would be able to both revive our business and find Mr. Langley to get our money back. Neither happened. All of which led us to Red Ridge. We not only needed their land, we needed their business and money too. When Marcus first called and needed Brian's services, we saw the perfect opportunity. Get rid of Marcus, pit Cade and Aiden against each other, come in and rescue the pack from themselves.

One could argue that we'd be doing them a favor. And we had less than a month to do it. Thirty days to vacate the property that my great-grandparents purchased decades ago. *Man, if I could get my hands on that son of a bitch Langley...*

"Have you talked to your dad recently?" Brian asked.

"About?"

"Our timeline. Are we still good with time?"

"If you call a little over three weeks good," I quipped.

Brian did his best attempt at a smile and leaned back in the chair resting his extra-long legs on the coffee table in front of him. I hated it when Brian tried to smile. The crazy-ass scar across his lip actually prohibits him from smiling properly so it always comes out looking sinister. That and his creepy eyes make him a freaky-looking beast. It wasn't hard to understand how he could strike the fear of God in just about anyone if he needed to.

"I'm not worried," Brian stated.

"Maybe you should be worried," I mentioned and then leaned in to add, "about Scarlett."

"What about Scarlett?"

"I have a feeling she's getting a little too attached to our poor Luke."

"What makes you think that?" he asked as he sat up in his chair. *Well, I guess that got his attention. And now that I have it...*

"Have you seen her around him? I tell you Brian, I think you need to send her home," I suggested.

A minute passed before he replied, "I think she can handle it, at least for a few more days. Luke is so upset with his dad missing. You can see it on his face. Let's let him lean on Scarlett for support and just when he needs her most, we'll send her away. It will crush him. Either that, or she can try to convince him to join us."

"No fucking way!" I snapped. "I have seen that shithead in action. He is way too loyal to betray his pack, and he's too damn lethal to let live."

"Then let's speed things up. Marcus is fading faster than any of us expected. Phillip is out of the picture. Luke is distracted. Cade and Aiden are nowhere near coming to an agreement. I could send Scarlett away in a few days, kill Luke, Marcus, and Phillip, and take over the pack. What's stopping us?"

"My father, for one," I noted.

"We can always say that we had to. That we were discovered." Brian shrugged and flashed another evil-looking smile.

Finally a plan with balls. "I'm in!"

CHAPTER 38

Scarlett

We were well into our third movie and I had been snuggled up next to Luke for a few hours, yet we'd hardly spoken. Since everyone arrived, we'd shared a few stolen glances but very few words. I couldn't gauge what was going on in his head or how he was handling his father's disappearance. I wasn't even sure if he wanted us all here, but the longer we sat here in silence, the less comfortable I was saying anything, so the silence stretched on.

Unfortunately, it only gave me more time to sink deeper into my thoughts, thoughts filled with regret and guilt, and Gavin had been blowing up my phone all day, which only served to repeatedly remind me of the mess I'd made of everything. I finally turned it off before we all met up to go to Luke's. But it didn't stop that sinking feeling in the pit of my stomach or the one question that had haunted me all day from popping into my head every few minutes: *What the hell am I going to do now?*

I had no idea what my next move should be. Should I leave like I'd planned? Tell Luke the truth and pray that my alpha didn't kill me for betraying our pack? Could I actually just stay and pretend I hadn't been lying to Luke this entire time? Maybe if I switched sides I could prove to Luke in the end that I didn't want to be a part of this. No, I knew he would hate me either way. But I could stay and do whatever I could to help him find his father and try to protect them from my pack. The truth was I had no idea what the right answer was or if there even was a right answer, but if I had to choose between doing whatever I could to help the Red Ridge Pack or tucking my tail and running, I was going to stay and help. But how was I supposed to face Luke and act as if I wasn't at fault for any of this?

I was shaken out of my internal what-do-I-do-now tirade when Luke began to run his fingers lightly up and down my arm. "Hey, you still awake?"

The sound of his voice instantly shot little jolts of electricity through my body, causing me to jump a bit, but I tried to play it off by sitting up and looking around. "Yeah, but it looks like everyone else is passed out."

Luke leaned up and paused the movie. "You hungry? Wanna head down to the kitchen?"

I looked his way and smiled, happy to hear that he felt like eating since I hadn't seen him eat much all day. "Sure. I'm always up for a late night snack." I stood, and as I followed him down the stairs, that sinking feeling in the pit of my stomach was quickly replaced with nerves now that we were alone…kind of, anyway.

On the way into the kitchen, I reminded myself over and over again to just act normal. That was what Luke needed right now. I needed to get out of my own head, get past all the shit rolling around in there, and just be there for Luke. He needed a friend, not a crazy pseudo-girlfriend who had a secret so big that it could fill the entire downstairs.

Luke headed straight for the refrigerator and let out a sigh. "Nothing in here worth eating unless you're up for takeout from a week or so ago." He checked the due date on the milk, and asked, "Cereal?"

When he turned my way with a half-empty gallon of milk in his hand, I nodded and watched as he headed over to the pantry to check out our options. "We got Cocoa Puffs, Apple Jacks, and some healthy shit my dad eats."

I opened up the cabinets I assumed would most likely hold the bowls and replied, "I'll take the Cocoa Puffs. Then I get chocolate milk too."

Taking milk and the box of cereal over to the table, he laughed. "That's what I've always said. My dad's been trying to shovel sugarless, whole-grain oats down my throat for years."

His smile remained, but it couldn't hide the sadness in his eyes. Guilt tried its damnedest to swallow me whole right then and there, but I somehow managed to smile back. I just hoped it looked genuine. As I set our bowls down, I replied, "I understand completely. My mother used to try to convince me that if she put fresh strawberries in some Special K that it would taste just as good as my Frosted Flakes. Yeah, not so much."

We didn't say much else as we chomped on our Cocoa Puffs, which only served to make the sound of our chewing ridiculously loud. A few times our eyes met, and we both laughed at our failed attempts to quiet our crunching. After his last bite, Luke sat there with a bowl full of chocolate milk and patiently waited for me to finish. When I'd fished out the last few stray puffs and stuck them in my mouth, he watched me chew and then asked, "Ready?"

He lifted his bowl to his lips and waited for me to do the same. With my bowl in my hands, I answered, "Ready." His smile made me smile, and then we were both trying not to laugh while be gulped down the chocolaty milk. As Luke reached for a napkin, he teased, "Damn girl, you look all kinds of sexy with a mustache." I shot him a dirty look and snatched the napkin from his hand to wipe my mouth. Chuckling to himself, he rinsed our bowls in the sink, and then I followed him into the living room.

After Luke started a fire in the huge fireplace that took up most of one of the walls, he grabbed a blanket out of a basket next to an oversized chair. I sat down on one end of the couch, and he spread it over my legs. He climbed under the other end of the blanket, and we sat facing each other, myself on one end and Luke on the other with our legs entangled in between. I hoped he couldn't feel the chill bumps that broke out over my body when his calf rubbed against mine.

Luke stared at the fire and appeared to be lost in thought. Without taking his eyes off the flames, he asked, "So, do you have any idea how long you're going to stay here?"

A lump formed in my throat at the thought of leaving him. I'd almost left today. I was supposed to leave last night. Yet here I sat, and I knew right then that I didn't want to ever leave. I could be content staring into Luke Stanton's eyes for the rest of my life, which was exactly what I was doing until Luke turned his attention to me and raised his eyebrows, probably wondering why I wasn't answering. "I'm not sure. I guess until my father decides it's time to leave," I finally replied.

"So what about your mom? Did she stay with your pack?"

His question caught me off guard, especially since my focus was on the way his leg felt resting against mine. My head snapped up, and the words flew out of my mouth before I had time to consider them. "She died." Immediately, heat rose to my chest and then up to my cheeks. Luke's eyes grew wide, and I knew that was probably the last thing he expected to come out of my mouth. From underneath the blanket, he ran his fingers over my leg, and with sad eyes, he said, "I'm sorry to hear that. My mom passed away too, but it was a long time ago. When did you lose her?"

"It's been almost a year now. But it still seems like yesterday. She was beautiful and perfect. She loved me like no other, but just like that she was gone." Tears stung my eyes, and I clenched them shut before a drop could fall. I felt like such a fool, but I had never said those words aloud. I had never spoken of her death. Everyone in our pack just knew; I'd never had to actually say it.

When I felt the couch shift, I opened my eyes. Luke sat up and pulled me toward him. "Come here, Scarlett. I didn't mean to upset you." He wrapped me up in his arms and laid my body against his. My head rested on his chest, and he ran his fingers through my hair. Nothing had ever felt so good.

"We don't have to talk about it. I wish I could say that I understand, but I don't. Not really. My mother died during childbirth, so I never got to meet her. All I know is that my father loved her like crazy. He never really recovered and has never let himself love another woman since. Instead, he poured everything he had left into being my dad and this pack's enforcer. I'm lucky to have him. He's always tried to love me enough for the both of them. I guess he felt like he had to make up for my mother not being here."

"He sounds like a really good guy, your dad. Mine has hardly looked at me since the night my mother died. He'll never admit it, but he blames me. She was on her way to pick me up from the movies when she was run off the road by an eighteen-wheeler. I'd begged her to let me go to a midnight movie, and I wouldn't let up until she said yes. My brother tells me all the time that it wasn't my fault, but she was out that night because of me, so I really can't blame my father for feeling the way he does."

Luke pulled his arms around me tighter and kissed the top of my head. "You know you can't blame yourself, right? It's not your fault. When I was old enough to understand why I didn't have a mom like everyone else, my Dad explained, in the best way he could, how she died. I carried that around for a long time, feeling like it was all my fault. It didn't matter that I was only a baby. If it hadn't have been for me, she would be alive, and my father would still have her. Even though he told me over and over again, that if that was true, then he wouldn't have me, I didn't listen. It took a long time to get past it, but somehow he finally got it through my thick skull. It wasn't my fault. And it wasn't yours either."

My heart swelled. His words meant more to me than he would ever know. I needed to hear it, even if I wasn't sure I could believe it yet. But maybe someday…

I kept my head on his chest, thankful he couldn't see my face. "You're right. It wasn't your fault, and I'm sorry you never got to meet your mother. I bet she would have been a wonderful mom."

"Yeah, I bet she would have too. So you and your mother, were you really close?"

"Very. My dad always favored Gavin, but it didn't matter then because I was a mommy's girl from the start. She was my favorite person in the world. My friends used to tease me and say that I'd rather hang out with her than anyone else. And it was true. We did everything together." My heart warmed as memories of my mother flooded my thoughts. It had been so long since I'd talked about her.

Luke ran his fingers through my hair as we lay there in silence. My eyes closed, and I listened to the beating of his heart, wondering if he was thinking about his dad. As if he could read my mind, he answered my question. "My dad and me are like that too. I hang out with him more than anyone, especially after Gage ran off. It's weird. He somehow managed to be my best friend and my dad at the same time, you know?"

Luke's voice cracked a little, and it made my heart hurt. I didn't look, but I wondered if his eyes were watering too. "Yeah, I know. My mom was like that too. I remember her helping me get ready for my first date. She forced me to go shopping with her and get my nails done. Then she insisted on doing my hair and makeup. I think she was more excited than I was. Then she hugged me, held my hand, and threatened to rip his head off when he dumped me a week later." I paused for a few seconds as I relived the moment in my head. "She would have really liked you, Luke."

I felt foolish saying it, but it was true. She would have loved him, but what really stung was the realization that she'd be so disappointed in the choices I've made. She certainly would have knocked my dad's head in for involving me in this.

Luke's voice broke into my thoughts. "You really think she would have liked me?" He sounded genuinely surprised as if he actually thought I was bullshitting him.

This time, I did look up. "Of course she would have. She would have loved you, Luke... And hey, don't worry. We are going to find your dad. I'm sure of it."

He didn't answer with words. Instead, he pulled me on top of him and kissed me fiercely. Every inch of our bodies melded together. As his hands made their way down my back, he kissed me harder, deeper. I couldn't help but moan as he grabbed my hips, pulling my body even closer. I felt him harden beneath me, and without a second thought, I rubbed myself against him. My hips rocked back and forth causing a desperate need to build inside of me. Luke's hands began to explore my body, but I wanted—no, *needed*—to feel his skin against mine, to feel his taut muscles tighten under my touch.

I pulled up his shirt, and his lips left mine but only long enough to pull his shirt over his head. My eyes took in his perfect physique as I ran my fingertips over his sculpted chest, down the ripples of his stomach, to the waistband of his jeans. I stopped there and looked up just in time to catch a wicked glint in Luke's eyes.

He sat up and as he pressed his lips to mine once more, his fingers slipped under the hem of my shirt. Slowly, he began to lift it up revealing my stomach, but before it got any further, a light came on upstairs and Cade's voice followed.

"Hey, Luke? Man, you down there?"

We froze, and all I could do was hope that he stayed put. Luke sighed and under his breath muttered, "Shit." Then he turned his head to the side so he didn't yell in my ear. "Yeah, I'm down here with Scarlett. Everything's fine. Go back to bed."

"All right, man. I'm gonna watch some TV 'til I fall back asleep. Let me know if you need anything."

Luke let out another deep sigh, and I buried my head in his chest in attempt to suppress a girlie giggle. Before long, he was laughing too. I rolled off of him and snuggled into his side. I rested my head on his bare chest, and we laid there without speaking for a while before Luke whispered, "Good night, Scarlett."

Running my fingers across his chest, I answered, "Good night, Luke." Then I closed my eyes and drifted off to sleep.

CHAPTER 39

Luke

Images of Scarlett's long, lean leg draped across mine as she slept soundly on my chest kept flashing through my mind causing me to move a lot slower than normal this morning. I hated to admit it, even to myself, but I really needed last night. I needed to be surrounded by friends. The mindless chit-chat and stupid comedies had helped. I needed to talk about my mom with someone who could relate and understand the guilt I sometimes still feel for my mother's death. Most importantly though, falling asleep tangled up in Scarlett's comforting scent somehow made me feel like things were going to be okay. She gave me hope for some kind of future, as cheesy as that sounds.

I had never slept with someone before—I mean actually *slept* all night together. We were both too emotionally drained from our conversation and not to mention nearly getting busted by Cade for anything more than sleep. Well, at least not until much later in the night. These were the memories I seriously considered might have only been a dream, that is until Scarlett woke up being shy and awkward this morning.

Sometime during the night, while we were sleeping on the sofa together under a warm, fluffy blanket, my hands began moving on their own. First, just slowly up and down her back. Scarlett responded instantly to my touch. Our eyes met in the darkness as we turned to face each other on the sofa only a moment before my lips crashed into hers. While our lips moved with fierce desperation, my hand was gently making its way down until I found the hem of her tank top. I slid my hand up under her top, loving the warmth of her skin. I wrapped my hand around her back and pulled her even closer to me as my tongue delved deeper into her mouth. With my hand at her back, I felt for the clasp of her bra and in one quick motion, unhooked it. I paused for a moment, giving her a chance to stop me, but instead she rocked her hips against me and made the sexiest little moaning sound I had ever heard. That sound alone made me want to slide it into home base, but I couldn't do that with Scarlett. For the first time, I wanted this to be just about her.

I pushed her tank top up, giving me access to her perfect breasts. I slid my hand up under her bra, and as my fingers toyed with her nipple, she held tight to my shoulder and continued to grind her hips against me. I'd never been so hard in my life. I kissed my way down past her neck. A sharp gasp escaped her lips as my tongue flicked over the peak of her breast. I was in heaven, taking my time, savoring each of those delicious breasts that I had been fantasizing about since I first time I saw them practically bursting out of the top of that sweater at the party by the lake.

Finally, leaving my mouth where it wanted to be, I let my hand travel down the side of her stomach, feeling her muscles twitch under my touch along the way. She was nearly panting, and I knew that it wouldn't take much to send her over the edge. Scarlett tensed just slightly as my hand dipped under the waistband of her yoga pants, and I urged her knees apart with my leg. Only moments after my fingers found their final destination, I felt her climax as my name passed her lips in a hushed growl.

I trailed little kisses back up her neck to her lips as I felt her entire body begin to relax. Suddenly, my eyes widened as I felt her hand leave my shoulder and quickly slide its way down my stomach. I knew where she was going, and I also knew what would happen between us tonight if she got there, so I stopped her.

"I just don't want to rush anything with us, okay?" I breathed into her ear.

Testing my resolve, Scarlett pushed herself against me, her palm rubbing my rock-hard erection while whispering, "You sure?"

Holy shit! Squeezing my eyes shut, I took a deep breath and sat up. Turning to face her on the sofa, I froze. She was propped up on some pillows, her hair was a mess, and her lips were swollen. The glow from the fireplace was casting shadows across her face. I swear she was the most beautiful person I had ever seen.

"You are the only thing I am sure about these days," I admitted.

The playfully seductive smile fell from her lips. She reached for my hand, pulled me back down, and cuddled up around me. That was how we fell back to sleep and that was how we were when we woke up.

I didn't want Scarlett to leave this morning, but she needed to go home and I needed to get over to Marcus's and figure out our next step. If the memories of last night were that distracting, I couldn't imagine what actually having her here by my side all day would be like. When Scarlett was near me, I couldn't help but feel a little happy even when everything else around me was falling apart, and feeling happy made me feel like shit. If my dad was out there somewhere suffering, I shouldn't be smiling; I certainly shouldn't be daydreaming about picking up where Scarlett and I left off last night. But there was a small part of me that knew that my dad would want me to be happy. At least that was what I was telling myself when the phone rang.

"Luke, the Santa Fe Sherriff's department called. They found your father's car. Noel and I are leaving now to go meet the Sheriff. Would you like us to pick you up on the way?" Marcus asked.

"Yes, sir. Thank you. Did they say anything about my father?" I asked.

"No, they didn't, but we may be able to find something in his car that will tell us what happened."

"Okay, sir. I'm ready when you are."

"We'll be there in five."

Finally, a lead. Making sure that I had my keys and cell phone, I threw on my coat and went to wait on the porch.

*****

"Since the car is registered to me as a company car, the police called me when they realized that it had been abandoned here. I made up a story about the employee who drives this car, getting so intoxicated on New Year's Eve that he forgot where he parked it. As luck would have it, the car was found in the back of a mall parking lot, very close to a nightclub. So if the sheriff asks, that's the story," Marcus explained as we pulled into the Santa Fe Hills Shopping Mall.

While Mr. and Mrs. Walker talked to the sheriff's deputy, I walked around the car looking for anything that could tell me where Dad was before he went missing. The car was unlocked, so I opened the driver's-side door and leaned in, trying to pick up on any foreign scents. All I came up with was my father's and the sweet scent that must have belonged to Michelle. I closed the door and stood out of the way while Marcus thanked the deputy. We all watched as he got into his patrol car and drove away.

The moment he was gone, Marcus erupted. "I knew it! I don't know which pack is fucking with us, but I will find out and when I do, I will make them pay!"

"Calm down, Marcus. We don't know that," Noel said.

I backed away as Marcus began to tremble. "They're after us, Noel. Don't think for one second that they aren't. They've taken Phillip. Hell, he's probably dead by now. I'll be next. They'll come after me, just like they did him. Then they will take the boys. They will pick us off one by one. They will come after you too, Noel. No one is safe," Marcus ranted. Noel grabbed Marcus by the shoulders, trying to calm him down.

I stood there frozen. Did he really just say that out loud? That some pack had killed my dad?

"Noel, you don't understand. We have to prepare our pack for the attack. We can't waste any more time…"

Waste any more time? Waste any more time? Is that what Marcus thinks we're doing? Wasting time? Is it wasting time looking for my father…his enforcer?

Tears stung at my eyes as my fists clenched, and the urge to beat the shit out of my alpha was almost unbearable. My eyes narrowed in on the rapid pulse in his neck.

"Marcus, you need to settle down—" Noel tried again, but Marcus cut her off.

"Let's get out of here. They're probably watching us right now," Marcus said, looking around wildly. "This could be a trap."

That was it. He didn't give a shit about my father. My father had been his enforcer since they were nineteen years old, and this was what he got for it. Marcus thought my dad was already dead, and it seemed he couldn't care less. He was more worried about himself at the moment.

I had to get out of here before I did something that could jeopardize the pack. I held my hand out to Noel with a look on my face that I hoped screamed *give me the damn keys before I kill someone.* Luckily, Noel was not a stupid woman. She stood in between Marcus and me and mouthed, *I'm sorry,* before dropping the keys in my hand.

Marcus was still looking around the parking lot for rival pack members and screaming about being prepared for war when I slammed the door the shut and drove away.

CHAPTER 40

Scarlett

My cheeks were flushed both from the cold and from the memories of last night when I walked through the back door. Before I went home this morning, I shifted into wolf form and went for a run. I needed to collect my thoughts before I faced my father. Things with Luke went further than I'd intended last night, and not just physically. The feelings stirring inside me were freaking me out. I knew before the night began that I had feelings for Luke, but now...now I was hooked, completely infatuated, and had moved well beyond the *like* stage.

I ran until my muscles throbbed, but it brought me no closer to an answer of what to do next. There was no way in hell that I would help my father, but I still didn't know how to handle the situation. I tried to convince myself that in reality, I hadn't really *done* much of anything, but the truth was that the intentions were there, and that I couldn't deny. I had come here to Red Ridge to help my pack, and while I hadn't actually played any real part in the plan, I had agreed to toy with Luke's emotions, get inside his head, and try to get him to back Aiden for alpha. Instead, the opposite had happened. Luke had most definitely gotten inside my head, and my emotional state was like a perfect storm, set on a course of complete and total destruction.

I tiptoed through the mudroom, silently chastising myself for being a chicken-shit, but I just wasn't ready to see my dad, or even worse, Drew. Relieved to find an empty house, I grabbed a bottle of water and a granola bar and hurried up the stairs. Tucked safe inside my room, I fell onto my bed. Immediately my mind was flooded with visions of Luke and me wrapped up in each other's arms on the couch last night. Warmth spread throughout my body, causing my cheeks to flush and desire to pool deep inside me.

While everyone I knew, even my closest friends, believed me to be *experienced* in all areas of life, the truth was that I'd hardly rounded second base before last night. Oddly enough, it was my own pack's enforcer, Justin King, who had supposedly had his way with me a couple of years ago. He tried, boy did he try, but I wasn't ready. I had to knee him in the balls to get his paws off of me, but that wasn't what he told the rest of pack. The next day, Justin claimed to be the proud owner of my virginity. From then on, everyone just assumed I was easy and didn't hesitate to treat me as such, though I couldn't deny that I was partly to blame. At the time, I was barely sixteen, and stupidly and blindly went along with it. Before I knew it, I was acting the part. While no other guy in the pack ever got anywhere near as far as Justin did, I started dressing in low-cut tops, short skirts, and tight jeans. Flirting became second nature, which only solidified my reputation, and nobody ever stopped to question who else I'd actually been with. It's amazing how much bullshit people were willing to believe.

Now, here I was, little virgin Scarlett, completely enamored with a guy I'd just met and had actually almost gone through with *it* last night. If he hadn't stopped us, I wasn't sure whether I would have or not, but if I had to guess, I was pretty sure that I wouldn't have said no. Being with him felt so right, which just made everything else so screwed up. I had to come clean. I couldn't run off into the night and pretend none of this had ever happened. Before I could talk myself out of it, I pulled out my phone to text Gavin.

> Hey I'm sticking around. I can't leave just yet. Don't try to talk me out of it. U just have to trust me. Stay put and I'll keep u in the loop.

I stared at my phone for a few minutes, awaiting Gavin's reply. I only hoped he wasn't packing up his car right now to come rescue me from Red Ridge. When my phone chirped, my heart practically leapt out of my chest. Hesitantly, I peeked at the screen.

> Fine I'll give u a few days but I'm
> ready to jump in the car at a moment's
> notice. Watch ur back Scar. Ur asking
> for trouble by staying there.

I hated to admit it, but he was right. Ditching Red Ridge would be my safest option, but I wasn't going to leave Luke. I had to do whatever I could to make this right, or at least try to. I needed to be honest with someone. I needed to talk to my dad.

Minutes and then hours passed as I waited for my father to return. I'd picked up my phone at least a dozen times to call him but knew that what I needed to say had to be done in person. So I waited...and waited. I'd showered, picked at my lunch, checked my email, and read a week's worth of status updates on Facebook and Twitter. Finally, at 6:05 p.m., the front door swung open. I was relieved to see that my dad was alone. I didn't need Drew here for this.

When the door closed behind him, I asked, "Hey, where ya been?"

Barely making eye contact, he replied, "Just had some business to take care of." He wandered into the kitchen and opened the fridge. He pulled out a beer, popped the top, and gulped down half of it before coming up for air. "What are you doing here? Don't you think you should be consoling Luke or something? This is the perfect opportunity to be his rock. He's vulnerable right now, which means he'll listen to you. Why don't you text him? See where he's at." He took another long swig of beer before the glanced out the widow. "It's about to rain, so you should head out soon."

I placed my laptop on the coffee table and dragged myself up off the couch. As I walked into the kitchen, I took a deep breath to try to calm the hurricane of nerves brewing inside me. "Dad, we need to talk. I don't want to be a part of this anymore. I can't. I care about Luke, and I don't want to hurt him. Before you ask, I haven't told him anything, and I thought about just leaving, but now that his dad is missing and…" I trailed off as soon as I saw the storm of rage flash across his face. Suddenly I saw what everyone else seemed to see when they looked at my father. While I always thought he was intimidating as hell, he never really looked scary to me. But now…Now I knew I'd made a huge mistake by trying to explain.

He took a few steps toward me and I backed up, cowering like a frightened puppy. Slamming his near-empty beer bottle down on the table, he roared, "You what? You really think you can just run off and there will be no consequences? You were asked to do one little thing. One measly little thing and now you're actually telling me you *care* too much. Give me a fucking break, Scarlett," He ran his fingers through his hair and looked around the room before his rage-fueled eyes landed on me once again.

His glare caused to me to back up a few more steps. "Dad…I'm sorry. I don't know what to do," I pleaded. "I don't want to hurt him. I want out."

"You don't want to hurt him?" He raised his chin and chuckled to himself. "You don't just get to decide that you want out, you stupid, pathetic child! I should have known you couldn't pull this off. You're too selfish, too weak to do what it takes to save our pack. Guess you plan to just let our pack die, like you did your own mother."

As his words sliced through me, my world grew fuzzy, and I found it hard to breathe, much less stand. Tears flooded my eyes, and when my back found the wall behind me, I slowly slid down to the ground. Wrapping my arms around my knees, I dropped my head and sobbed. I heard my father move and then felt him standing above me. For a brief moment, I thought he might reach down and gather me in his arms like he used to when I was a little girl. But that didn't happen. He grabbed my hair and pulled my head back to force me to look at his. He stood above me, my hair entangled in his hand, and stated flatly, "You don't have the right to call yourself The Fixer's daughter, you weak-minded piece of trash. Now get out of my house before I force you out. You have a job to do. So get your pathetic self together and do it!"

He released my hair, allowing my head to fall, and headed back to the fridge to help himself to another beer. I scrambled up off of the floor and hurried toward the door. I pulled it open and for a moment, watched as the rain poured down from the sky. I couldn't turn around to get an umbrella and my keys were on the table in the kitchen. So, I grabbed my coat from the coat rack, covered my head with the hood, and ran out into the rain.

CHAPTER 41

Luke

After leaving Santa Fe, my day went from bad to worse. I drove all the way back to Red Ridge in pouring rain and a blinding rage. I was so pissed at Marcus, and as much as I tried, I could not calm myself down. I couldn't believe how little Marcus actually cared about my father considering Dad had been his friend and enforcer since before I was born. Marcus just gave up hope completely, decided he must be dead. I doubt he would bother continuing to search for him, so I guess I'd be on my own then.

My mind was racing a mile a minute when the small grocery store on the edge of town caught my eye, and I remembered there was zero food in the house. Dad always did the grocery shopping, but I figured I should stop to pick up a few things to keep me going for a while.

I was wandering aimlessly up and down the aisles lost in thought when Michelle, dad's girlfriend, walked up and rested her hand-held basket on her hip, "Honey, are you all right? You look kinda out of it."

I snapped out of it and answered, "Oh yes, ma'am. I guess I'm just tired."

Smiling, she glanced inside my basket to find it practically empty. "Where's that handsome daddy of yours? I usually see him doing the shopping."

Thinking quickly, I explained, "He had to go out of town. Some emergency business trip."

"And he didn't have time to shop for you, huh?" she teased and took my cart. She placed her basket inside and started walking. "Well, we can't have you starve, and I don't think you should live off of Fritos and bean dip while he's gone. How about I help you out?"

Michelle was such a nice woman. Simple and genuine, the kind of woman my father deserved, but I knew he would never allow himself to truly have. I felt guilty for lying to her, for making her believe that my dad was safe in some hotel on business when the truth was that even his own alpha thought that he was dead.

Things got even more uncomfortable when we got to the front of the checkout line and Taylor was at the register. I didn't even know that she worked there. Guilt washed over me when I realized just how little I knew about this girl. I never did call or text her after I stood her up New Year's Eve, and if the look she was giving me was any indication, she hadn't forgiven me.

"Well if it isn't Luke Stanton," Taylor said, oozing attitude.

Michelle looked at me and smiled, surely knowing that I had done something to piss this girl off. I decided that the best thing to do was to remain silent and get out of there as fast as possible.

I just stood there and watched as she rang up the groceries, ignoring the fact that she was shooting daggers at me with her eyes the entire time. After I paid, and she handed me the receipt, I finally looked at her and blurted out, "Taylor, I really am sorry. See you at school after break?" Then I grabbed the cart and took off out of the store, hoping Michelle had followed since her groceries were in my cart as well.

My quick trip to the store didn't exactly go as planned. As if things weren't complicated enough. I was already angry with Marcus and worried sick about my dad. Now I felt like an ass for standing up Taylor and guilty as hell for lying to Michelle, who obviously cared about Dad. Next time, I'll just starve…or go eat at Gage's.

"I can't thank you enough, Michelle, really," I told her as I walked her to her car.

"It's no big deal, honey. You better get home before it starts raining again. If you need anything while your daddy's gone, you call me, okay?"

After we packed up her car, I thanked her once more and as soon as I turned to head toward my car, rain began pouring from the sky with a vengeance, freezing cold rain that stings your face and burns your hands. Without hesitation, I ran to the car, threw my bags in, blasted the heater, and drove home as quickly as possible in the downpour.

After I pulled the car into the garage and put the groceries away, I did a complete search of my father's car. I couldn't find a single damn thing in there that would help me find my dad or even help me figure out what may have happened to him. The more I searched the more frustrated I became. After that, I tried to pull myself together, but my emotions were all over the place. I went from angry to sad to helpless to numb in record time. While in the stage of numbness, I made myself dinner, took a shower, and then sat in the living room staring at the weather channel on TV. I needed to figure out my next move, but I couldn't focus. All I knew was that Marcus may have given up searching for my father but that didn't mean that I would.

When I finally decided that my brain couldn't handle being tortured anymore, I turned the TV off and planned to go sulk in bed. I was halfway up the stairs when the doorbell rang. I paused in mid-step, and contemplated ignoring it, then decided that probably wasn't a good idea given how my luck was running lately.

I peeked through the peep hole, vowing if it was another impromptu sleepover, that I wouldn't answer, but when I saw Scarlett soaking wet and shivering on my doorstep, I swung open the door and pulled her inside. "Holy shit, baby. Get in here. What are you doing out in this weather?"

As soon as I shut the door behind her, I grabbed a blanket and wrapped it around her. I rubbed my hands up and down her arms to warm her and noticed she wasn't only shaking uncontrollably because she was cold. She was sobbing.

"Are you crying?" I asked like an idiot. Of course she was crying. "Come here," I said reaching for her. She weakly protested, claiming that I would get wet, but she was in no condition to argue with me. I tugged her into my arms, my T-shirt immediately soaking through. Feeling the shock of the cold cotton against my skin, I hurried us over to the fireplace and sat on the brick hearth, bringing Scarlett down on my lap.

I tucked a loose strand of cold, wet hair behind her ear, kissed her icy cheek, and asked, "You wanna talk about it?"

She lifted her head like she was going to say something, but once our eyes met she buried her head in my shoulder once again. I could feel her shaking sobs begin to quiet as I ran hand up and down her back. Soon Scarlett lifted her head again, and she wiped her eyes with the back of her sleeve, "I'm sorry Luke. I shouldn't be here."

"Don't be sorry. I'm glad you're here. What's going on?"

"I just got into a really, really bad fight with my dad."

I fought back the urge to run out of here and punch her father in the face for hurting her, and it took every bit of self-control I could muster to stay put. I looked her over, looking for any sign that he'd gotten physical but didn't see anything suspicious. That is until I looked into her eyes. They were full of fear. Complete and utter terror. "He didn't hurt you, did he?" The thought of that bastard putting his hands on her made my chilled skin burn red hot with the need to rip him to shreds.

Scarlett placed her still-cool palm on the side of my face and said, "No, he didn't hurt me. Not like that."

Relieved, I covered her hand with mine and brought hers to my lips. "Want to tell me what happened?" I asked as I continued to rain little kisses along the inside of her palm.

"No," she replied as a wobbly smile spread across her face. "Tell me about your day."

I took a deep breath and lowered our hands to my leg. As we sat there by the fire together, I told Scarlett everything. I told her about the Sheriff and my dad's car, about Marcus's meltdown, and about seeing Michelle and Taylor at the grocery store. I told her how the worst part had been the way Marcus had been convinced that my father was dead and had switched his concern from finding my father to finding out which pack was after us.

As soon as I mentioned that Marcus believed that my father was dead, Scarlett broke down again. Tears poured freely from her eyes, and I was at a complete loss. I had absolutely no idea what the hell to do. This is one of those times when not having a mother, sisters, or any other girls in my life really showed. The way she just sat there crying into her hands scared the shit out of me. I wanted to fix this for her, but I had two problems. I didn't know what was wrong or what to do about it. So, I broke down the situation. First, she was still wet and would surely feel better in some dry clothes. That was a problem that I could solve.

"I'm going to get you some dry clothes," I muttered before shifting her off my lap and leaning over to kiss her forehead. "I'll be right back." I stood up and walked over to the stairs. I stopped when I got to the landing and looked back, she was still in the same position. Now I kind of felt like I was abandoning her when she needed me. Shit! I considered go back but had promised her dry clothes. God, this was confusing. Taking the steps two at a time, I hurried into my room. I opened my dresser drawer and pulled out a T-shirt for me and a long-sleeved thermal for Scarlett.

I pulled my shirt over my head and hurried into my bathroom to grab Scarlett a towel when I heard her soft, hesitant footsteps on the stairs. My heart pounded wildly in my chest as I turned and walked back into my room and stood there listening to her walk down the hall toward my room.

"I got cold," she said when she saw me standing there. She looked so lost and sad that it tore at my heart. I couldn't stand to see her that way, and I only knew one way to make her feel better. I had promised myself that I would take things with Scarlett slowly, a promise that would surely be broken if she continued to look at me that way. Whatever was passing between us was too intense, and if she didn't look away soon, she would be out of those wet clothes faster than anticipated.

Without breaking eye contact, she asked, "Can I come in?"

"Oh sorry, of course," I muttered as I moved aside so that she could enter.

She wandered around my room, picking up pictures and looking at the books that lined my bookcases. She smiled when she noticed a picture of my father and me when I was about eight, but all too soon, her face fell and she looked sad all over again. I wanted to take her mind off whatever had caused that look, so I moved toward her and said, "You know something, you are the first girl who has ever been in my room."

Scarlett stopped what she was doing, her hands dropped to her side, and she looked at me with raised eyebrows "Seriously?"

"Another first," I whispered.

"What does that mean?" she asked, now looking thoroughly confused.

I crossed the room to be near her. "It's nothing. I just realized I've been experiencing quite a few of firsts with you," I admitted, enjoying the delicate blush that crept up her cheeks. We were now standing toe-to-toe, the chemistry between us nearly visible and my bed only inches away.

My eyes traveled up her still-damp jeans to the half-zipped hoodie and her T-shirt that clung to her chest. Immediately, images of last night flashed into my mind. My eyes roamed their way up past her neck to her lips. I paused there and watched as she drew her bottom lip into the warmth of her mouth, then bit down gently on it. There was no hiding how completely aroused I'd become in that moment. As soon as my eyes reached hers, I couldn't hold back any longer.

My lips met hers, gently at first, but grew more intense within seconds. Without breaking our kiss, I slid her hoodie off her shoulders leaving her in only a thin v-neck T-shirt. My lips traveled down her neck to the swell of her breasts as my hands found the hem of her shirt. In one smooth motion, I lifted her shirt over her head, wrapped her in my arms, and lay us both on my bed.

Scarlett ran her hands up my shirt and let out a small whimper as her fingertips swept over my heated skin. With a new sense of urgency, Scarlett tugged at my shirt until I allowed her to pull it off of me. Our kisses reached a new level of desperation as she rubbed herself against my erection, and I knew that if she wanted me tonight, there was no way in hell I could slow us down.

My hand found the top of her jeans, and after I unbuttoned them, I slid down the bed and helped her remove them. As I made my way back up, I took my time exploring and tasting her entire body. When I came to a certain highly sensitive spot, Scarlett froze.

"A first?" I smiled, looking up at her. I paused for a moment, giving her a chance to stop me if she wasn't ready, but she didn't. Instead, she nodded. In record time, her sexy black panties were on the floor next to her jeans. She threaded her fingers in my hair and let her head fall back against the bed. I took my time, enjoying every moan, whimper, and shutter that came from Scarlett's delectable body.

When I kissed my way back up to her face, she looked worried. "Baby, what's wrong?" I asked, nuzzling my face in the crook of her neck.

"I've never...I mean...this *is* my first."

"You're a virgin?" I asked cupping her face in my hands so that she'd look me in the eyes.

She bit her bottom lip again and then murmured, "Yeah."

I slid off to the side of her and propped myself up on my elbow.

"Luke, don't."

I gently kissed her lips before I said, "We should slow down and wait until you are ready."

"I am ready," she said, reaching for me.

I tucked her hair behind her ear and kissed her neck. "Scarlett, baby, I want you to be sure, because in a way it's my first time too."

"What do you mean?" Her eyes locked with mine, and I couldn't believe what I was about to admit, but it was the truth.

"I've never been with anyone that I truly...cared about."

Scarlett smiled, and her eyes softened as she ran her hand down my face. "You're shivering."

"You seem to have that effect on me," I said before kissing her gently on the lips. Scarlett put her hands on my chest, and before I realized what she was doing, she'd rolled me over to my back and shifted her body so that she was lying on top of me.

"I want you, Luke Stanton," she whispered breathlessly as she pressed herself against me.

The moment those words left her lips, I'd flipped her on her back and was looking down into her big, brown eyes. "You already have me, Scarlett. I'm all yours."

CHAPTER 42

Drew

I'd overheard the argument between Brian and Scarlett last night. Well it wasn't as much of an argument as it was an awakening for Scarlett, I'd hoped. But when she ran out of here last night and didn't come home, I knew we were in trouble. There was only one place an upset Scarlett would run: straight into Luke's arms. Originally, that was exactly where we wanted her to be, but now it had become the last place she needed to be.

I'd spent half the night listening to Brian retell the evening like I wasn't in the other room to hear the whole thing and the other half waiting for Scarlett to return. She needed to be convinced that what she thought she felt for the meathead wasn't real. It was fabricated. We fabricated it. It was part of the plan. She just wasn't the one who was supposed to fall for it; he was. I knew Scarlett was getting too attached. I warned her, and I warned Brian. If she ruined this, if she ended up putting the future of my pack in danger, I would...

The lock on the front door shifted, so I stood ready to knock some sense into this girl if I needed to. "We need to talk," I said flatly when Scarlett walked through the door.

Scarlett, looking like she had just been busted replied, "What do you want, Drew?"

I took another step toward her, well aware that my nearness made her nervous. "I heard what you told your father last night."

"And?" she asked, wrapping her arms around herself.

"Have you lost your mind Scar? Didn't we just have this conversation? I clearly remember discussing just how much Luke is going to despise you when this is all over."

Scarlett tried to walk passed me, but there was no way I was letting that happen. I grabbed her arm and flung her up against the wall, causing a picture that hung nearby to crash to the floor. Trapping her between my arms, I got up in her face and took a deep breath. I could smell the sex they had last night and probably again this morning. That combined with the fresh scent of fear I was causing turned me on.

I ran the tip of my nose down her neck and inhaled deeply again before I spoke. "You listen to me, Scarlett. I don't care about your feelings for Luke. I don't care if you think you love him. I don't care if you have suddenly grown a conscience and decided that what we are doing here is wrong. It doesn't matter to me. All that matters is my pack. If you care about your father, your brother, Luke, you will keep your big mouth shut. Do you understand?"

Scarlett tried to duck under my arms, but I grabbed her tightly by the arms before she could escape. She attempted to wiggle out of my grasp, so I tightened my grip, digging my nails into her skin. "If I find out that you have said anything, I will pick up that phone and end Phillip's life."

Scarlett's eyes widened and tears pooled in her eyes.

"I'm glad that something finally got your attention. Now, if you don't want Luke to end up blaming you for the death of his father, you need to keep your end of the bargain and your mouth shut."

The first of many tears fell from her eyes as she pulled free and rushed passed me. I knew she wanted to run to her room and lock herself away, so I blocked her path to the stairs. She took off through the house and out the back door. I had said all that needed to be said, but decided to chase her down was just for the fun of it. Maybe since she wasn't the flirty little virgin tease anymore, I'd just have to show her what it was like to be dominated by the alpha.

Scarlett was clearing the back patio when I grabbed her by the back of her jeans. She whirled around, and with both hands on my chest, she pushed me back, yelling, "God damn it! Drew Barnes, I swear to God! You better back the fuck off of me, or I will—"

"You'll what? I could bend you over and take you right here on the patio, and you wouldn't be able to do a damn thing about it," I warned, cutting her off. Suddenly, a movement in the trees behind Scarlett grabbed my full attention.

"What?" Scarlett asked, sensing that something was wrong.

I mentioned toward the woods with a nod of my head. Scarlett turned and saw what I was already focused on. A wolf. Not an ordinary wolf. A werewolf, who was close enough to have heard Scarlett call me Drew. A wolf whose identity and scent, from this distance, couldn't be detected.

Scarlett turned back to me with a look of pure panic in her eyes.

"Go inside and take a shower. You reek," I said coldly.

I stood there in the backyard and zeroed in on the wolf, who surprisingly stood stock-still staring right back at me. Finally it raised its nose into the air and ran off in the direction of the lake. Only then did I go inside.

CHAPTER 43

Scarlett

I'd been locked in my room for hours. After I took a quick shower, I'd curled up in the middle of the floor and hadn't had it in me to move. Ever since I'd spotted the wolf in the woods, my mind had been in a whirlwind of fear, confusion, and an outright panic. In under an hour, I went from dancing on cloud nine when I woke up in Luke's arms; to murderous rage when Drew threatened Phillip's life; to being completely panic-stricken after being caught red-handed by a mystery wolf. It could have been anyone, and if he heard what I thought he had, I was in some deep shit.

When I ran to Luke's last night, I had every intention of telling him the truth. He deserved to know everything that I knew. He deserved to know that I suspected that my pack had his father. That I believed that he was either already dead or that they were holding him for insurance. But I knew my pack well, and I knew that if they could use someone to get what they wanted they would, which meant there was a very good chance that Phillip was still alive. I wanted to be strong for Luke. I was willing to risk my life to help save his father. I knew when the truth left my lips it would mean a death sentence for me.

But my father was right. I was selfish and even more than that, weak. When I saw the broken look in Luke's eyes, I couldn't find the words. I couldn't do it. But not because I was scared of what my alpha would do when he found out I'd betrayed my pack. The truth was that I was terrified Luke would never look at me again the way he looked at me when I stood there dripping wet in the doorway of his bedroom.

My skin broke out in chill bumps as I remembered the way his eyes devoured every inch of my body, the way I melted into his arms, they way I pushed all thoughts aside and allowed myself to get lost in the moment. How could something be so right yet so wrong at the same time? I wanted him. I needed him, and I didn't want my first time to be tainted by the lies I'd told or the truths I'd chosen to keep hidden, but it was.

I closed my eyes, envisioning our night together. The gentleness of his touch, the fire in his eyes, the fierceness in his kiss. Nothing had ever felt more perfect. I had been so wrapped up in the moment that everything else in the world just faded away. But then the colossal shit storm that I'd created all came to a head as soon as I saw Drew's wicked grin this morning. It was like he knew exactly what had happened and planned to use it to his advantage.

Now I was stuck. If I told Luke the truth, Drew would have Phillip killed, and there wasn't a single part of me that didn't believe him. He'd do it just to spite me. Then again, if I knew Drew and his father, they would use Phillip for all he's worth first and then probably kill him anyway. God, what the hell was I supposed to do? Odds were they'd kill me too.

I needed to talk to Gavin. No, if I called him, he would surely come running out here to my rescue and probably make everything even worse. I couldn't drag him into this mess; I needed to figure this out on my own. I'd screwed up royally, and though I was quite sure there was no way out of it, I needed to decide the best way to proceed. I should have told Luke the truth, but I didn't. I should have never slept with him, but I did. Yet there was a huge part of me that didn't regret it. I wanted to. More than anything, I wanted to give myself to him. There was no denying that I was falling in love with him, which made it hurt so much worse knowing he could never love me in return if he knew the truth. And he would, sooner or later. And that was why it was a mistake. I was hiding too much. There were too many lies entwined in this twisted web I'd woven.

But there was nothing I could do about any of that now. All I could do was accept the fact that I'd fucked up and now needed to figure out what to do and somehow manage to not get anyone killed in the process.

Lost in thought, I practically jumped out of my skin when my father began pounding on my door. "Scarlett, unlock this damn door. You've been in here all day."

I scrambled over to the door, sure he wouldn't hesitate to knock it off its hinges if I didn't act fast enough. Slowly I pulled the door open and stared into the cruel eyes of my father. There was no love there, no concern, no sympathy.

He grabbed my arm and yanked me through the door and into the hall. "You need to get your shit together. You look like hell." When I didn't respond, he continued. "You have ten minutes to clean up and head over to Luke's. Slap a smile on your face and get to work. We need to know what's going on."

Tearing my eyes from his gaze, I turned to head back into my room, but he wrapped his hand around my wrist, pulling me to a halt. "Listen carefully, Scarlett. I'm trusting that you'll do the right thing here. You better keep your mouth shut. If you even think about telling Luke or anyone else why we are really here, I won't be able to save you…or Phillip Stanton. Be smart about this. Play your part, and you just might get out of this alive."

I didn't respond. There wasn't anything to say. My own father just admitted that he wouldn't stop our alpha from killing me. When it came down to it, his pack was more important that his own child. I just stood there in the hallway, completely numb. Without another word, he walked away.

I did what he asked. I got dressed, pulled my damp hair into a ponytail, and put on a bit of powder and mascara. I stepped back from the mirror and looked myself over. My eyes were sad, bloodshot, and puffy. I put a few drops of Visine in my eyes and dabbed a bit of concealer under them. After I added more powder, some shimmery eye shadow, and eyeliner, I looked a little less pitiful, but none of it hid the sorrow lurking behind all of the makeup.

When I walked into the kitchen, both Drew and my father stopped what they were doing and stared at me. I didn't make eye contact or say a word. Instead, I grabbed a frozen pizza out of the freezer and a two-liter of Coke from the fridge, and I walked out the front door.

CHAPTER 44

Luke

Scarlett showed up with a frozen pizza and some soda claiming that she wanted to make me dinner. Scarlett didn't need a reason to come over, and I would have called and asked her to come over after my meeting tonight anyway, but I had a feeling that she came over so early because she needed to get away from her house, her father in particular. I still didn't know what they'd fought about, but it must have been pretty bad. It sucked that things were so bad for her at home, and I wished that she felt like she could share that with me. I guess I couldn't blame her though. Our relationship was still so new and there were plenty of things that I hadn't told her either.

We ate in an awkward silence sitting next to each other at the kitchen table. My eyes rarely left her face but her eyes were clearly avoiding mine. Occasionally our hands would accidentally touch. A few times our legs brushed up against each other. Something unsaid but mutually felt hung in the air. It was thick and all-encompassing, and if left unaddressed it would tear at us both.

Scarlett got up to throw our paper plates away, but I stopped her. I took her hand and led her to my room. Still no words were spoken as we both climbed on to my bed and lay down facing each other. I knew how I felt about Scarlett, but knowing it and actually saying it out loud were two different things. I had never said those words before, and for reasons I couldn't put into words, I felt like I didn't deserve for her to love me in return. But maybe it was because my dad was gone, and I might never have the chance to tell him, I felt like I needed to tell Scarlett how I felt about her before it was too late.

Pushing aside all the confusion and anxiety surging through my body, I finally released the words that had been consuming my mind, body, and soul. "I'm in love with you, Scarlett" I admitted softly.

Scarlett's eyes widened for a moment, then clinched shut as her face blushed and her breathing became more rapid.

"Scarlett, are you okay? I didn't mean to freak you out. I should have just kept my damn mouth shut," I told her, reaching out and taking her hand. When I did, Scarlett opened her eyes. Her beautiful brown eyes were filled with tears, but a small, hesitant smile appeared before she breathlessly asked, "Really?"

I wrapped my arms around her and pulled her tightly against me. "Oh yeah, I'm sure. There's not a doubt in my mind. I love you, Scarlett Reed."

Her lips crashed into mine. She kissed me with need and desperation as she rolled her body on top of mine, pulling back only once, and only long enough to say, "I love you too."

*****

"Are you sure you don't want to come with me?" I asked as I got ready to leave for my meeting with Marcus and the elders. I pulled Scarlett against me one last time and breathed in that delicious scent of hers that had worked its way into my dreams and into my heart.

"I don't think that's a very good idea," she replied, and for the first time in my life, I think, I actually pouted, but just a little and surely it was a manly pout. She lifted up on her tiptoes and nibbled on my bottom lip with her teeth, and I took the opportunity to envelop her in my arms and devour her perfect mouth. Pulling her hips flush against mine, I made sure she could feel just how much I wanted her again. With eyes blazing with desire, she teased, "Keep that up and you won't make it to the meeting." After a playful peck on the tip of my nose, she whispered in my ear, "Call me when you get home and I'll come back over—if you want me to that is."

I answered by kissing her until her legs gave out, and she had to lean against me for support. Then I had to force us out the door, or she would have been right and we would have never left the house.

When I pulled up in front of Scarlett's house, she leaned over to kiss me goodbye. My hands reached over to cup her cheeks, and I stopped her about an inch away from my face as I mouthed, *I love you*. She leaned in, and her lips gently caressed mine before she whispered, "I love you back." I wanted nothing more than to pull her back into the car and ravage every inch of her perfect body as I watched her slide out of the seat. But with a serious amount of self-restraint, I watched as she hurried inside.

I drove to the Walker house in a lovesick haze.

*****

I was the last to arrive at the meeting, and it didn't go unnoticed. "Finally, we can get started," Marcus grumbled and tromped heavily into the formal dining area, which had apparently been turned into a makeshift conference room. A few of the elders ignored Marcus's haste and came over to check on me.

I assured them that I was fine, and yes, I was worried, but sure that everything would turn out okay. The lies slid off my tongue, leaving a bad taste in my mouth, but I knew it was what they needed to hear. Seemingly appeased by my response, they followed me into the formal living room. Looking around at the small select group— Marcus, Noel, Brian, Cade, Aiden, Aiden's grandparents, and Shari's grandparents—I could assume we were here to discuss what to do next about my father. Maybe I was wrong about Marcus. But as soon as he began, I knew I'd been right all along.

The room grew silent as we all gathered together, but the silence was suddenly broken by the sound of Marcus's fist slamming against the console table. "We must prepare the estate for an attack! Immediately!" Marcus yelled. "We have become too comfortable, too human-like here in this pathetic little town. We are unprepared. And let me tell you all! A war is coming! We need to get everyone trained for combat. We must stand together and fight. Fight until every last one of the mutts who think they can take over my pack is slaughtered, torn to shreds, completely annihilated!"

We all looked around at each other. I wasn't so sure he wasn't completely off base, but I did think he was overreacting. And he was leaving out a huge part of this: my father.

"I agree, Dad, but let's—" Cade tried but Marcus cut him off.

"No buts, Cade. We must be ready," Marcus said. He turned to Brian, "What have you learned from your connections?"

"There hasn't been any more chatter about a pack trying to take over, and I'm sorry, but I've heard nothing about Phillip," Brian explained. He looked directly at me. His steely eyes tore through me and a ripple of nerves shot up my back.

I knew that wasn't good news, but there was no time to dwell on it because Marcus erupted once more.

"Damn it, Brian. You call yourself a fucking 'fixer?' What good are you even doing here? So far, you have been of no help to me at all. Your connections are useless," Marcus spouted, his face turning multiple shades of red. His mouth opened, surely to lash out again, but instead he began grasping for air.

He picked up a bottle of water and took a long sip, but as soon as he swallowed the liquid, he started choking uncontrollably. Stumbling forward, he grabbed a nearby end table and leaned over. With his fingers gripping its edge so hard that his hand was shaking, he tried to suck in some much-needed air, but his knees gave out as his coughing continued. Cade and Aiden both rushed over to help him. Marcus attempted to stand before his sons reached him, but when he did, we were all taken aback. His eyes had rolled back in his head, and his mouth was foaming like some kind of rabid wolf.

Noel screamed as Marcus fell backward on the floor and began to convulse and flail. Cade hurried over to hold his mother back as Aiden's grandfather shouted for someone him to find the pack's resident physician. Aiden shot out the door, but the rest of us watched as Brian dropped to his knees and held Marcus's head still so that he wouldn't hurt himself. The rest of us stood back in silence and shock. Without even realizing it, I'd begun backing up until I reached the wall. I had to shove my hands into my pockets to keep them from trembling. Our pack was truly falling apart one member at a time.

CHAPTER 45

Scarlett

I'd pretty much taken up residence in my room anytime I had to be in the god-awful place I currently called home. My mission: to avoid my father and Drew at all costs. I was lying in bed staring at my phone and willing it to ring or chime or something to alert me that Luke was ready for me to come back when the sudden sound of someone pounding on the front door sent my pulse racing. I jumped out of bed and peeked out the curtains to see if I could tell who it was, but there wasn't a sign of anyone, but the doorbell rang repeatedly and the door was taking a serious beating.

For a moment, I'd decided it would probably be in my best interest to ignore it, but whoever it was on the other side of that door was determined to get inside. If I waited much longer, I feared the person might resort to breaking windows. My heart pounded erratically in my chest and my gut warned that whatever the person was there to do or say, it wasn't going to be good.

As I crept down the stairs, the pesky phone in my back pocket finally decided to chirp, which caused my entire body to jerk violently, and if it hadn't have been for the lifesaving banister, I would have surely tumbled straight down to the tile below. I stopped to regain my footing and attempted to calm my nerves, but as soon as I pulled my phone from my pocket and glanced at the screen, my chest constricted and scurried away to go cower in the corner.

It's Cami. I know ur in there.
Open the damn door. We need to talk.

Holy Mother of God! She knew! Why else would she be here? This was obviously not a social call. She had to know something. Oh God! The wolf! *Please, please, please don't let that be it!* I smoothed back my hair and tried to reassure myself. *It's okay. I can do this. I just need to play it cool.*

With shaky fingers, I started to reply *ok* to her text, but then shook my head at my stupidity and shoved my phone back in my pocket when it dawned on me that it would make much more sense to just open the damn door like she'd asked. Dread filled my bones, and again I toyed with the idea of running back to my room and hiding, but I knew I had to do this. I needed to know what she knew, and if it was what I thought it was, if she had told anyone else.

Before I swung the door open, I planted an innocent smile on my face and slowly counted to ten. Time to face the music. I turned the knob, ready to greet my persistent visitor, but as soon as I opened the door, my smile quickly faded, and I couldn't seem to stop my feet from backing up to get away from the very angry werewolf on my doorstep. Cami was tiny by werewolf standards, but the rage in her eyes promised she could do some serious damage to a full-grown man if she needed to.

As my feet continued their retreat, Cami pushed her way inside. In fact, she marched right passed me and into the living room and through the kitchen. After inspecting the remainder of the downstairs, she met me back in the foyer and asked, "Are we alone?"

Completely bewildered, I looked around as if Drew or my father might suddenly appear out of thin air. "Yeah, we're alone." My voice sounded weird. Way too panicky. So much for playing it cool.

Cami stared me down for a moment as if searching for the right way to begin, and I fought back the urge to shout, *just say it!* When she finally spoke, her voice was even, completely confident, without an ounce of hesitation. "I'm not even going to ask what you are really doing here and give you a chance to lie. It was me in the woods behind your house. I heard you call your so-called brother Drew Barnes and saw the horror in your eyes when you saw me standing there. Then when Drew stared me down as if warning me— no, threatening me—to ignore what I'd heard, I knew I couldn't just let it go."

Cami took a deep breath and waited, maybe to see if I'd respond. To deny it. Try to make her believe that what she heard was wrong. But I knew better. She knew more. There was no question in her voice. She wasn't fishing for information. She already had all the facts she needed.

My gaze hit the floor. I couldn't stand to look at her. Not when crushing guilt and regret had invaded my body from head to toe. Cami reached into her pocket and pulled out some folded pieces of paper. "You guys hid your tracks well. No Facebook, no Twitter, no Instagram. What? Did you delete it all before you came here? But you should know you can't get rid of everything, especially when you're the son of the CEO of a sinking company. After some digging, I found this article: 'Nathaniel Barnes, CEO of NRB Incorporated, Takes a Major Hit.' And look here at the pic. There is Drew Barnes standing next to his father, the alpha of your pack."

I just stood there gaping at the papers in her hand. What could I say? There was no way to talk myself out of this one. Cami shoved the rest of the pages against my chest. I took them from her hand but didn't look at them.

She let out a deep huff and continued, "Well look at them. I guess you couldn't exactly expect the rest of your pack to delete their Facebook and Twitter too. There are some really good pics of you, Drew, and even the real Gavin."

Finally, somehow I mustered up the courage to finally speak. "Cami, let me explain." I'd planned to go on, spill my guts and finally come clean, but she didn't let me. She stepped forward, got right up in my face, and seethed, "I'm not the one you need to explain to. It's Luke you're going to have to face. He deserves the truth even if it kills him. He deserves so much more than your lying, deceitful ass. And just so you know, I hope he rips you limb from limb for what you've done."

My eyes filled with tears, so I clinched them shut and tried to swallow the lump in my throat, but it didn't help. I could hardly breathe, and before I knew it, I had slid to the floor. My body practically convulsed as I tried sucking in huge gulps of air between sobs. I'd messed up everything, and now I was going to lose it all. Luke, my family, my pack, and probably my life. But I only cared about one thing, and the thought of losing Luke tore through my body like a tornado ripping to shreds everything in its path.

I could feel Cami still standing above me, but I couldn't look up. I couldn't do anything but sob uncontrollably. After an excruciatingly long few minutes, Cami toed my thigh with her boot and said, "Come on. Get up. And get yourself together. We need to go meet Luke. And don't try anything stupid because he's expecting us. I warned Cade if we weren't there in 15 minutes that he better coming looking for us. Plus, I have Allison watching your house to make sure we make it to Luke's safely."

Her words were like daggers and shook me out of my wallowing mess of emotions. My head shot up, and for the first time since she'd arrived, I looked straight into her eyes, completely shocked that she actually believed that I would try to escape or worse, try to hurt her.

Surprisingly her expression softened a bit. "It doesn't look like I have anything to worry about, I guess. I certainly didn't expect you to break down right here in the foyer." She reached her hand down to help me up. "Come on, Scarlett. Time to finally put an end to all the lying. It's clearly tearing you apart."

Somehow I made it to my feet, and on shaky legs I followed Cami to Luke's. Allison stood and watched as we made our way toward her, and when we approached, she didn't say a word. She simply turned and opened the unlocked door. I followed them inside to find Gage, Cade, Aiden, and Teagan all standing around in the living room. One face among the crowd was missing, but as soon as everyone turned to watch us enter, Luke stood up, concern filling his sad, heartbreaking eyes.

I stood there in front of them all, my focus solely set on Luke, and finally admitted the truth. "I know which pack is plotting against you."

CHAPTER 46

Luke

"It's mine. That's why we're here," Scarlett confessed as she lowered her eyes to her hands. When she finally looked up again, it was directly at me. "My father wanted me to get close to you and convince you to back Aiden for alpha."

"Wait, wait, wait," Aiden interrupted. "Maybe you need to start from the beginning."

A sudden chill entered my bones at the same time as my palms grew damp. *Did I really want to hear this from the beginning?* When my hands began to tremble, I clinched them tightly into fists. I knew that whatever Scarlett was about to say was going to break me, and I hated myself for allowing that to happen. I stood and moved to the back of the sofa, but my position did nothing to make me feel any less vulnerable.

"I will tell you everything I know, but first, please believe me when I say that I was purposely kept in the dark. I had no idea what my father's true intentions were. I would have never agreed to help him if I did," she said.

"Of course," Cade answered for all of us. I couldn't say anything.

"My pack is in serious financial trouble, and we are about to be forced off of our land. When we came here so my dad could help out with that crazy guy werewolf hunter," Scarlett paused and let her eyes wander over to Teagan, "I guess my dad saw an opportunity."

"He saw a pack divided, an easy target," Cade stated flatly.

Scarlett nodded. "I can only assume that when we returned, our alpha and my father quickly devised a plan to take your pack over. From what I'd heard in bits and pieces, they want your land and your business."

"And that plan was?" Alli asked.

Who cared! I needed to get out of this room. It was bad enough that I had been used by Scarlett and her pack, but to have it exposed in front of all my friends was humiliating. I could tell that Scarlett wanted to talk to me alone, but there was no way that was going to happen. Since the day I became interested in girls, I'd never dated the same one for more than a couple of months, and in a matter of a few days, this girl made me fall in love with her. How's that for fucking karma?

"I'm pretty sure the plan changed along the way without me knowing about it. I guess Drew was right after all. I am naïve," Scarlett murmured.

"Who the hell is Drew?" I asked, finally managing to find my voice but doing little to control the emotion behind it.

"He is our alpha's son. He has been pretending to be my brother, Gavin."

Jesus! This just keeps getting more and more twisted! I tried pacing up and down the back of the sofa, anything to calm the hurt and fury that threatened to explode from my fists. The desperate need to hit someone, to destroy something consumed me, and I wasn't sure how much more I could take.

Scarlett stood there shifting her weight from foot to foot, her face pale and her eyes bloodshot. She looked so lost and alone standing before us, and I silently cursed myself for wanting to hold her. Damn her! How could she do this to me? How could she look me in the eyes and tell me she loved me? I hated her for making me love her.

"My real brother wouldn't have any part in this. He tried to talk me out of it, and I wouldn't listen. He is still trying to get me to come home," Scarlett continued.

"What was Drew's part in this?" Aiden asked.

"As far as I was told, he was just supposed to cause trouble between the two of you, but now that just seems too simple. He must be doing something that I don't know about."

"Besides torturing you?" Cami added looking from Scarlett to me.

I tried to pretend like it didn't kill me inside that this guy was messing with Scarlett. I stopped and gripped the edge of the couch before I exploded right then and there.

"What does she mean?" Teagan asked when I didn't.

"Nothing, he's just an ass." She stared at the floor, and I knew there was more.

Cami's eyebrows shot up as she spoke. "It's not nothing. I heard him loud and clear, Scarlett. He was manipulating you, threatening you. He threatened to rape you, for God's sake. Don't try to protect him. I would hate to think what would have happened to you if Drew hadn't seen me in the woods."

Scarlett's dejected eyes looked at me, then at Cami. "I wasn't supposed to fall for Luke. I was just supposed to get him to fall for me. I made the mistake of telling my father how I felt." Scarlett turned to me, "I told him how much I cared about you. That I didn't want to be a part of this."

"Why were you supposed to get Luke to back me and not Cade?" Aiden asked.

I didn't think that it was possible for Scarlett to look anymore uncomfortable, but she suddenly did. "They felt that you were the weaker brother; the one that they could manipulate the easiest. They banked on the pack falling apart if you took over. I'm sorry, Aiden. I'm just trying to be honest," she said.

I laughed. I didn't know why. None of this was funny. Apparently, I was no longer thinking clearly.

"It's okay," Aiden told her.

"Are you doing something to make Marcus sick?" I asked coldly, my emotions shifting in the blink of an eye.

Scarlett stiffened. "I don't know anything about that, but I wouldn't put anything past them right now. Not anymore." Scarlett stood up and walked over to where I was. She tried to reach out and take my hand, but I jerked it away. "You have to believe me Luke. I meant every word I said to you. I still do. I wanted out of this whole thing, even if it meant never seeing you again. I told my father and Drew that I just couldn't do this anymore."

Taking another step back, I asked, "Then why are you still here?"

She took a step back too and wrapped her arms around her waist. "They told me if I left or if I told you about us, if I betrayed them, they would kill your father."

I turned and my hands found the couch in front of me. I held on as my world spun in circles. I was only vaguely aware of Cade ordering Gage to take Scarlett home and make sure that she was safe once she got there. I tried to focus of the back of the couch, but as soon as I did, I heard the snapping of the wood frame. Cami, Teagan, and Alli were ushered out of the house just as the first piece of sofa was ripped off and thrown across the room. The first was followed by the second, then the third. I didn't stop until the entire leather sofa was in pieces and scattered around the living room. I grabbed a lamp and launched it at the fireplace just before I picked up the end table it was sitting on and hurled it at the floor to ceiling bookshelf.

I all but collapsed into the closest chair I could find. My hands were a bloody mess from the wood and nails of the sofa, and I was drenched in sweat. I took a deep breath and surveyed the damage I had just inflicted on the poor room. My father was going to be so pissed. *My father*...I pushed my way passed Cade and Aiden and hurried into the bathroom to clean up my battered hands. It was then, standing in front of the mirror, that I noticed the tear streaks down my face. Great, not only did I completely lose all self-control in front of everyone, apparently I cried too. An enforcer shouldn't be seen tearing apart furniture or crying. EVER! Suddenly, it occurred to me that with Dad gone, and me over the age of eighteen, that I was the acting enforcer. Maybe someone should start looking for a replacement.

CHAPTER 47

Scarlett

The cold air hitting my tear-streaked face as we walked out of the house made me shiver uncontrollably. Pulling my coat tighter around my body, I had to focus on putting one foot in front of the other. All I wanted to do was curl myself into ball and cry until I had nothing left. Gage put his hand on my arm, and I stopped and turned around to face him. I didn't want to look at Gage, but I couldn't stop myself. He was Luke's best friend in the world and he must hate me now too, but when our eyes met, there wasn't hatred in his eyes. Instead of yelling at me like I expected him to, he pulled me to his chest and let me cry into his sweatshirt.

When a small hand touched my shoulder, I looked up to find Teagan giving me a sympathetic smile. She pulled me from Gage, trying her best to console me. I didn't know why she bothered after what I did to her family, but she did. I heard a loud crash from inside, and my head jerked up. Alli flinched as she stared through the window. I peered inside just in time to witness Luke completely destroy his living room.

Seeing the destruction caused my knees to buckle. I did that to him. This was all my fault. He'd finally let someone in, and I fucked him over. He would never heal from by betrayal, and I'd never forgive myself for hurting him. Underneath all that intimidating muscle, Luke had a huge heart with so much love to share. Knowing that he would probably never trust someone enough to love again completely ruined me. There on the porch, I sat on my knees, covered my face with my hands, and sobbed.

"Omigod!!" Alli shrieked as she grabbed my arm and dragged me back into the house.

In the middle of the demolished living room, Cade and Aiden were going at each other for real. A series of punches and grunts was the only sound heard as skin met skin repeatedly. This was no alcohol-fueled fight. Both were at their full power and neither was holding back this time. They were both were bleeding heavily as they wrestled each other to the ground. Without warning, Aiden freed himself from Cade's grasp, backed up, and transformed in the blink of an eye. Seeing the change, Cade transformed in midair as he launched himself toward his brother. The two giant wolves battled in the already annihilated room, hell-bent on destroying one another.

"Where the fuck is Luke?" Gage yelled as he backed us all up against the wall to keep us from getting in the way of the two battling wolves.

Gage shouted at them, pleading with them to stop, but it seemed to only fuel their desire to tear into each other. Then Gage seemed to realize the fight was impossible to stop and gave up to let the two brothers battle it out.

I flattened myself against the wall and watched in disbelief as they clawed and bit at each other's body. Alli and Teagan were clinging to each other, fearing for the safety of their mates. They cried out repeatedly, begging them to stop. Needing to comfort my friend like she did for me such a short time ago, I reached out and rubbed my hand up and down Teagan's back.

Aiden swiped his paw out and his claws made contact with Cade's chest. With his claws driven deep inside, he dragged them forcefully down the length of Cade's chest, and instantly, Cade let out a yelp as blood began to ooze from his fresh wound. Alli hid her face in Teagan's arm. With Cade clearly injured, Aiden appeared to have the advantage, but then Cade caught Aiden's shoulder between his massive jaws. He sank his teeth down into the flesh and jerked his head back. It was Teagan's turn to scream and hide her eyes from the bloody scene.

As if it was just any other day, Luke casually walked out of the downstairs bathroom and leaned against the wall as he watched the fight. With no sign of emotion on his face, he appeared completely indifferent. He simply crossed his arms over his chest and watched on, never looking my way.

As soon as Teagan noticed Luke, she grabbed Alli's arm to get her attention and together they rushed over to beg him to put an end to the fight before it was too late.

Without taking his eyes off the fight, Luke shrugged. "Sorry, but I'm sick of the bullshit. Let them fight it out. This has to end one way or the other. Now's as good a time as any." There was no hint of feeling in his voice. It was flat and monotonous as if he couldn't have cared less, but I knew the truth. He did care, and it was killing him to watch this whether he chose to let it show or not. And I couldn't blame anyone other than myself.

Teagan and Alli continued to frantically beg Luke to stop the fight. His eyes softened as he took both girls into his arms and whispered something to them. Whatever he'd said appeared to be gentle and reassuring and somehow managed to get both Alli and Teagan to calm down a little.

At least until a loud yelp reverberated from Aiden's chest. All of a sudden, he was pinned under Cade, and Cade's mouth was holding him down by his throat. I sucked in a deep breath, fearful that Cade had gotten so carried away that he would bite down, but Cade held his position just long enough for Aiden to divert his heated gaze. Just like that, the fight was over. Cade slowly released his hold on Aiden and watched as Aiden rolled over, then slowly backed away.

Cade Walker had staked his claim as the future alpha of this pack, and Aiden had no choice but to step aside.

As both brothers shifted position, for a moment no one in the room moved. Then their mates rushed to their sides. Seeing the love between them shattered what was left of my heart and caused my tears fall all over again. I took one more look at the love of my life and turned and ran out the door.

CHAPTER 48

Luke

The fight was over, but I just stood there. I couldn't move. I'd never felt more detached. I'd just stood by while the two guys I was supposed to protect ripped each other apart. And I didn't care. I didn't stop them because I didn't care enough to do so. I was done. In my head, I knew I should have been disappointed with my behavior, but I couldn't seem to feel anything at all.

Completely impassive, I stared at the front door for long after Scarlett had left; something inside me was lost the moment Scarlett walked into my house to confess that everything between us had been a sham.

She was gone. Whatever we had was over. I was alone. It was odd to feel this way because I had kept myself alone my whole life, but now I felt empty.

I pushed off the wall and walked away to give the guys a few minutes alone with their mates. After chugging a beer, I grabbed some sweatpants from the laundry room to give the guys something to wear. By the time I walked back into the room, the girls were gone and the guys were finishing up tending to their wounds. Luckily, it wasn't anything that a few dozen butterfly bandages couldn't handle.

The tension was still thick in the air, but the decision had been made. Cade was the next alpha...end of story. I always knew that if this came to blows, Cade would win. Marcus was going to shit a brick, and I couldn't even find it within myself to be happy about that. Whatever. I no longer gave a shit who became alpha. Hell,

Aiden could take over as enforcer if he wanted to. At this point, I'd gladly hand over the position on a fucking silver platter.

I walked over to a sulking Aiden and a smirking Cade and tossed them the sweats. Assuming I should being doing something, I continued into the kitchen, grabbed three more beers and said, "Let's go into my dad's office."

"What are we going to do with this information?" I asked as soon as we were all seated. Neither of them answered.

My eyes shifted back and forth between the two of them, waiting for one of them to speak up, knowing it should have been Cade since he'd just secured his position as alpha. To my surprise it was Aiden who opened his mouth first. "Do I even need to be here?" Aiden finally muttered, drawing a growl from me and one hell of a dirty look from Cade.

Cade turned to face his brother and said, "I know you don't believe this or even want to hear it right now, but we need you. Just because I will become alpha doesn't mean that I can do all of this on my own. I need my enforcer *and* my brother by my side. So Luke, you need to get your head on straight, and Aiden, you need to get over this shit quick because, like it or not, we are in this together."

Knowing Cade was right and seeing the doubt on Aiden's face, I added, "Those assholes have my father, and according to Scarlett, he's still alive. We're not going to sit here and behave like scared little bitches. I need to get my father back and then I want to make the Crescent Hills Pack suffer. Cade's right, we need your help."

Aiden sat back in the chair and was obviously trying to take it all in. "Well, we can't take this to our father. He's just not himself, and I don't trust the elders to keep this from him either," Aiden said.

"Agreed," Cade replied. "I need to get Dad home and tell Mom that he shouldn't have visitors. It is completely possible Brian is the one causing Dad's episodes."

"Should we at least warn Marcus about Brian though? I'm not the asshole's biggest fan, but I hate leaving him so vulnerable," Aiden pointed out.

I looked to Cade, who looked back at me. "It can't hurt to warn Mom. She'd be more willing to listen than Dad," Cade added.

"Marcus is going to be fine. He's one tough son of a bitch," I said before finishing off my beer. "But don't tell him I said that."

Aiden offered to stay and help me clean up the mess, but I wouldn't let him. I did ask him to apologize to the girls for me if I scared them with my crazy tearing-apart-furniture bullshit. They both attempted to play down the situation assuring me that it was their fight that upset their mates, but I knew my behavior had started it all. And if I had done my job, Aiden and Cade would have never been able to take it that far. But now that a decision had been made, maybe it was all for the best.

Except for the part where Scarlett Reed held my heart in her hand and crushed it all to hell.

Aiden headed out, but for some reason, Cade asked to stay for a while longer. We hung out at the kitchen table and had another beer. Cade downed half the bottle, then said, "Scarlett promised that she wouldn't let her father or Drew know that she told us."

"And you believe her?" I asked.

"Yeah, I do, and to be honest man, the more I think about this whole thing, the more it just doesn't add up. There has to be more to the story."

I didn't know what to say. She'd screwed me over. I couldn't get past that in order to wonder if there was more. But then my thoughts turned back to what Cami had said about Drew, about how he'd threatened Scarlett, threatened to rape her, told her if she didn't follow orders that he'd kill my father. Maybe there was more to it. My vision blurred, and I wasn't sure if I wanted to cry or break something.

All I knew for sure was that I wanted to kill Drew Barnes.

Cade stood up, sucked down the last of his beer, and chunked the bottle in the garbage. "Well, listen. It's late. Tomorrow morning at sunrise we'll meet here and figure out how the hell we're going to get your dad back."

I shook my head. It was all I could manage. The day had drained me of every ounce of energy I had.

As Cade was leaving, I felt like I should say something to him about the fight. So even though it felt awkward as hell, I reached out to shake his hand and said, "I'm not sure if congratulations are in order or not. Either way though, I'm glad it was you. I have always been your enforcer. Any other way wouldn't feel right."

"Thanks Luke. That means a lot," Cade replied, pulling me in for a man-hug. "And thanks for not stopping the fight. Aiden may not agree, but it was better this way. Behind closed doors, you know?"

I nodded and Cade left. I closed the door behind him, turned out the lights, grabbed another beer, and headed to my room. I tried to think about the positive parts of today. My dad was alive and we knew where he was. We knew what to expect from the Crescent Hills Pack so we couldn't be ambushed, and best of all, we finally had our new alpha.

I could only focus on the positive for so long. The damage I'd done to the living room could be repaired, but my heart had been broken. The ache in my chest kept reminding me of what I'd lost today.

All of those sappy breakup songs suddenly held new meaning for me. I'd always avoided relationships because I felt like I'd be the one to screw it up, the one to hurt someone else. I never considered what it might feel like to be the one who got hurt. Now I'd be sure to never let it happen again. This kind of pain wasn't something I was likely to forget anytime soon.

CHAPTER 49

Drew

Last night Brian told me that he needed my help getting Marcus home from the infirmary today. I thought that seemed weird. I mean, why me? Why not Cade or Aiden? I guess Brian didn't want them to know how bad off Marcus really was.

I didn't realize how bad he was either. Marcus was a fucking wreck. He looked like a shadow of his former self. Thin and pale, he definitely didn't look like the alpha I met just a short time ago. The pack doctor seemed puzzled by Marcus's mysterious illness though he didn't admit it.

"Cade came by earlier, but Marcus was asleep. I told him that we should have some answers soon," the doc told Mrs. Walker.

"Answers?" Mrs. Walker asked.

"Yes," the doc replied. "I sent a sample of Marcus's blood out to a friend of mine for testing. Hopefully, we'll at least be able to rule some things out if not figure out exactly what is causing his affliction."

Mrs. Walker smiled, but the smile appeared forced. "That's great news. Thank you, Dr. Walters." When she turned around, the glare she shot Brian was hard to miss. What was I missing here?

Marcus was sedated for his own protection but just until he was safely at home. I wasn't complaining because it made him easier to move, and we didn't have to listen to him rant about bullshit nobody wanted to hear. I still wasn't sure why Brian wanted me there to help, but I didn't ask. As soon as he was settled, I got out of there.

I was halfway down the driveway when I remembered that I'd left my phone sitting on the table by the front door of the Walker house. I didn't bother knocking since I'd just left and neither of them had bothered to see me out. I slowly turned the knob and opened the door just enough to step inside and reach my phone, but I froze when I heard Mrs. Walker and Brian speaking in hushed tones.

"Noel, that was way too close. Marcus almost died."

"I know, baby. I'm sorry."

Baby? Baby!

I opened the door a little more so I could see what the hell was going on in there. I couldn't believe what I was looking at. Brian and Mrs. Walker were locked in an embrace that was far from innocent.

"I just want this whole thing to be over so we can finally be together," Mrs. Walker told Brian.

"There is nothing I want more than that. We just have to be careful. We can't risk anyone finding out about us," Brian replied, and what happened next made me want to puke. I mean Mrs. Walker is a definite MILF, but when Brian's hands grabbed her ass and pulled her against him as he kissed her, softly at first and then like he was trying to eat her face off of her body, it seriously made my stomach churn. It was gross. Just plain nasty. The moment she started unbuttoning his shirt, I grabbed my phone and got the hell out of there as fast as I could.

As I hurried back to our temporary home, I began to wonder what other secrets Brian had been keeping from me and just how much of this operation I truly knew about. One thing was for sure, his secret was coming out. I wanted all the details on that sordid affair he was having with the alpha female of the Red Ridge Pack, and he was going to tell me everything. Even if I had to beat it out of him, he was going to tell me the truth. The whole truth.

CHAPTER 50

Scarlett

Rolling over and throwing my covers back took every ounce of energy I had, but I needed to get out of this bed. I needed to go to the bathroom, needed to take a shower, needed to eat something or at least drink some water before I became completely dehydrated. I hadn't been out of my bedroom for two days and had spent just about every minute of it huddled under my covers.

After spilling my guts the other day, the last thing I'd wanted to do was go back to the house from hell, but I didn't have anywhere else to go. I contemplated leaving it all behind and heading back to Crescent Hills, but I couldn't get up the nerve. A tiny part of me still held out hope that Luke would want to see me again, if only to get some closure. But as the hours turned to days, I knew it wasn't going to happen.

On the bright side, Brian and Drew decided to go home for a couple of days. I didn't know why, and they didn't bother to tell me. All I knew was that after the fight, I sneaked into my house, hoping to avoid them both because there was no way that they wouldn't see right through me. As soon as I entered, I heard them in the throes of a heated argument behind closed doors in the office. Then the next morning, there was a knock on my bedroom door. I pretended to be asleep, and after they left, I received a text from my father letting me know that they'd headed home and a reminder to keep my mouth shut. Too late for that, but at least I would be alone.

When I sat up and threw my legs over the side of the bed, I instantly became light-headed. My mind grew hazy, and my world began to spin, so I closed my eyes and fought back the nausea in my stomach. I'd never thrown up in my life, but the churning in my gut and bile rising in my throat was unmistakable. I reached out for my nightstand, needing some kind of support to help me to my feet. When I broke out in a cold sweat, I knew I needed to get to the toilet as quickly as possible. With all the strength I could gather, I managed to hoist myself to my feet and stumble into the bathroom. Without hesitation, I dropped to my knees and vomited. My entire body convulsed as I dry-heaved repeatedly, but there was nothing in my stomach to throw up besides some nasty, liquidy gunk.

Remaining on my knees, I reached up for the cup sitting beside the sink and filled it with water. After gulping it down, I pulled off my clothes and somehow dragged my limp body into the bathtub. I turned on the water, plugged the drain, and laid back. Breathing deeply in and out, I tried to relax as the lukewarm water filled around my body. My heart raced and sweat dripped down the side of my face even though I was submerged in water that was just this side of warm.

I remained in the tub until the water turned cold. Chill bumps covered my body and my fingers and toes looked like prunes, but at least I no longer felt like I was going to pass out. I figured it'd be in my best interest to get out now in case my insides went to war again.

Slowly, I sat up and grabbed onto the sides of the tub, and tried to lift myself out but didn't get very far. Failing miserably, my pitiful body splashed back down into the water. After a few minutes and a firm you-can-do-this talking-to, I'd constructed a new plan and was determined to get the hell out of the bathtub even if it killed me.

Again I sat up, but this time, I turned on my side and latched both of my hands onto the same side of the tub to use for support as I made it to my knees. When I'd successfully made it halfway up, a weak smile spread across my face. It was the first time I'd felt a semblance of anything positive in days, but it was just enough to push me toward my goal. Finally both of my feet were planted on the fluffy bathmat. I couldn't remember a time I'd worked so hard at anything.

Painstakingly slow, I dried off, pulled my hair back in a messy bun, and brushed my teeth. I needed food and more water. It was the only way I'd get some energy back. That had to be the explanation for my weakened state. Werewolves may not get sick, but apparently, they can dehydrate and starve to death. As I tried to remember the last time I'd actually eaten, I looked in the mirror and decided that two days in bed, broken hearted and guilt stricken, did not look good on me. I'd been beating myself up for forty-eight hours straight, and it showed. Dark circles were under my puffy, red-rimmed eyes, and for the first time in my life, I was pale. Like vampire pale. I turned away from the mirror, more disgusted with myself than with my appearance, and headed to my room.

I grabbed the nearest sweats I could find, dressed, and headed for the stairs. Just the sight of them made me want to cry. I could hardly get out of the bathtub. How the hell was I supposed to make it down the stairs? My shaky legs decided that I could do this before my brain agreed, and I wasn't even halfway down before my head was spinning again. I almost gave in and sat down, but I reminded myself that everything would be fine if I could just get something to eat.

One step at a time, I made it to the kitchen. I grabbed a bottle of water out of the fridge, a banana from the counter, and some crackers from the pantry. I headed toward the table but decided that some fresh air might do me some good. My feet felt heavy as I trudged out to the back porch, but when I opened the door and the cold air hit my face, I'd never been more thankful to be outside.

My body flopped down into the nearest chair, and I let out a huge huff. I opened the water and gulped down half the bottle before I began nibbling on the crackers. I closed my eyes, waiting for the moment I'd spontaneously feel better, but Luke's tormented face filled my mind instead.

It was the same vision that had plagued my thoughts and dreams since I'd admitted my part in my pack's plan.

I didn't know how my heart, which had been shredded into a million pieces, still managed to beat inside my chest. I was broken, completely crippled, and my never-ending supply of tears filled my eyes again. I hated myself for hurting him. Hated myself for betraying the only guy I'd ever loved. Nothing would ever be able to change that. I'd fucked up, and now I had to live with it. But that wasn't what killed me the most. It was the fact that Luke had to live with it too. And for that, I'd never forgive myself.

The sound of the back door opening startled me, but I didn't turn around. There was only one face I wanted to see and where my body might have been failing me, my sense of smell was not. I sat the crackers down on the table and asked, "Oh joy, you're back. What do you want, Drew?"

I heard his footsteps and then felt his body directly behind me. He leaned down until his lips grazed my ear and the warmth of his breath mixed with his clean, earthy scent triggered my stomach to churn once again. I felt his fingers in my hair and cringed. As he gently pulled my bun loose, he whispered, "What the fuck do you think you're doing, you pathetic little whore?"

As if his words could somehow singe my skin, I flinched, but his hand immediately wrapped itself around the back of my neck to hold me in place. His hushed tones grew louder and harsher as he continued. "Did you hear me, you stupid bitch? What are you doing here looking like shit instead of with Luke? Why isn't he following you around like your little lap-dog? What the hell is going on and why do you look like you haven't slept in days?"

When I didn't answer, he forcefully shoved my head away and began to pace back and forth. "You better start talking, Scarlett! You better not have screwed this up! Do you hear me? I know for a fact that something is up." I sunk down in the chair, covered my face with my hands, and began to weep. It was the last thing I wanted to do, but I couldn't control it, and I knew it would only serve to piss Drew off even more.

Drew stopped pacing, and even though I couldn't see him, I could feel him standing in front of me. Fear crept up my spine, and I knew right then that this wasn't going to end well. "I saw Cade and Gage sneaking around our pack's property. Why the hell were they there, Scarlett?"

My head shot up upon hearing those words. "What?" tumbled out of my mouth as a mixture of shock and terror swallowed me whole.

Drew's eyes narrowed and a tick started in his jaw. "You didn't! Tell me you didn't tell that piece of shit the truth! Tell me you didn't ruin everything!" he raged.

I covered my face with my hands again, fearing he'd be able to discern the truth in my eyes.

His hands gripped my wrists tightly as he pulled my hands away from my face. I opened my eyes to find Drew's face only inches away from my own. Seething with rage, his venomous eyes stared into mine as he awaited my response. His grip tightened and I tried to pull away. He wasn't letting go.

I shook my head back and forth and finally found my voice. My fear for myself turned to fear for Luke and what Drew might do if he suspected that Luke knew the truth. My voice sounded strong even if my body did not as I shouted, "Back the fuck up off of me, Drew! I didn't say a damn word. They know nothing! Now let go of me before you regret it!"

I'd barely finished my sentence before Drew yanked me up out of the chair by my throbbing wrists and pulled me toward him. His lips were only millimeters away from my own. "What are you going to do, Scarlett? How the hell do you plan to make me regret it? Because I can think of a few ways to make you regret whatever it is *you* may have done. One of which involves me bending you over that railing and——"

Before he'd finished his sentence, before I'd considered the consequences, I'd done it. I spit in his face. Spit in my future alpha's face! Drew forcefully shoved me away, and I stumbled back but managed to stay on two feet. In the state my weakened body was in, it was a wonder I didn't fall to the ground.

I looked back up at Drew just in time to see the back of his hand flying toward my face as he growled, "You fucking bitch!" When he hit me my body flew back and I landed on the ground.

I lay there for a moment in a crumpled heap before I glanced up to see the storm raging in Drew's eyes as he stalked toward me.

Outright panic tore through my limp body as I inched backward in some pathetic version of a crab walk. Drew could have caught up with me easily, but he slowly prowled my way, his rage-filled eyes tormenting me with each step as if this was all a game to him. I had to get out of there. I was no fool. My chances were slim, and I was easy prey, but I had to try.

I turned over and was back on my feet with surprising ease considering how I bad I felt. Without looking back, I took off running through the trees, shifting form in mid-stride. I'd managed to make it into the thick brush, but a hellacious howl warned me that Drew wasn't far behind. My heart raced as I considered my options. I couldn't out-run him, definitely couldn't out-fight him, so my only option was to out-smart him.

Spotting a thickly wooded area ahead off to the left, I took a sharp turn but stumbled a bit on some loose branches. I'd regained my footing quickly, but not before razor-sharp teeth clinched down around my hind leg. What could only be described as a shriek escaped my mouth as Drew's fangs sank straight down to the bone, latched on, and didn't let go.

My entire body jerked back all at once as I collapsed to the ground, but it was no longer the bite causing my pain. I managed to lift my head enough to see a thick branch deeply lodged into my thigh. Blood poured from the entry wound, and I knew I needed to get it out so that I could heal. Otherwise, I'd bleed to death.

My heavy head fell back to the ground as a dark shadow cover me. I looked up at what would most likely be the last thing I'd ever see. My blood dripped from Drew's muzzle as he snarled. I couldn't watch. There was murder in his eyes, and I knew this was the end. Slowly, my eyes closed.

The last thing I remembered was Drew's hot breath on my face as his strong jaw wrapped around my neck as I silently prayed that one day Luke would forgive me.

CHAPTER 51

Luke

I couldn't remember the last time I laid around all day and did absolutely nothing. I mean I literally didn't do anything, except feel sorry for myself and check my phone every five minutes for an update from Cade. Yesterday morning, Cade and Gage took off for Crescent Hills to see if they could find any sign of my father or information regarding the impending attack of our pack.

I demanded that they let me go with them, but Cade insisted that I stay here, claiming I was too "emotionally invested" to not do something stupid. Asshole. After Gage and Aiden had to physically restrain me from beating the shit out of Cade, I finally relented. Cade was right. I'd likely jeopardize the mission the second I saw anything suspicious. So I was left here for Aiden to babysit, though he thankfully chose to stay out of my hair 99 percent of the time.

After Cade's last text, which said they were heading back and had come up empty, I had pretty much given up hope of ever seeing my father again.

The pain in my chest from Scarlett's betrayal had only been getting worse as each minute passed. I'd never thought in a million years that it would be her who broke my heart. I was so worried about hurting her, about doing something that would cause her to hate me that I never stopped to consider that she had the power to do the same to me.

I'd only made it downstairs once all day today. My mouth felt like sandpaper, and I desperately needed a bottle of water from the kitchen, maybe two. Otherwise, I would have stayed put. I didn't know why, but I just felt tired and weak and had no interest in getting up, especially since there was nothing I could do to help find my father. Maybe this was what depression felt like. I would have stayed downstairs if there was still a couch down there to lie on. It took all the strength I had to walk back up all those stairs. I didn't remember making it back to the couch in the TV room, but somehow, I must have because I woke up there a while later when the doorbell rang.

I waited for a while to see if whoever it was would just go away, but no such luck. If the incessant ringing was any indication, the person outside was obviously growing more and more impatient. Taking a deep breath, I pushed myself up and let my feet fall to the floor. A weird wave of dizziness flowed through me as I stood up, and I had to sit back down and lower my head to my hands.

"Luke? You up there, man?" Aiden yelled. Apparently he just decided to let himself in. I could have sworn I'd locked the door, but it didn't matter how he got in. At least I didn't have to make it all the way down the stairs again.

"I'm upstairs," I called out. As soon as I lifted my head, an unfamiliar feeling rolled through my gut, and I felt as though I may throw up.

When Cade and Aiden turned the corner, I tried my best to appear normal.

"You look like shit," Cade announced as soon as he saw me. So much for looking normal.

In response, I just huffed and then tried to lie down and turn over to get comfortable, but my body didn't want to cooperate. I ended up on flat on my back after letting loose a series of moans and groans.

Then I noticed Cade and Aiden exchanging a couple of looks that I didn't understand, and it pissed me off that they were leaving me out of their silent conversation. "What? Just say it."

"Say what?" Aiden asked, playing stupid.

"Whatever you guys are talking about with your eyes," I said.

Aiden smiled, but he pretty much always smiled. Cade, on the other hand, looked grim, even more grim than usual. I didn't like that. It made me feel like things were about to get worse and really, how the hell could things get worse?

"You realize what's wrong with you, don't you?" Aiden asked as he plopped down in a chair.

I looked back and forth between Aiden and Cade as the realization struck me. *It can't be true. No way! We can't be.*

"Breathe, Luke," Cade demanded. I automatically obeyed and filled my lungs with air but instantly started choking on it. Cade reached down and pulled me up by my arm. Sitting up, I was able to catch my breath, but my head kept spinning.

"This can't be happening?" I mumbled.

Aiden shrugged. "You feel sick?"

"You haven't had any contact with Scarlett for a few days, right?" Cade asked.

I nodded in answer to both questions. Cade sighed as he sat on the other end of the sofa and said, "It seems so, but there is only one way to know for sure. You have to go see her. If you feel better just being near her, then I'd say you found your mate."

"But she lied to¬—"

"Doesn't matter," Cade interrupted. "Do you love her?"

I did not want to have this conversation with Cade and Aiden right now. I closed my eyes and laid my head back on the sofa behind me.

"It won't go away just because you want it to," Aiden stated, propping his feet up on the coffee table like this was no big deal. "It doesn't work like that."

"How exactly does it work then, Einstein?" I asked, sounding harsher than I intended.

Cade's furrowed his eyebrows and replied, "Look man, if you two are true mates, then you have to be together. Period. And you didn't answer my question. I realize that it's not very manly to sit around and talk about your feelings, but it's a fairly simple question when you think about it. Do you love her?"

"Yes," I reluctantly admitted.

"Then that's all that matters…"

"No, it's not. She lied. She betrayed me and our pack," I argued.

"Do you really think she had a choice? Luke, come on. You know how things work in packs. We've all had to do things we didn't want to do for the sake of our pack," Cade reminded me.

"That doesn't make it any easier to swallow," I muttered. This couldn't be the only way. Yes, I loved Scarlett. Even after everything she did, I still felt it deep inside my chest. If she walked through that door right now, I honestly didn't know what I would do or say. I'd felt empty for two days, but along with that empty feeling came hurt and betrayal. I didn't know if I would ever be able to trust her again.

"You need to go to her," Aiden said.

When I shook my head, he urged me to reconsider. "You look like shit, and I know how badly you must be feeling. Cade and I have both been there, and she's probably just as bad off as you are. I remember seeing Alli so sick and thinking that she was going to die. It scared the shit out of me seeing my sister like that."

I looked over at Cade and the look of absolute guilt and horror on his face tore at my insides.

Aiden's eyes shifted to Cade's as he said, "Sorry man, but it's true."

"No, he's right. I let my dad keep me away from Alli when I needed her and, more importantly, she needed me. She suffered because of me. Don't be that stubborn, Luke. Go to her. She has no one. If you are mates, you will know it instantly. It will haunt you for the rest of your life if you let it get any worse because eventually, you will have to face her," Cade said.

Shit! It didn't seem like I had a choice in the matter. I had to go to her. I should have never left her alone for the past two days in the first place. Honestly, I wasn't sure I would have, but Cade saw Brain and Drew in Crescent Hills, so I figured she'd be safe while they were gone. However, there was a good chance they'd be back soon, and I needed to make sure they didn't find out what she'd told us. I'd never forgive myself if they hurt her.

My decision made, I struggled to sit up, and as I took a moment to allow the room to stop spinning, I asked Cade, "So what happened in Crescent Hills? Why do you think Brian and Drew were there? You really didn't find out anything?" Aiden shot Cade another one of those looks that spoke volumes. Unfortunately I didn't speak the language, so I threw a pillow at him. "Damn it! Will you two stop that? It really pisses me off."

Aiden chuckled to himself. "Cade thinks he saw Kendall there."

"Shut up, man! I should have never told you that. It wasn't her anyway, so just drop it," Cade snapped.

I smiled for the first time in days, but I couldn't help it. Seeing Cade's cheeks redden was priceless. "Kendall, huh? You sure it wasn't her?" I asked, unable to hide my amusement. I wished I could have seen it. I bet he almost shit his pants.

Cade grimaced. "Positive. And I have no idea what Brian and Drew were up to, but how about we go see what we can find out? I'm pretty sure they are heading back today."

With a bit of renewed energy at the thought of seeing Scarlett and maybe getting some answers, I forced myself up off the couch and threw on some jeans and a hoodie.

"So you're going over there?" Aiden asked as I headed for the stairs.

"Yep," I answered without stopping.

"You gonna wait for us or what?" Cade asked as he trailed behind me. "I think it's about time we had a word with Drew and Brian. Don't ya think?"

Aiden, following close behind Cade, said, "First thing's first. Let's find Scarlett. Luke isn't in any shape to help until we do. Then we can make a plan to interrogate Brian before we beat the living shit out of Drew."

Cade chuckled. "Good idea, Aiden. Come on. I'll drive."

CHAPTER 52

Drew

"Oh God, no! Holy shit! No! No! No! What have I done? Jesus Christ, Scarlett! Look what you made me do! You stupid, stupid bitch! This is all your fault. You made me do this to you! Do you hear me? You did this!" My entire body shook as I looked down at the mangled mess I had made of Scarlett's body. Dropping to my knees, I concentrated on breathing in and out before I flipped the fuck out.

I'd never meant for things to get so far out of hand, but she wouldn't stop running from me. Now, I didn't even know if she was still alive. Cautiously I reached out to feel for a pulse. The moment my fingers made contact, her body shifted from wolf to woman. A girlie shriek flew out of my mouth as I jumped away from Scarlett's naked body, and immediately, I looked around to make sure no one had heard. Thankfully, it didn't appear that anyone had witnessed my wussy-ass reaction or anything else that had happened here.

Even in this form, she didn't move. That was a bad sign. She was a bloody wreck, but I didn't see any wound that she wouldn't be able to heal from. I stood there just gawking at her limp body wondering why the healing process hadn't already begun. It wasn't until I reached down and turned her on her side that my stomach lurched, and I knew that what I saw was bad news. When I'd chased Scarlett down, she fell hard onto her side and a thick fallen branch impaled itself in the side of her upper thigh, just below her hip. It was lodged in there good too. I couldn't tell how deep, but judging from the dark, red pool of blood around her injury, it was not a superficial wound. I'd never seen so much blood in my life, with the exception of in those stupid slasher movies. I still needed to check for a pulse, but with that much blood all around, I was too afraid to touch her.

What I really needed to do was get her to a doctor, but what would happen to me when they found out that I was the one that caused this? No, no doctor, but I couldn't just leave her there. Could I? I must have paced back and forth for a solid ten minutes while Scarlett lay there bleeding out, trying to decide what to do. Finally, I built up the nerve to place my fingers below her nose to see if she was breathing. After I determined that she was still alive, I slowly placed my hand on the branch and gave it a slight tug. The stick shifted, but so did the flesh around it, all bloody and oozing and...*holy shit!* I turned and lost it. Completely lost it. I couldn't stomach the sight of her wound. I just couldn't do it. I dropped all the way to the ground and hung my head over my knees as I hyperventilated.

While I tried to focus on slowing my breathing, my mind raced, and the more I thought about it, the more sense it made to just let her die. She'd been causing nothing but trouble anyway. She probably told Luke the truth, and if he had any sense at all, he wouldn't want anything to do with her now. She'd betrayed her pack, so we wouldn't take her back. In fact, my father would probably have her killed if she ever returned. I'd actually be doing the bitch a favor if I let her die, but I couldn't just leave her here out in the open.

I scanned the area for a place to hide her. I found a small ditch not far off, so I held my breath, lifted Scarlett off the ground, and carried her to it. She appeared to be near dead already. I laid her down in the ditch and felt for a pulse. Nothing. Without a second thought, I quickly covered her body with a bunch of leafy branches and brush until she was completely hidden.

As I stood back to inspect my work, I swallowed a lump in my throat and fought back the sickening feeling in my gut. I knew what

I'd done was wrong, but it was what was best for my pack. I had to put the pack first. If that meant that Scarlett had to be sacrificed, then so be it.

I tried to cover my tracks the best I could, but any werewolf worth a shit would be able to scent me out, but there was nothing I could do about it now. Besides by the time anyone realized that she was missing, I would be long gone. With one more quick look around, I shifted and ran back to the house.

CHAPTER 53

Luke

The moment the thought that Drew or Scarlett's dad might hurt Scarlett entered my mind, I couldn't get to her fast enough. Don't get me wrong, I was still pissed at her, and I really didn't know if things with us would ever be the way they were, mated or not, but the need to see her safe was all-consuming.

We were halfway to her house before I realized I hadn't showered in two days. Guess it didn't matter now. I could get my shit together once I knew that Scarlett was okay. We pulled up in front of her house and another one of those vicious combinations of nausea and panic swept through me. Not thinking clearly, I jumped out of the car and dashed up to the porch.

"Scarlett!" I yelled as I pounded on the door. Unable to wait for an answer, I placed my hand on the doorknob and turned. To my surprise, it opened, and I hesitantly took a step into the house.

"Scarlett," I said just loud enough for someone inside the house to hear me. When she didn't respond, I flipped the on first light switch I came to. That light was followed by every one I could find as I ran through the house calling her name. Panic quickly consumed me as I flew through each empty room.

"The house is empty," Cade said as I walked back down the stairs, but I knew that already. My heart stopped when the backdoor opened and Aiden stepped inside looking grim. "I think you guys need to see the patio."

I pushed passed Cade and hurried outside. The sight of the patio furniture over turned and flung around haphazardly sent chills down my spine. My hands clenched into fists at my side, my mind raced through one bad scenario after another, and I felt the sting of tears in my eyes. Something bad happened here. Scarlett was in danger.

"Don't jump to conclusions," Cade said.

I turned around and stared him down as if he'd just made it to the top of my hit list. Did he really believe it was possible for me not to jump to conclusions?

"I know it looks bad, but it won't do anyone any good to go crazy without knowing," he corrected himself. "Let's go back to my car and wait for someone to come home. It doesn't look like anyone has left for good, so someone has to come back eventually."

"I'm going to take a closer look in her room, and I'll meet you in a minute," I mumbled as I walked away from the horrible scene on the patio. I needed a minute alone, some time to get my emotions under control before I played the sit-and-wait game in the car with Cade.

I walked into her room again, and as I fell back onto her bed, I was inundated by her scent. It completely consumed me. When I breathed her in again and again, my stomach eased, and the headache that I had for past two days vanished. Just being in the room where she'd been made me feel better, stronger. And I knew exactly what that meant.

*****

Cade shot me an odd look as I got back in the car. "Find anything?"

I wasn't quite ready to admit what had been confirmed while I was inside. "Nah. Where'd Aiden go?" I asked since he was no longer in the backseat.

"I told him to go on home and we would call him when someone showed up," Cade explained before he proceeded to look me up and down. The knowing look on his face made me want to tell him to piss off. "So I guess it's true, huh? She really is your mate?"

The car became instantly stuffy, and I would have done just about anything to get the hell out of there. I tugged at the collar of my hoodie and rolled down the window.

"Sorry man, it's just that your color is back, and you're holding on to one of Scarlett's shirts for dear life," he noted. I looked down and couldn't believe it. I hadn't even realized that I had picked it up off her bed. I stared out the window at her house and confessed, "Shit. I can't believe this is happening."

We waited and waited, but nobody came home. As the minutes passed, Scarlett's scent had faded, and the headache and nausea returned with a vengeance. I needed to find her. Sitting here waiting was a waste of time. There had to be something else I could be doing besides waiting in this damn car.

My mind raced with all of the possible horrific things that could have happened to Scarlett, and those images left me feeling desperate and helpless. My palms were slick with perspiration, my eyes blurred, and the sound of Cade texting on his phone was enough to send me over the edge. I wanted to crawl out of my skin.

Just when I thought that I might have to use the last of my energy to crush Cade's phone into a thousand pieces, a car I didn't recognize came speeding straight toward us. Cade and I exchanged a concerned look as the car screeched to a halt. We both hopped out of the car, and a tall, lean guy about our age got out and started yelling.

"Which one of you is Luke?"

I took a step toward him, and the guy actually pushed me. Ballsy move. He may have been a few inches taller than me, but he wasn't nearly as built. Needless to say, I didn't move, but the piece of shit tried and tried again.

"Where the hell is my sister?" he shouted, this time getting right up in my face.

So this was the *real* Gavin, Scarlett's real brother.

"Tell me where she is or I swear I will take your ass down!" Gavin ordered, trying to push me again.

Scarlett's brother or not, this guy was starting to piss me off, and I didn't have time for him, nor did I feel up to showing him just how unlikely his threat to "take me down" would be. I grabbed him by the collar of his shirt and flung him up against Cade's car. "Gavin, right?"

He didn't respond right away, so I grabbed his shirt again and gave him a little shake to make sure he was listening. "Listen to me, Gavin. I don't know where she is, but I need to find her too. And I'm not going to hurt her. I swear, I would never hurt Scarlett, but she's missing. I need to find her, and I need you to help me."

His eyes went wide with shock, but he still didn't say anything, so I shoved him back and grunted. "Are you just going to stand there or are you going to help me find your sister?"

I stepped back and let Gavin straighten himself up before asking, "When was the last time you heard from Scarlett?"

The shock was gone and replaced with obvious skepticism. Gavin crossed his arms over his chest defiantly. "Why the hell should I tell you? Hell, maybe you are the reason she's missing."

I looked over at Cade, and the bastard was texting. Texting! And smirking. I grabbed the phone out of his hand and shouted, "Who the hell are you texting? And stop fucking grinning. It's not going to be funny when I have to tell Scarlett that I beat the shit out of her brother."

Cade snatched his phone back and said, "For you information, I was texting Aiden to tell him to get his ass over here." Then he chuckled to himself and nodded toward Gavin. "Just tell him and get it over with."

I froze. Hell no.

"Tell me what?" Gavin asked, his eyes darting back and forth between Cade and me.

"Jesus Christ, Cade!" I snapped.

"Tell me what? Is this about Scarlett?" Gavin demanded.

"It's nothing," I muttered as I glared at Cade.

"You tell me then," Gavin urged Cade, and I suddenly felt like a chicken-shit.

Cade rolled his eyes at me and said, "Scarlett and Luke are true mates."

"Yeah, right." Gavin laughed. I rubbed my hands over my eyes and through my hair. This was turning into a disastrous night. Gavin looked at me and asked, "He's kidding, right?"

When I didn't say anything, he looked horrified and then said, "I don't know whether to shake your hand or punch you in the face."

"Don't hit him. He's in a bad mood. He'll probably hit you back," Cade joked.

"Listen, I haven't seen Scarlett in two days. I feel like shit. She probably feels just as bad as I do, and I need to find her. So, have you heard from her or not?" I demanded.

"Holy shit," Gavin stammered as his eyebrows shot up as if something important suddenly occurred to him. "Holy shit, shit, shit shit...she hasn't retuned any of my texts...I thought that you did something to her...oh shit...Luke, dude," he stopped and turned to Cade. "Will he really hit me?" he asked.

Cade took a few steps to strategically position himself between Gavin and me. "You better just say what you need to say," Cade warned. I was trying to remain calm for Scarlett, but with the way Gavin was acting, I was having a really hard time doing so. Just in case I really didn't like what he had to say, I shoved my hands into the pockets of my jeans.

"Okay, just remember, I thought that you were the bad guy. When I hadn't heard from her, I thought you must have found out and your pack had done something to her. I thought she was in danger." Gavin stopped and looked over at his car before he continued. "The last time I talked to Scarlett she told me about your father, so when I decided to come find her, I brought him to trade," he admitted.

I looked at Cade. "What the fuck did he just say?"

"He's in the car," Gavin clarified.

Sucking in a deep breath, I ran over to Gavin's car and sure as shit my dad was unconscious in the back seat. "What the hell is wrong with him?" I demanded as I pulled the door open and reached inside to feel for a pulse.

"They've been keeping him sedated," Gavin explained as he walked to the other side of the car. "I gave him a pretty big dose before I stole him, not enough to do any permanent damage; just enough so he wouldn't wake up on the way here and try to kill me."

A deep growl rumbled in my chest before I could stop it. "Dude," Gavin said to Cade, "the man is huge. You can't blame me for that."

"Did anyone see you take him?" Cade asked.

Gavin shook his head. "I wouldn't be here if they did. No one even knows where I am. I was worried and thought Scarlett needed my help. And well, I needed a bargaining chip. So, I stole your dad and came straight here. I swear no one knows where I am."

I looked at Cade and I knew he was thinking the same thing I was. We could use this to our advantage, and quickly, if we came up with the right plan. With perfect timing, Aiden showed up. Cade explained everything, and Aiden agreed to take my dad and Gavin to my house and make sure that no one saw them. I could tell that Gavin didn't like our idea because he wanted to help find his sister, but after I assured him that I would do whatever it took to make sure she was found, he finally agreed that keeping his presence here a secret was vital.

Before they left, I asked Gavin, "Would Drew hurt Scarlett?"

He wouldn't meet my eye and looked at the ground. "I hate to say this, but I wouldn't put it passed Drew or my father. Drew is an evil son of a bitch, so yeah, I'm pretty sure he would." He turned to leave, but stopped and turned back around. This time he looked me in the face. "Hey Luke? I'm really sorry about your father...about everything. I tried to talk Scarlett out of coming here, but she was determined to help my father."

Gavin looked away as if trying to decide if he should continue. He took a few steps toward me and must have decided to lay it on the line. "Look man, she'd probably hate me for telling you this, but he's barely spoken to her since our mom died. It's been really hard on her, and when my dad asked her to help, she didn't want to tell him no. She just wanted him to love her again. To know that he still cared about her. The bastard knew it and used it to get her to agree to all of this. I know it's not an excuse for Scarlett's part in everything, but she really cares about you. She wanted out. She didn't want to hurt you, but she couldn't get out of it without hurting you or getting your father killed. She was stuck. I'm sorry, man."

I nodded my head and held out my hand for him to shake. "You don't know how much I needed to hear that. And thanks for saving my father. I know you only brought him back to save your sister, but you brought him back, and that's all that matters. But you do realize that you can never go back if they find out that it was you."

He shrugged. "I did what I had to do."

I glanced over to Cade.

"Well you are always welcome here," Cade assured him.

Gavin looked off in the distance again. "Thanks, man. Now go find my sister. Oh and if you happen to beat the shit out of Drew in the process, just icing on the cake."

With Gavin, my father, and Aiden gone, Cade and I got back in the car to wait. And we didn't have to wait long. Only seventeen and a half minutes later, a light switched on inside the house.

CHAPTER 54

Drew

"What the fuck? Christ, I'm coming," I yelled at the asshole pounding a hole in the freaking front door. I didn't need that shit. I needed to get my things and get the hell out of this place. When I saw that it was Luke I decided to let the stupid meathead pound away for a bit longer. No need to rush. Plus I needed to get my game face on.

"Scarlett!" Luke yelled just before I opened the door for the giant jackass, who would have very likely taken up residence on our porch if I hadn't. Our eyes locked. I smiled and stepped aside. "Luke, come on in." It was clear he was trying to appear calm but he was seething with rage.

He took one step inside and asked, "Where is Scarlett?!"

Think fast, damn it. My hand shot up to cover my mouth, and I looked at him with what I'd hope portrayed pity. "Oh, man. Didn't she tell you? She left. Went back home."

Luke took a step closer and popped his knuckles in an attempt to intimidate me. I tried not to let it show, but it worked a little. The dude was a beast.

"I'm going to ask you one more time, *Drew*. Where the hell is Scarlett?" he growled.

Oh, well that changed things. So he knew. Good. I could work with this. No more games then. I was tired of having to play nice with this trash anyway.

"Like I said, *Luke*, she went home," I repeated, stepping up to him just to see what he would do. He actually smiled, and I knew immediately that was not a good thing. Luke grabbed me by my shirt and swung me around until my back was facing the open front door.

"She did not go home, Drew. You and I both know that," he said as he took a few steps forward, forcing me to step back until we were both out on the front porch. "Save yourself a lot of pain and tell me where she is."

"I don't think she wants to see you, man. At least, she didn't mention your name when she was begging for her life—ugh, fuck!" I shouted. I didn't even see his fist coming before it crashed into my face. I should have expected it, but I thought I would have had a little more of a warning. I reached up and lightly touched my nose, knowing immediately it was broken and bleeding like crazy. I tried to keep my voice calm, but it was hard. The beast was strong, and I could tell that punch was just the beginning.

"What did you do, Drew?" he demanded pulling me in close.

I laughed. I knew he was going to hit me this time. I watched his jaw clench and his eyes darken as he prepared to slam his fist into my face again, so I braced for impact. Pain shot through my jaw as my knees buckled from underneath me. Coughing, I scrambled back up to my feet and stepped away from Luke. I looked around and saw Cade standing by his car, arms crossed over his chest, a smug look on his face. I knew a secret about his mother that would wipe that look right off his face, but I figured I'd save that little bombshell for just the right moment. Turning my attention back to Luke, I spit blood onto the ground. Trying to fight him was useless since I was clearly outnumbered and Luke was freakishly strong, but I could cause him pain unlike any he'd ever felt before. "Come to think of it, Scarlett did mention your name. She called out for you once, but that was before I fucked all thoughts of you out of her pretty little head."

Before I could even prepare for the blow, Luke made contact. "Ugh!" I doubled over. Son of a bitch, that hurt! I had never been punched in the stomach before, and I never wanted to again.

Desperately trying to hide the pain, I forced a smile on my face and laughed. As soon as the sound left my lips, I was hit again. This time I tried to defend myself, but I think that just pissed him off more.

"Tell me where she is, Drew, or I swear to God I will kill you," Luke warned.

It was time to unleash the big dogs, and hurt this bastard more than his fists could ever hurt me. I groaned and sputtered as if I'd had all I could take. "She's gone, Luke." I tried to look serious, but failed miserably as laughter bubbled up inside of me again. "She's dead. I killed her. I watched as the life drained from her eyes."

"Liar!" Luke roared and grabbed me by my throat.

"Go ahead Luke. Kill me. I dare you! My dad will fucking destroy you! He will annihilate this entire godforsaken pack!" I tried to yell, but my air supply was limited. "Do it, Luke! But nothing is going to bring that backstabbing bitch back to life!"

It was in that moment that I began to feel the true strength and wrath of Luke Stanton. Pain shot through every inch of my body. I felt every punch, every kick, every stomp from the top of my head to the bottom of my feet. My vision was blurred, not only due to the nonstop blows to my skull, but because of the stream of blood pouring from a cut somewhere above one of my eyes.

I knew the end was coming. I felt myself slipping in and out of consciousness. Somehow I ended up on my knees, and I vaguely remembered looking up at Luke as he prepared to end my life. But as luck would have it, Cade stopped him. He didn't have to pull him back. His words were enough. "Luke, we need him. To find Scarlett's body."

Luke's shoulders slumped as he took a few steps back, and the rage in his eyes was replaced with grief. I grinned through the pain and said, "I knew it. I knew you would come to your senses, Cade. Besides, you're too much of a pussy to actually kill someone."

CHAPTER 55

Luke

I'm not sure how it happened, but somehow Cade managed to stop me from killing Drew. I was only vaguely aware of walking away. My ears were ringing, and after the adrenaline rush wore off, wave after wave of nausea crippled my body. I stumbled away and rested my hands on a nearby pine tree in the yard just in time to completely lose it. I'd vomited for the first time in my life yesterday, but that was nothing compared with the constant convulsions my body was going through today.

As I tried to catch my breath, Drew's words sank in. *Scarlett was dead! No! She can't be dead! I don't believe it! I can't believe it!*

I turned to see Cade holding Drew down. Cade saved him today, but one day soon, I would get my hands on him again. I'd just have to make sure Cade wasn't around when I did. The desire to wrap my hands around Drew's throat and squeeze until the ache in my chest subsided was nearly too much to ignore.

Out of the corner of my eye, I saw Aiden making his way back here. He took one look at Drew and asked, "I take it he didn't cooperate?"

I glared at him. "Really?"

Aiden held both hands up in a mock surrender then walked over to speak to Cade.

"Can you do something else for me?" Cade asked Aiden.

"Sure," he replied, his voice flat.

"Will you take this douche bag to the lodge and lock him up in the cell? I need to organize a search party to find Scarlett," Cade said while handing the nearly unconscious Drew over.

"Sure thing," Aiden said as he flattened Drew to the ground and dug his knee into his back.

Cade walked to the trunk of his car and came back with a couple of large zip ties to bind Drew's arms. Just in case.

Once they were gone, Cade pulled out his phone and started making the calls. I couldn't keep my knees from trembling. I made my way back to the front porch and all but collapsed on the steps. Sitting with my head in my hands, I listened as Cade called everyone and told and retold the story. If I had to hear him say that Scarlett might be dead one more time, I might have to kill him.

Before long, Gage pulled up in front of the house. Cade said something to him, but I didn't have the will to listen in. Gage looked over at me and froze. He was my best friend and could always read me like a book. He saw it on my face. The anger. The hurt. The sadness. Gage didn't say anything; he just sat down next to me while we waited for everyone else to show up.

I had wanted to go ahead, but Cade ordered me to wait and give him a little time. He said that if I went alone in "my condition" that they would end up searching for the both of us. Another one of those dizzy spells only proved Cade's point.

Mrs. Wright was next to arrive along with Alli and Teagan. Mrs. Wright was all business. She told Cade that he needed to call his mother and fill her in as well as and warn her about Brian. We all gathered around while he made the call, but Noel didn't answer. I didn't like the feeling that gave me in the pit of my stomach. I knew Cade wanted to go find his mother, but I also knew that he would stay and search for Scarlett first. Cade left his mom a message detailing what was going down on the estate and Brian's involvement in it all.

By the time we had split up and decided where to start, Aiden and few others showed up to help. I was done with waiting. Without a moment of hesitation, I changed from man to wolf and took off to find my mate.

I ran straight off the back patio into the woods behind the house. The moon was full and its light seeped through the trees casting shadows on the ground. It wasn't long until I picked up her scent. At first I panicked. The fear of finding her was almost as great as the fear of never seeing her again. I quickly shook that thought out of my mind. No, she needed me. I took a deep breath and tried to clear my head of everything except her scent. As I slowed to barely a walk, things began to grow silent. All I could hear was the crunch of leaves under my paws. My breath was visible in the frigid January air. I looked to the skies and saw a few snowflakes beginning to form and settle on the trees above me.

I scanned the area and then my nose hit the ground. Blocking everything else out, I followed the faint smell to the left. As her scent got stronger, an eerie feeling seeped into my bones. Cade silently came up behind me and stepped up to my right. When he looked at me, and I knew he felt it too. She was close. Her scent seemed to be everywhere. It surrounded us, but it was wrong. Forced. Unnatural. It was like someone, Drew, purposely spread her scent to throw us off.

I walked around in a large circle, keeping my eyes closed and focusing on where her scent was strongest. When I opened my eyes, I knew. I dashed over to a small ditch and then shifted immediately. It felt wrong to find her as a wolf. I would need to hold her, to touch her one more time.

I scanned the area until I saw the spot I was looking for. I hurried over and fell to my knees. Frantically, I cleared away the branches and leaves until I saw the first of the blood. With tears filling my eyes, I pushed away the rest of the debris that Drew had piled up on top of Scarlett.

She looked dead. Her body was cold, her lips a horrible shade of blue, her beautiful eyes closed to the world. I pulled her to my chest and held her as my tears fell.

Now standing behind me, Cade asked, "Does she have a pulse?" His words prompted me to action. I felt along her neck, hoping and praying to feel something under my fingers. I held my breath and waited…there! I'd felt it. It was weak and barely noticeable, but it was there.

"She's still alive!" I cried.

"But why isn't she healing?" Cade asked.

I quickly laid her back down and began examining her body for the cause of this. Once I turned her on her side, I gasped. The branch protruding from her upper-thigh made my heart lurch. I wanted so badly to just yank the damn thing out, but I didn't have anything to staunch the bleeding with, and from the looks of her, she didn't have much more to lose.

Suddenly Teagan was kneeling down on the other side of Scarlett holding a blanket in her arms. I looked up to see that everyone had now gathered around us. Cade was pulling on a pair of sweatpants, and I knew it was for Teagan's benefit. She wasn't a were, which understandably made her quite uncomfortable around a bunch of naked guys. I was just grateful her modesty made her decide to follow us with clothes and blankets.

Teagan knelt down next to me and said, "Okay Luke, on three you pull that out of her leg, and I will press down with the blanket."

I nodded.

"One…two…three."

It was deep, but it came out easily and whole. Teagan didn't even flinch when I pulled out the branch. She just did her job.

Quickly I lifted Scarlett into my arms, careful to hold pressure on her wound, and ran back to her house.

By the time we got there, a car was waiting to take us to the infirmary. I held her the entire way. I couldn't put her down. She was my mate. She had to make it. She had to. I needed her. I loved her. I pulled her close, kissing her face, and whispered, "Scarlett baby, you have to come back to me. I need you to open your eyes. I love you. You can't leave me yet."

CHAPTER 56

Scarlett

My entire body felt numb. My eyes were closed, and to be honest, I was scared to open them. Terrified at what I might see, where I might be. But they didn't stay closed for long once the familiar scent of Luke assailed my senses. At first, I thought I had to be dreaming, maybe even in heaven, until I heard his light breathing.

My eyes fluttered open and took a moment to focus. I was in the infirmary. I was safe. And healing. It felt like my head weighed a ton as it dropped sideways in search of Luke. His head popped up, and his red-rimmed eyes were filled with unshed tears. He shot up from the chair next to my hospital bed and took my hands in his. "Scarlett, thank God you're awake. Are you okay? Are you in pain? Do I need to get the doctor?"

All I could do was shake my head. There were no words. The lost look on his face left me completely speechless. I couldn't do anything but lie there and stare into the deep brown eyes of the guy I thought I'd never see again. Not only did I think Luke would never speak to me, but I truly, without a doubt, believed my life was over. My battered body lay bleeding in the woods covered by branches and brush for what seemed like days, though I wasn't really sure how long I was out there. I was in and out of consciousness, in excruciating pain, and too weak to do anything other than lift my head a few inches off the ground. Every time I shifted even the tiniest bit, my vision would blur and I'd black out. It wasn't long before I was begging for death, begging to be taken out of my misery.

But now here I was. I was alive, and there was so much to say, but I had no words.

Luke's eyes left mine and then his hands were gone, leaving me feeling cold and empty. I wanted to reach out and stop him. Tell him not to leave me, but I couldn't. I watched as he walked over to a counter along the wall, grabbed a glass, and filled it with water from a small plastic pitcher. He opened a straw that was sitting nearby and stuck it the cup. He turned back toward me, and our eyes locked again. He held out the water and said, "You should drink something." Then he placed the straw near my lips, so I took it into my mouth, slowly taking in the cold water.

The liquid ran down my throat, and nothing had ever felt so good…well, almost nothing. After a few small sips, Luke put the cup down on the table next to my bed and moved back over to the chair. He watched me closely but didn't say anything else for a few minutes. Silence filled the air. I guess neither of us knew what to say. His eyes no longer held the cold, hard stare they did the last time I saw him, but I still couldn't read him. And the fact that he wasn't speaking was making me more and more anxious.

I took a moment to look around the room and examine my condition. My leg was elevated and wrapped with heavy bandages. Everything else seemed to be cuts and bruises, maybe a broken rib or two, but all were well on their way to being healed. My leg was the obvious culprit of the severity of my condition. It was then that I remembered the branch that had lodged itself deep into my thigh when I was trying to get away from Drew.

Drew! Where is Drew? Does Luke know how I ended up bleeding out in the woods? What had happened while I was gone?

My heart rate increased as fear enveloped my entire being. I couldn't explain it other than my flight response kicked in. Ignoring the resistance from my battered body, I shot up in the bed but couldn't hold in the pained gasp that escaped my lips when everything shifted. Luke jumped up from his chair, taking my arm in one hand and placing his other behind my back to steady me. "What are you doing, Scarlett? Are you okay? You should lie back down."

My eyes searched Luke's face for any evidence that he knew what had really happened. "Where is he? Where is...Drew?"

His eyes softened as he spoke. "Just lie back down. Please just try to relax. But we do need to talk." I let him guide my body back down to the mattress. He adjusted my pillow under my head and then carefully repositioned my hurt leg. Once he was satisfied that I was comfortable, he sat back down in the chair and placed his head in his hands as he took a few deep breaths.

This wasn't going to be good. I could feel it in my bones, and I tried my best to mentally prepare myself for what he had to say. No matter what it was, I knew it was going to hurt like hell, way worse that anything I'd suffered thus far.

Luke didn't look up before he began. Though his hands no longer covered his face, his focus remained on the floor below as he spoke. "I know that it was Drew who attacked you and left you for dead in the woods. We have him."

He finally looked up, and his eyes locked with mine. "I met your brother. He came for you, and...he brought my father with him." Immediately my eyes filled with tears as I shook my head in disbelief. It wasn't that I doubted that what Luke was saying was true; I just couldn't believe what I was hearing. I wanted to reach out for him, but I didn't. I wasn't sure if he wanted me to, and I couldn't handle it if he didn't let me.

I laid my head back on my pillow and closed my eyes trying to keep my tears at bay, but that didn't stop them from rolling down my cheeks. His father was back. After everything that had happened, that was what was most important. His father was alive.

But how did Gavin end up with Phillip?

My eyes flew open and my body tensed. Any ounce of relief I'd momentarily felt was zapped away in an instant. Gavin was in danger. Our alpha would kill him if he found him. "How? Why was Gavin with Phillip? Are they safe? Are they okay? Where are they? Where's Drew? My father? You have to make sure they are safe. Hidden! If my father finds out—"

Luke jumped out of his chair and grabbed my hands. "Shhh. Calm down. Everything is fine. My father and Gavin are safe. I told you we have Drew. Please, Scarlett, calm down." Luke left one of his hands wrapped around mine, but with the other, he began running his fingers through my hair. He tucked a few strands behind my ear, and then with his thumb, wiped away my tears. "When you didn't return his calls, your brother thought that we had found out what was going on and that you were in danger. He took my dad and planned on trading him for you. What he didn't realize was that it wasn't our pack that put you in danger. We have Drew in a cell at the lodge, but we are still looking for your father. As far as we know, he doesn't know that Gavin or my father is here."

Luke leaned down and kissed my forehead. His lips lingered there as he inhaled deeply. "God, Scarlett. I thought I'd lost you." Without a second thought, I threw my arms around his neck and pulled him toward me. I needed to be close to him, at least for this moment. After that, I'd be forced to face whatever followed. Relief washed over me again as Luke's arms wrapped around me too. Holding me tightly, he whispered, "I should have never left you alone."

I pulled away but only so I could look into Luke's eyes. "I'm so sorry, Luke. I know you will probably never forgive me, but you have to know how sorry I am. There are no excuses for what I did. I was stupid and naïve and I just needed my dad to…No, it doesn't matter. I should have never come here. I should have never agreed to any of this. Everything just got so screwed up, and I didn't know what to do. I fell for you, and Drew knew it. I wanted out. I wanted to tell you the truth, but he said he'd kill your father. I thought I was keeping you safe, keeping your father safe. I just didn't know what to do, didn't know how to make it right. I screwed everything up, Luke, and I'm so sorry."

He swallowed hard before he leaned down to rest his forehead against mine. Instinctively, my eyes closed, and I breathed him in, wanting to hold on to this moment forever. It may have been the last time he held me, and I didn't want it to end.

I felt Luke take a breath before he spoke. "I know, baby. And I forgive you...for everything. I love you, and I never want to live without you, so please say you still love me too."

Completely shocked, my eyes sprang open, and I said the only thing I could think to say. "What?"

Luke laughed as he cupped my face in his hands and smiled. "Say you still love me, Scarlett."

My heart pounded in my chest, and I couldn't believe what I was hearing. This couldn't be real. He loved me. He forgave me. He didn't want to live without me. I needed to answer him, but all I could seem to do was stare at him in disbelief.

"Say something, will you?" Luke urged, and it was enough to snap me out of me my stupor. I nodded my head and finally answered him. "Of course, I love you, Luke. More than anything in this world. I love you, and I never want to live without you either."

Without warning, Luke's lips crashed into mine as he kissed me hard. Needing him closer, I wrapped my arms around his neck and pulled him toward me until his chest laid against mine. I parted my lips and welcomed his tongue as he deepened the kiss. I lost myself in the taste of the guy I never thought I would taste again. His fingers ran down my sides, back up, and then entangled themselves in my hair as he kissed his way down my jaw line, my neck, my shoulders, and then back up to my lips. He gently sucked on my bottom lip before he pulled away, leaving us both breathless.

He looked into my eyes and said, "You don't know how glad I am to hear you say that. Say you're mine, Scarlett."

My heart swelled as I vowed, "I'm yours. No matter what. I'm yours, for as long as you'll have me."

He smiled like he knew something I didn't before he kissed me again. Then he pulled away and said, "Don't freak out, but I hope you're sure about that because you're my true mate, Scarlett Reed. And that means you're mine forever."

CHAPTER 57

Luke

Scarlett's eyes widened and a smile that completely melted my heart appeared on her beautiful face. I couldn't resist pressing my lips to that smile. I knew things were still not right on the estate, and Scarlett and I had a long way to go before we could get back to the place we were. So yeah, there were plenty of problems yet to be solved, but it all seemed doable at that moment. Sitting with Scarlett, my hands touching her face, my lips caressing hers, all felt right in my world again.

I reluctantly pulled back when I heard footsteps stop in front of Scarlett's door. "Come on in," I said.

Cade and Dr. Walters walked into the room. I probably should have moved out of the way so the doc could check on Scarlett without having to work around me, but I couldn't. She was mine, and even though I knew the doc had to touch her, I didn't like it. The doc unwrapped Scarlett's bandages and she winced. A growl escaped my body before I could stop it. Scarlett reached for me and pulled me against her whispering, "Don't worry…I'm okay."

The doctor apologized and rewrapped her leg. He explained that it was healing nicely and that if I wanted to take Scarlett home, she should be fine. Scarlett nodded, and I told him that I would take her to my place. I also asked him to stop by my house and check on my dad. Cade pulled the doctor aside and told him that he had to keep Phillip's return a secret for now. The doctor agreed and went to get his things.

"Aiden and Gage are over at the lodge guarding Drew. He's healing pretty fast and should be much better by tomorrow," Cade said after the doctor left the room.

Another one of those unexpected growls rose out of my chest. I didn't give a shit about Drew's condition. "Two more minutes alone with him and he could be out of the picture for good." Scarlett gave me an apprehensive look, and I shrugged. It was just a matter of time anyway. I would get my hands on him again.

Cade placed his hand on my shoulder. "I understand, Luke, but we still might need him. I'm calling a pack meeting. My house. First light. I want my dad there, and he can't be moved. I stopped by the house, but it was quiet. Dad was sleeping in his room and Mom was asleep in the guest room upstairs. There's been no sign of Brian, so we can't afford to wait any longer."

"I'll be there. Are you going back to your house?" I asked.

"No, I'm going to check on Aiden and Gage, and then I'm going to try to catch a few hours of sleep at Alli's," Cade said. He started to leave, but stopped in the doorway and turned around to say, "I'm glad you're better, Scarlett. We were all worried about you."

*****

As soon as I carried Scarlett into my house Gavin came rushing over. Ever since I'd found her in the woods, my protective instincts were in overdrive, so as her brother approached, it took a great deal of self-control not fling him out of the way. Somehow Scarlett must have recognized my possessive reaction to his nearness, so she assured Gavin that she was all right and asked him to give her a minute to get settled. Fortunately he stepped back and waited until I carried her upstairs and put her in my bed before he came up to see her.

While I didn't want to leave her side, I decided it would be best to give them some privacy for a moment, and I really needed to check on my father. After kissing Scarlett on the forehead, I walked over to the door. "I'm going to see how my dad's doing. Can I get you something from the kitchen, baby?" I asked before I left.

She smiled brightly and nodded her head. "That would be great. I'm starving." I returned her smile before heading downstairs.

When I stepped into my dad's room, the doctor was just finishing his exam. "Your dad's going to be just fine when the drugs wear off. Unfortunately, he was given a pretty heavy dose, so he's been in and out of consciousness and will be extremely groggy when he wakes. It might take some time for him to get back to normal, but don't worry. He'll be back to his old self soon."

"Is there anything I can do for him?" I asked.

"You're already doing it. He's comfortable. He's resting. That's it. I started an IV just to keep him hydrated. When he comes around, don't let him yank it out."

As soon as the doc left, I sat down next to my father and grabbed his hand. Before I realized what I was doing, I was spilling my guts, telling him everything that had happened since he disappeared. I knew that he probably couldn't hear me, but I didn't care. I told him about the fight between Cade and Aiden, about seeing Michelle at the grocery store, and about Scarlett. For the first time in my life, I told him how much I loved him and how thankful I was to have him in my life, how I couldn't imagine a world without him and how much it hurt to think for one second that I'd never see him again. I told him things I knew I would never say if he were awake, but it felt good to say it all out loud. Before I left, I squeezed his hand and promised we'd make the bastards who'd hurt him pay. Then I stood up, made sure he was comfortable, and left.

I was warming up some soup in the kitchen when Gavin came in. "Thanks for letting me talk to Scar alone," he said.

"Thank you for bringing my dad home," I replied as I prepared a tray of food for Scarlett. "I'm sorry about roughing you up back there."

Gavin just shrugged it off as if it was no big deal.

"Can we start over?" I asked, holding my hand out to him.

Gavin smiled and shook my hand. "I would like that."

"Listen, make yourself at home. Eat whatever, drink whatever; our house is your house. The guest bedroom is upstairs across from mine."

"Thanks, Luke," he said. I nodded and carried the tray upstairs.

I made a big fuss about feeding Scarlett. She kept insisting that she was more than capable of feeding herself, but I wanted to do it. Finally I set the spoon down and looked into her eyes. "I almost lost you. Let me take care of you tonight. Tomorrow you can do it all by yourself, but not tonight. I need to do this. Please?" She understood and indulged my need to be her caretaker.

It was getting late and I needed to be up with the sun, but I didn't want to fall asleep. I wanted to lay awake all night and watch her. When she yawned and tried to wiggle herself under the covers, I stood and lifted her up. I pulled the covers back and helped her change from the infirmary gown to one of my T-shirts.

"You coming to bed?" she asked when I just stood there watching her. "Yeah," I said. I slipped my jeans off and pulled my shirt over my head. She smiled up at me. "Don't get any ideas, girl. You almost died tonight," I told her as I climbed into the bed and wrapped my arms around her.

She sighed and then buried her face in my chest. "I love you, Scarlett," I whispered into her hair. She lifted her eyes to mine and said, "I love you too, Luke."

CHAPTER 58

Scarlett

My eyes fluttered open the next morning when I felt Luke stir. I was still snuggled up to his chest and his arm was still wrapped around my body holding me close. We must not have moved all night. Stretching my arms up over my head, I yawned and immediately noticed that I felt considerably better today. The numbness had subsided, and I no longer felt drained. In fact, my energy level seemed back to normal, and although my leg still ached a bit, I knew with the help of the crutches the doctor left, I could get around just fine.

I propped myself up on my elbow to find Luke staring down at me with desire shining in his deep brown eyes. A grin spread across his lips, and I wanted nothing more than to wrap myself around him and beg him to make love to me. But I knew better. As much as he may have wanted to, Luke wouldn't do more that kiss me until I was completely healed.

He learned over and kissed me chastely before he pulled away to ask, "How are you feeling?"

"I'm great, actually. Completely rejuvenated, and my leg barely hurts." I reached up, placing my hand on Luke's cheek. "I want to go with you to the meeting this morning. I need to be there."

Before he even answered, Luke was shaking his head. "No way. You need to rest. I don't want you involved in any of this. We still haven't located your father, and I need you safe."

I sat up and faced him, pleading with my eyes for a moment before I spoke. "No, what I need is to be there. I need to face your pack. Explain my actions. Explain my part in all of this, why I did what I did. If I'm going to stay here, if I'm going to be your mate, I need them to hear me out. They have every right to hate me, but I have to try to make this right. I need to be honest with them all, Luke. I don't want to hide."

My eyes fill with tears, so I looked away, not wanting him to see me cry. Luke swept my hair over my shoulder and gently touched his lips to my neck before he inhaled deeply. His lip grazed my shoulder as he pleaded, "I just need you safe, baby. I can't risk losing you again. Please. I couldn't handle it if anything happened to you."

I reached over to cup his face in my hand and guide his lips to mine. Melting into his embrace, I parted my lips and slipped my tongue out in search of his. If I could have crawled on top of him, I would have. Instead, I had to work within my limits, so I rolled onto my good hip and ran my fingers down his bare chest and across his rippled abs. When his body shuttered against my touch, every part of me filled with need and I wanted him so badly that it hurt. My body begged to make him physically claim me as his own, and I cursed my damn leg from preventing it from happening.

His fingers threaded themselves through my hair as his lips, his mouth, his tongue ravished my own. I pressed my chest against his, needing to be even closer. Luke pulled away but only slightly and looked into my eyes. "Baby, I want you so bad. It's literally going to kill me if we don't stop." The hunger in his eyes only intensified the desire coursing through me. I didn't want him to stop. I never wanted him to stop. His lips were only a breath away, so I moved in for at least one more soft kiss; but as soon as our lips touched he entangled his fingers in my hair once more, pulled me against him and devoured me all over again.

A knock on the door broke our frenzied need, and we pulled away from each other, both breathing heavily. We straightened our clothes, and I ran my fingers through my tangled hair before I called out, "Come in."

Gavin cracked the door open and joked, "Are you two decent?" He peeked inside and chuckled as if he knew exactly what had been going on just before he interrupted. "Sorry guys, but Luke, we need to get going if you want to be early."

Just as Luke started to get up, I placed my hand on his arm to stop him. "I meant what I said. I want to go. I can explain better than any of you what my pack is up to." This was my last-ditch effort to convince Luke to let me go, so I played the last card I had. "Plus, if you really want me safe, then you'll want me with you. I'll be safest by your side. I know you won't let anything happen to me."

Luke didn't respond, but it was clear the wheels were turning in his head. I turned my attention to Gavin, and with my eyes, I tried to relay a help-me-out-here message. Without the luxury of words, I wasn't sure he'd understand, but just as I'd hoped, he had heard me loud and clear. He nodded his head once and said, "You know, man, she's right. She'll be safer with the rest of us than here alone. I think she should come."

Letting out a heavy sigh, Luke got out of bed and reached out his hand to help me up as well. "Well, I guess we better get you ready, then." Once he'd gotten me to my feet and my crutches under my arms, he whispered, "Promise you won't leave my side."

After I reassured Luke that everything would be fine, I told Gavin to give us five minutes and then plastered a smile on my face that I hoped hid the anxiety building inside me. I was about to face all the people that I'd set out to deceive. But I needed to do this. That I knew, but it didn't make me any less freaked out about the whole thing.

*****

We arrived at the house just as Cade, Alli, Teagan, and Alli's parents showed up. A sickening feeling crept through me that I couldn't explain. It was eerily quiet as we all acknowledged each other, but only with a few head nods and small smiles. Nobody spoke as we all followed Cade up the driveway to the front door.

Once inside, the house appeared to be empty. The lights were off, and Noel was nowhere in sight. Cade flipped on a few lights and looked around. "My mom's probably in the bedroom with Dad. It's early so maybe they're still asleep. You all hang out here. I'll be right back."

Cade headed through the living room toward a hallway that must have led to the master bedroom, and after Luke told my brother to keep an eye on me, he hurried to catch up with Cade. Maybe he sensed something was off too.

Seconds later, there was some commotion coming from the direction they had headed, which was quickly followed by muffled voices, and then a thunderous wail erupted from the bedroom. Without a word, we all rushed down the hall.

Gavin helped me hobble hastily behind them, but before we made it, someone else let out an ear-piercing shriek. Gasps and sobs and stifled words came from the bodies filling the doorway that were blocking my view. Slowly they filed into the room. Gavin walked ahead of me, and before I could see what was going on, I heard Cade calling out to his father, repeating, *No, no, no.*

My brother moved to my side so that I could get into the room. I couldn't make sense of what I was seeing at first, but when realization struck, my eyes widened in shock as I let out an anguished cry of my own. Gavin put his arm around me as I watched in horror as Luke attempted to pull Cade off of his father's dead body.

CHAPTER 59

Drew

My face still throbbed from the beating I took from that assface meathead last night. But that's okay because one day soon, he will be the one begging me for mercy. Mercy that would never in a million years come. Killing his stupid bitch was just the beginning of the pain I'd planned on unleashing on him once I got out of here!

The morons they had guarding me refused to acknowledge me. As much as I tried to get them riled up, it was useless. They refused to utter a single word in my presence. I thought for a moment that Aiden would give in and start cussing me out or something, but nope. They just sat there and stared at me like I might suddenly acquire super human powers and burst through the iron bars.

I looked over at Gage, who was picking at the toe of his boot. "Hey man, aren't you bored as hell? It's driving me insane. Got any cards? I could totally handle a game of Texas Hold'em right now." Gage didn't look up. He just continued picking away at his damn boot. "Fine, no poker. How about Go Fish? Solitaire?" No response.

Oh my God. I'm going to die of boredom. Brian better be trying to figure out how the hell to get me out of here.

I heard the doors open upstairs and I thought, *finally someone different to look at*! But my excitement was short lived, and I instinctively backed up to the far wall of my cell as the entire pack began to file into the room. From the look of them, something serious had gone down. *What the hell did Brian do?*

The girls had red, teary eyes, while the guys marched in looking like they were out for blood. My blood. Their reaction couldn't possibly be over Scarlett. They didn't even know her that well.

I made every effort to appear unfazed, but no one spoke and that alone took my anxiety to a whole new level. They all just stared at me. Finally a woman walked over to Aiden and Gage and pulled them aside to whisper something to them. I tried to pick up what was being said, but I couldn't hear clearly. I did, however, pick up on their body language. As the woman spoke, Aiden's back straightened and his hands closed into clenched fists. When he looked back over at me, he had nothing but rage his eyes. *This is so not good!*

My heart attempted to leap out of my chest when Luke and Scarlett walked in the room hand in hand and stopped right in front of my cell. I swallowed down my disbelief and tried to recover quickly. I threw my hands in the air and declared, "Ahh! She lives!"

I watched as Luke pulled her tightly to his side. I couldn't believe that he would forgive her. It was pathetic really. There was no way in hell I'd ever forgive something like that. Unless…

The epiphany it hit me like a ton of bricks. Scarlett did look sickly the last time I saw her, and even though Luke managed to pummel me with ease, he too looked like death-warmed-over and wasn't nearly as strong as he was when he took on Aiden and Cade at that New Year's Eve party. Holy shit! They were mated!

I laughed my ass off right there, locked in a cage surrounded by an angry mob that surely wanted to see me dead. But it was just so damn funny that I couldn't help it. This whole situation was hilarious. Or maybe I really was starting to lose my mind.

I finally got a hold of myself and wandered up to the front of the cell. Looking Scarlett square in the eyes, I sneered, "Damn girl! We told you to screw him, not mate with the son of a bitch! You really can't do anything right, can you?"

Luke actually growled at me, and Scarlett had to take his arm and pull him away when he tried to reach for me through the bars. I was about to make a smart-assed comment about Scarlett already wearing the pants in the relationship when Cade came busting in the room. I'd never thought he looked all that tough, but the look on his face was nothing short of murderous rage. He stalked over to Aiden and yanked the key to my cell from his hand. Within seconds, my cell was open and a very angry Cade was in my face.

I tried to consider my options here. Yes, I was a decent fighter. If I was 100 percent, I could probably take Cade, but I had just been beaten within an inch of my life, and Cade wasn't my only problem. The entire pack was watching my every move. There was no way I was getting out of here alive.

"Sit," Cade ordered, pulling me by my hair and shoving me down into the chair in my cell.

Cade circled me, obviously trying to calm himself down a bit. "I'm only going to ask you this one time. Where is my mother?"

His mother? Oh! I couldn't have hidden the grin on my face if I had tried. I figured the damage was done, so I went ahead and gave in to my laughter.

"You think it's funny?" Cade shouted. "You sick bastard! My father is dead, and my mother is missing and you think it's funny?"

They actually went through with it. Brian and Noel killed Marcus Walker. Good! "Oh yeah, it's hilarious. And I'm laughing because you're about to learn that your mother is a fucking whore!" I said.

"Ugghhh." My head was whipped back by the force of Cade's hand. He actually backhanded me like I was his damn bitch. I stood up and spit blood at his feet. "You hit like girl!"

Cade pulled his arm back, and I prepared myself for the punch he was about to throw, but his phone began to ring. He looked torn. I could see how badly he wanted to hit me, but at the same time, he was so worried about his mother that I knew he would stop and answer that call.

"You might want to answer that," I said, my voice dripping with sarcasm.

Cade stepped out of the cell and pulled his phone out of his pocket. Gage shut the door to my cell and turned his attention to Cade. Confusion spread across Cade's face as he stared down at the name displayed on the screen of his phone. He looked from his phone to me and then back down at his phone, and I knew right then that I was going to be all right. Overcome with relief, I began laughing like a madman because I knew exactly who was on the other end of that call.

The phone continued to ring, so through my laughter, I advised, "You better get that, Cade. You of all people should know how testy she can get."

Cade answered and put it on speakerphone. "Hello?" he asked tentatively.

"There's my girl! I knew you'd find me! I miss you, baby," I shouted loud enough for her to hear me.

"Cade Walker, if you touch one hair on my man's head, I swear to God you won't live to see another day!" she warned with nothing but conviction in her voice.

Cade's jaw dropped. He looked around at the faces in the room before he uttered, "Kendall?"

"Actually, dipshit, I go by Avery now. New pack, new name, new man. A true alpha this time." She paused for a moment, probably waiting for Cade to reply, but he must have been too freaked out to respond. "Cat got your tongue, Cade? Well, let's just cut to the chase, shall we? If you ever want to see your mother again, I suggest you prepare yourself to make a trade. Drew for Noel, no negotiations. Otherwise you'll be an orphan by nightfall."

Every pair of eyes in the room shifted their attention to me and the shock on their faces was priceless. All I could do was smile. I knew my girl would come to my rescue, and I couldn't help but call out, "I'll see you soon, baby!"

CHAPTER 60

Luke

My father didn't take the news of Marcus's death as I expected. I thought he would react as Cade did, bursting with rage and the desire for revenge. Maybe it was because he was still suffering from the effects of the sedative or maybe he was even stronger than I thought. Either way, I figured I'd never know what he was feeling inside in that moment. Hiding his emotions was his specialty.

My dad didn't say a word. Instead, he sat motionless in his bed, his head bowed, his hands still in his lap, as if he hadn't heard us when we told him that Brian had murdered our alpha. But when I looked closer, I saw that his eyes were clenched shut, and I realized that he was struggling to keep it together. Marcus was no longer the alpha of this pack, my father no longer his enforcer.

As I looked around my father's bedroom, the next generation of leaders looked back at me. Cade and Allison, our alphas. Aiden, Teagan, and Gage would no doubt become trusted advisors. And now I was the enforcer. I knew it would happen one day. I just didn't expect it to be so soon, and I certainly didn't expect to have the support of a mate behind me.

As if she somehow sensed I needed it, Scarlett laced her fingers through mine, and when our eyes met, she gave me the strength I needed to get through this. Her eyes said it all. She believed in me. She loved me. She was going to be by my side every step of the way.

"Cade, Luke, Aiden," my father said softly, "it is up to you all, to not only save Noel, but seek vengeance for our alpha's demise. We must show the Crescent Hills Pack that we are once again united and strong."

"We will, sir," Cade said as he stood up. "You have my word."

Letting go of Scarlett's hand, I stepped in to stand at my alpha's side. Aiden didn't hesitate to step up as well, and we all came together ready to do whatever we had to do to make Crescent Hills regret the moment they decided they could take down our pack. This was far from over, but together, we were going to make it right.

ABOUT THE AUTHORS

Sara Dailey and Staci Weber have been friends and coworkers for so long that they finish each other's sentences and answer to either name. They both have an addiction to romance novels, sweet white wine, and sexy rock stars. They both live in League City, TX, with their husbands and kids. *Web of Lies* is their fifth novel together.

Boroughs
Publishing Group

Did you enjoy this book? Drop us a line and say so! We love to hear from readers, and so do our authors. To connect, visit www.boroughspublishinggroup.com online, send comments directly to info@boroughspublishinggroup.com, or friend us on Facebook and Twitter. And be sure to check back regularly for contests and new releases in your favorite subgenres of romance!

Are you an aspiring writer? Check out www.boroughspublishinggroup.com/submit and see if we can help you make your dreams come true.